budge

Budge

A novel by

Tom Osborne

ANVIL PRESS :: VANCOUVER :: 2012

Anvil Press Publishers Inc.
P.O. Box 3008, Main Post Office
Vancouver, B.C. V6B 3X5 Canada
www.anvilpress.com

Library and Archives Canada Cataloguing in Publication

Osborne, Tom, 1949–

    Budge / Tom Osborne.

ISBN 978-1-897535-99-8

    I. Title.

PS8579.S36B83 2012   C813'.54   C2012-905379-1

Cover design: Rayola.com
Cover illustration: Shawn O'Keefe
Interior design: Heimat House

Represented in Canada by the Literary Press Group.

Distributed in Canada by the University of Toronto Press and in the U.S. by Small Press Distribution (SPD).

The publisher gratefully acknowledges the financial assistance of the Canada Council for the Arts, the Canada Book Fund, and the Province of British Columbia through the B.C. Arts Council and the Book Publishing Tax Credit.

Printed and bound in Canada.

budge:
to cease resistance
to move; shift; stir

*For Liza & Garette
& their diligent fostering
of the non-terrible*

&
*to my mother,
who raised six of us and
killed none*

WANDA OSBORNE
1924–2011

Of Hobbies and Destructive Behaviour

LOUELLA DEBRA POULE, at age thirty-four, is changing her life. Louella Debra Poule, at age thirty-four and of looks considered by many to be pretty when maintained, a prettiness that hints of past childhood days of skinny bare legs at play in water sprinklers, days of varied and brightly coloured dolls arranged around a child's table awaiting imaginary tea and cookies, days of stuffed teddy bears and bunnies and leopards and tigers and other toy animals scattered about and left underfoot in all rooms of the house, the favourite being a bedraggled alligator with most of the stuffing gone, and everything made all the more cuddly and innocent and presumed to last forever by the insulating power of naught more than sweet girlhood dreams.

"You must attempt change, Louella," says prison counsellor Jane. "Eradicate destructive behaviour."

And Louella listening to the faint ticks emanating from the baseboard heater, staring ahead at prison counsellor Jane's office wall and letting her gaze follow the criss-cross pattern of the dull green–painted cinder blocks.

"You might think of a hobby when you get out, something to fill your time. Do you know what a hobby is, Louella?"

And one is sure one does, conjuring images of butterflies speared on pins, handmade birdhouses displayed in rows along a garage wall, postage stamps arranged on a grid-lined page . . .

"I think I do," says Louella.

I.

How It Works

THE DAY JIMMY FLOOD mutters, "I think I can get me a helicopter," and Ginger Baumgartner nods out next to him with a face-plant onto the kitchen table, and Marco Da Silva beside her reaches out an arm to lift her head to scoop two caps of heroin out from under her cheek, and Blacky Harbottle cuts the high-grade stuff on a cheap kitchen scale with whatever he can find that's white and powdery to make it go further on the street, and Louella Poule looks on through aqueous, drug-pinned eyes as Melody Tenbrink tosses her cookies in the john adjacent the kitchen after smoking her modest rock of crack, this becoming the day the delicate bar graph that mandates the ups and downs of a drug addict's existence will dip even lower for everybody just mentioned (if that's possible).

For this is the day the Cuban and the Mick are at the front door, fists about to pound, then not, deciding instead to put two pairs of boots to it, with the ensuing crash alerting those wasted in the kitchen at the back of the house, who as one jump to their feet (all save Ginger Baumgartner) and Louella Poule grabs a jacket, using it as a catch-all at the edge of the kitchen table, Blacky Harbottle scraping scales, dope, baggies and ashtrays, coffee cups and newspapers and half-eaten doughnuts and anything else on the table over the edge and into the jacket catch-all, a .22 pistol tossed into the collection at the last minute, and Louella Poule bundling it all up and making for the open kitchen window to dump it out directly on the head of the plainclothes narc huddled there, and so at this moment does Time, for all the inhabitants of the house and for Louella Poule especially, thus appear to stand still, then lay its misappropriated self down along the kitchen floor as if to say, *"I can do no more, I've plumb run out, you poor goddamn goombas . . ."*

SO, HOW IT WORKS: let the front main door of the house on St. Catherines Street on Vancouver's upper east side fall inward under force to the darkened inner hallway, unnerving sound of wood splintering as doorstops, door jambs, door casings fly; hinges, deadbolts, and strike plates airborne, and more timber screeching as two pairs of large-sized Daltons belonging to the Cuban and the Mick kick out in perfect unison to bring that door down, and in.

The two cops sing: *"O Paddy, dear, and did you hear the news that's going around . . ."*

And these two are none other than the Cuban and the Mick, two plainclothes narcotics officers of dark and questionable reputations on the streets, judged no better than the criminals themselves by most of the druggies they routinely hunt down and bust, beat, and rob. The so-called Cuban, real name Peter Manfred Rourke, of rotund, hairy six-foot-five frame and swarthy complexion, not a Cuban at all, but in reality part Black Irish would anyone believe, and with pirate's eyes sunk deeply into dark sockets above a black scraggle of beard. And the Cuban's partner, the so-called Mick, real name Ruben Gerald McFadden, who is, in fact, also part and even more Irish but of the fairer set, of hair light brown leaning to red and topping a lankier frame built tall and wiry with eyes of a psychotic hue of pale blue, slightly bulging especially when enraged, as they often are, and he who is thought to be even more dangerous than the bigger, meaner-looking Cuban. And as is the pair's MO and spirit for their job, it is not an uncommon occurrence for them to break into Irish song in honour and pride of their ethnic heritage, and this occurrence is most often manifested while in the heat of any bust, as they are now.

They sing: *"The shamrock is forbid by law to grow on English ground . . ."*

And so it's on this very note and lyric the Cuban and the Mick gain entrance to the hallway that leads to yet another door of the house on St. Catherines Street, and this door, too, is sent crashing inward off its supports with hinges and screws, spiral and ring-shank nails, and cement-coated sinkers pinging off the linoleum and cheap wall panelling of the main inner room, and all this destruction and violence notwithstanding the fact that often enough the doors assaulted by this team are unlocked and unbolted in the first place, but such are the temperaments and aforementioned spirit of the two narcs, and what would be the fun of gaining entrance through doorways by time-honoured conventional methods when one has the credentials to simply shout the word *police*, and have licence to lay waste to all that lies in one's path?

"No fun at all, we thinks," would be their answer if ever asked, they being, in their own minds at least, an answer in themselves to that great question from the public: What to do about crime?

"Kill them all," might say one.

"But spare the wee ones," might say the other.

And "Unrestricted authority," would definitely say both.

And it's just before this uncomfortable and sudden upheaval of life in the house on St. Catherines Street one might say things had been going surprisingly well for the owner, one Blacky Harbottle, who had become almost optimistic about his life before this event. True, there have been drug and contraband busts before, but not for some time. Business has been good, as one has been flying under the radar so to speak; from the drug suppliers to dealers, they have been behaving themselves. But now this.

"But now what, exactly?" Blacky Harbottle may say to himself, even knowing well this sort of thing and much worse can come with the bleak territory of the illegal life, Blacky Harbottle of a hard-trimmed red goatee, hockey-stick sideburns, and hair hanging long and wet-looking, a shock of bright red. There is nothing black or dark anywhere around this head to support the moniker *Blacky*. Even the eyes are light coloured, blue-green and set into a middle-aged face somewhat heavily creased, each crease perhaps reflecting, to the knowing eye, a life of under-the-table scams, crooked business dealings, and a predisposed talent for the hatching of subversive plots. And there's something else there, too, that may suggest to the knowing eye something of the mystical, perhaps some underlying belief in and fear of the greater intangibles of the universe, and something on top of that of being a whiz at cribbage and pinochle. All that and an innate flair for drug running.

And even Jimmy Flood, Blacky Harbottle may further acknowledge to himself, a long-time associate and cohort, has been pulling his weight, quite a feat considering what a fuck-up he is. Of course, this evaluation of others by Blacky Harbottle is hardly fair, especially in the case of Jimmy Flood. Jimmy Flood has not had the advantages of one Blacky Harbottle, nor been endowed with a comparable intelligence, although Jimmy Flood is not stupid, as Blacky Harbottle may point out, but runs more along the lines of foolish and somewhat immature, and being a drug addict doesn't help. "Of course, I do drugs, too," might say Blacky Harbottle. "But mine is a more *renaissance*-type habit. I mean, Jesus, I can still read a fucking book once in a while even when I'm using!" Suffice to say a more unlikely relationship might not be easily imagined, but Jimmy Flood does know the street, as Blacky Harbottle does seem to know how to conduct business, however illegal. In fact, as fate would have it, the two met when a younger Blacky Harbottle was just venturing into the lucrative world of crime by running illegal numbers on the NFL and printing up his own betting sheets.

"Spied this guy running the printing press in back of the shop," as Blacky liked to tell it. "Weird, skinny freak. Was gettin' some bogus business cards made up for my bogus consulting firm, Dicom Industries or something, which was a complete fuck-up by the way. Never did get off the ground even for one score. Anyway, Flood was the only guy in the shop at the time, an' I got him to start printing numbers sheets for me. I booked odds on NFL games each week, paid Flood a flat rate for each set of sheets. Did well, actually."

But now, *right* now, how well will anybody be doing, what will be the upshot of this terrible day, or, more accurately, the workings of but a few mere moments of this terrible day when the delicate balance of one's existence is upended? Because the fact was that the main and earlier part of this day had been more than satisfactory— money had been acquired—a large drug deal successfully transacted—and there'd been enough for all and sundry to get royally wasted. In fact, as one's memory may have it, everyone was feeling pretty darn good, except maybe Ginger Baumgartner, who was being sick in the can. Yes, all was well and wonderfully good until the doors started coming in and a window or two began tinkling shards of glass across the floor and then half nelsons and full nelsons and sleeper holds and chokeholds and the occasional body slam from the Cuban and the Mick seemed to befall the entire cast just minding their own business sitting around one's sorry kitchen table in the house on St. Catherines Street. And who could explain why everyone except Louella Poule would get off with naught but assorted bruises and a modicum of humiliation, while she is to be suddenly locked up, given drug then gun charges, and eighteen months plus a day, and tucked away to come down off drugs cold turkey, writhing on the bottom bunk of a two-woman cell and wringing a sweat-soaked blanket into tight little knots, and all this not to mention the mind-bending constipation that comes with sudden drug withdrawal, and forced to smuggle a spoon out of the mess hall and then to dig gingerly up one's backside in the dark of night just to help things get going?

"And who on god's fuckin', freaking earth could explain something like that, I'd like to know!" Blacky Harbottle might likely say, eyes raised to the ceiling, arms flung out to his sides, and whisky splashing freely onto the carpet from the forgotten glass in one hand.

2.

The Right Thing to Do

WHEN FIRST INCARCERATED, Louella had followed truck, toed the line, said little to anyone, kept her hands in her pockets, and fashioned a confident don't-give-a-shit shuffle. And wrestled hard with the knot of fear pitting her stomach.

Eyes were the biggest problem, she found, avoiding them anyway. There were too many of them, some unfriendly, some too friendly, some just plain angry-mean-I'll-kick-your-ass-for-nothing types. All kinds of images of the joint had filled her mind when she was sentenced, having taken the fall for the .22 handgun charge because the gun was Jimmy Flood's, her sort-of boyfriend, and he already had a rap sheet and would have done a lot of time with that charge on him. And it was an expected thing on the street that she take the rap for him and get less time, only eighteen months, the stand-up thing to do, and in her numbed state of mind she at the time had almost welcomed the negligible opportunity to be something of a hero. Blacky Harbottle originally took the fall for the drugs, it being his house, and, well, his fucking drugs, but all the others got off. (Blacky Harbottle, harbourer of numerous and varied reputations, one being that he had a shitload of horseshoes up his ass at any given time, would, in fact, serve only fourteen days before being released on some vague technicality.)

Understandably, Louella Debra Poule, upon hearing about all these developments, will know there is something intrinsically wrong with this picture, her being the only one of all of them charged and convicted, but she is too drug-sick and generally bummed-out by the whole affair to efficiently evaluate the right or wrong of it. Simple survival becomes the priority, survival for however long she had to serve. Some good news is she's headed for a minimum-security facility, somewhere in the Fraser Valley. The word *minimum* makes it sound not all too bad. Her first night there's a fight in the dining area over a place in the food line, two girls going at it with food trays, and some girl takes a bad beating later in one of the johns. But it's not all shit and hullabaloo, for there are signs that some kind of friendship and loyalty can exist in a place like this, as Louella overhears a short, pockmarked girl mumble to a friend in passing, "My old man's coming over the fence tonight. Gotta go..."

And Louella had heard from girls and guys on the street that this phenomenon did take place and not infrequently, guys actually coming over the fence *into* prison for the sake of getting booze and contraband to their girlfriends—throw a blanket over the wire along the top of the fence, shinny up, and toss the goods over. On this level, prison life could be thought of as being somewhat educational: how to make moonshine out of any mixture of fruits or vegetables, if left to fester long enough; how to hide things when there's nowhere to hide things; how to make a designer shank; or how to trust the rare few and mistrust the rest.

But it turns out to be, at best, crushingly dehumanizing, Louella Debra Poule afloat in the realms of the unreal, the main unreal being, for her, having to suddenly go without dope. There's no lack of drugs to be had in the place if one has the means, but the angles and jailhouse politics that go along with it just don't seem worth it. When one is forced to kick cold turkey, one might as well try to go all the way with it, maybe come out the other side clean or, at the very least, peacefully dead. But for those who try it, the senses will be stretched, every noise in the place will seem to have an echo of itself permanently attached, so it's never completely quiet, the echoes reverberating along the corridors, off and through the cinder-block walls, constantly re-energized by echoes of echoes as one climbs the stairs between floors staring at each step ahead at eye level, rubber no-slip strips along the edges that remind one of more innocent high school stairwells, but in these stairwells the odd shoulder or hip brushing by, nudging, and one is immediately left wondering, was that an accident or challenge, who's pushing who, and *whattayagonnadoaboutit*? And everywhere the place heaves and rattles with bits of conversation and comment, relentless and intrusive expressions of the soupy mess of personalities confined together, often taking the form of arbitrary and sporadic shouts, whoops, curses, laughter, screaming, and crying that long after they've stopped, continue to roll through the mind like hardened stones, like, who *is* pushing who?

So, how it goes...one's paranoia grows, that's a given. Wraps itself around the gut and envelops one's shoulders, like a yoke, restricting the body and leaving the mind to fend for itself, the mind wondering who to talk to, who to stay the fuck away from. Simple, really.

"You got a cigarette?" from the upper bunk already taken, glimpse of dark brown hair, dark brown eyes. Just a question, right? Nothing threatening about someone wanting a smoke, for Christ's sake. And Louella Debra Poule taking the lower bunk, not yet made up, and dutifully rummaging through her bag, looking for them goddamn smokes to give two to her new cellmate, like putting money in the meter, helping the poor, deciding it's the right thing to do.

3.

Of Commemoration and Possibilities

UPON THE DEATH of her mother six months after her sentencing, Louella Debra Poule (recommended on good behaviour and what was considered by the review board as pursuing sincere inroads to rehabilitation) is allowed to attend the funeral, under guard, of course. A female sheriff's officer accompanies her, dressed (Louella is relieved to see) in street clothes and not too disposed to engage her in too much conversation or an overkill of condolences (for which she is also relieved).

"Sorry for your loss," the officer says. And, "You okay?"

Louella says she is okay, thanks, realizing down deep in some closed-off part of her being she's not really, but it will not all manifest itself until some later time. And she standing a moment outside the unmarked police car. And gazing down the grassy slope of the cemetery grounds, a small crowd gathered there at the bottom under a white awning affair tethered to aluminum poles held steady by thin, white ropes pegged to the ground.

"Okay, Louella?"

And the two of them walking down the slope, past polished granite headstones, some tinted blue, some red. And some shiny black with silver lettering. But most appear a speckled grey: some plain, some engraved with crosses, cherubs or floral wreaths, conch shells, doves, intricate ivy lacing. Olive branches. And being careful not to walk on the many markers set in the ground, Louella moving her feet carefully, for not everyone likes or can afford a headstone, one figures. And many of these markers dressed in bronze reliefs with various designs; a lighthouse perched on rocks; a mountain scene, forest, and lake; a dogwood tree on one and on another the shiny bronze portrait of a child. And nearing the white awning, so many unfamiliar faces, Louella Debra Poule, under guard, her own and that of the legal system and standing precariously close to the edge of this open grave, the open grave of Rosemary Elizabeth Poule. Blackbirds shrieking high in a tree. Someone in the crowd coughing. And it's a relief to see Aunt Inga looking over from under a flowered Sunday hat.

It's a fair-sized gathering, which surprises Louella for some reason, mostly women over fifty and a number of reluctant-looking husbands. Dew sparkles on their shoes; the priest drones over the grave. And Aunt Inga's second husband, Horst, is spotted there behind Aunt Inga, his dark hat pulled over his eyes. Louella follows Aunt Inga's lead, tossing a handful of dirt on the coffin as it's lowered.

After the burial she's allowed to partake of tea and cake (no alcohol) back at Aunt Inga and Horst's, where a larger crowd has gathered, but again, most are unfamiliar.

"I'm relieved to see your escort has the tact not to wear her uniform," whispers Aunt Inga. "It's never any fun having to parade one's indiscretions before the public eye."

"She's okay," says Louella and later traverses the yard in quiet, watched from the patio by her escort, who attentively partakes of tea and cake, and accepts a bottle of sparkling lemon-flavoured spring water.

Louella traverses the yard again, feeling anxious, awkward, not one's self, although she'd be the first to acknowledge that who "one's self" would actually be at this moment she has no real idea. One has been drug-free since being locked up and has attended group meetings in the joint with other girls who want to get straight. One has also sought out counselling there, and it all seems to have helped some. But here, now, on the "outside," it seems one has almost forgotten how to carry on a conversation—how to greet people—how to *talk*. And now Momma's gone and it hasn't sunk in yet, nothing has, and it's a revelation that this is the first real funeral one's ever attended, as an adult anyway. There's been no lack of deaths in one's own crowd over the years—overdoses, accidents, homicides—but there was a significant lack of funerals attended. There was Chico Barber—that was a funeral, sort of, one could say maybe. Poor old Chico died sitting right there in the second-hand easy chair in his living room, overdose, and they had all banded together on the living room floor at the feet of the body and shot up the rest of his heroin. Got good and wasted and talked about Chico, with his head tilted back against the chair, eyes half closed and mouth open, heart not beating, blood no longer flowing. Until Blacky Harbottle mentioned the fact that everyone had forgotten: that Chico had, in fact, been a total asshole. And everyone stopped talking about him, crashed for the night there in Chico's apartment, and in the morning took anything of cash value and let the authorities know by an anonymous tip where the body could be found.

Louella approaching a corner of the yard now and startled by the salty-sea smell that wafts up from the ocean shore below, the water visible through the trees. There are very few true smells in lock-up. There's the smell of fried grease permeating the eating area. And, of course, the ever-present and various odours of people. Oh, and disinfectant. Plenty of disinfectant.

She stands a moment by some blue flowers.

"My African lilies," says Aunt Inga coming up from behind. "Horst is drunk, I'm afraid, and thankfully we're almost out of food. Your mother's friends weren't really mine, although they seem like a nice bunch."

"I don't know any of them," says Louella.

"Well, how could you," says Aunt Inga, twisting free a lily. "Here. Take this. Put it in a scrapbook or something. To commemorate this day."

"Commemorate? I can hardly fucking comprehend it."

"No tears?"

"Are people talking?"

"No. People handle loss in different ways."

"I'm not handling anything."

"We can talk about it."

"Not now, I don't think."

"Heavens, no, my dear, not now. You're too distraught, although you may not know it. Some other time, when you're ready."

"What do you know that I don't, Aunt Inga?"

"Most everything, I suspect, my dear. Come, your guardian says it's time to go."

AUNT INGA WILL ARRIVE to pick her up the day of her release, a hot summer day in late June, a vapour trail visible across the sky, heat waves roiling off the pavement. Uncle Horst sits quietly in the back seat.

"You look good, Louella," says Aunt Inga. "Horst insisted I bring him along for the occasion. I don't expect you to talk much, my dear, time to integrate and all that. You'll stay with us a week or so to help acclimatize yourself to life on the outside. Just a little joke, love. You've done what was required of you. Fulfilled your obligation to society, in my mind, anyway. Today's a new day. Isn't that right, Horst?"

"Yes. A new day," says Uncle Horst, not unpleasantly.

"Full of possibilities. New horizons! New heights!"

"Yes, possibilities ..." echoes Uncle Horst. "Heights..."

"Thank you, Horst," says Aunt Inga. "We'll be home for a drink soon."

And Louella leaning back in the front passenger seat, pressing her head into the rest and clutching her prison-issue tote bag against her thighs.

"One of the girls was stabbed last night," she says. "They attacked her with fountain pens."

"Dear god," says Aunt Inga, easing the car forward. "What a terrible thing, Louella."

4.

"The Hills Where Peace Was Made"

IN THE TOWN of Wetaskiwin, Alberta, about a half-hour's drive south of Edmonton and at four thirty in the morning, stands a very angry man.

On the other side of the counter in the town of Wetaskiwin, Alberta, and facing the first angry man stands another angry man. One man is of Burundian descent (the Hutu tribe to be exact) from the small African country of Burundi that borders the other African countries of Rwanda, Zaire, and Tanzania. The second man is of possible Irish-Ukrainian descent but is a naturalized Canadian citizen, from Canada, a larger country bordering the Atlantic Ocean, the Pacific Ocean, and the United States of America. The one immigrated to Canada from Burundi in 1998 to escape a violent civil war in that small African country; the other has lived in Canada all his life. One was an economic adviser for agricultural development before being forced to immigrate and take a menial job such as all-night clerk in an all-night Petro-Can gas station convenience store on Highway 2A in Wetaskiwin, Alberta. The other has never really bothered to work. One is well educated; the other is "educated enough," he supposes. One is forty-seven; the other is thirty-seven. One has a gun; the other has not.

Outside the store and waiting in a car with the motor running is another man, also a naturalized Canadian of possible Irish-Ukrainian descent and younger brother to the angry naturalized Canadian standing in the store. This third man, the naturalized Canadian brother, is not angry, however. This third man is, well, a dreamer. Butch Truman, younger brother to Gordy Truman, one of the two angry men in the store. Butch Truman dreams. He dreams of having things, all kinds of things, things he thinks will make him happy. In fact, that's why he and his brother are in Wetaskiwin in the first place, home of the famous Wetaskiwin Water Tower ("the oldest functioning water tower in Canada"); they're here because of his dreams. That's why they'd checked out Wetaskiwin's Dan Simpa Used & Collectible Auto Mart the afternoon of the day before after driving down from Edmonton, and that's probably why they are now at this all-night gas station convenience store: some part of some part of one of his dreams. That and the fact they'd scored some crack earlier, smoked it, scored some more, smoked that and so on, and now they are needing another part of another part of one of his dreams. And Gordy had said he'd take care of it.

Inside the all-night convenience store, Claver Hakizimana, Burundian immigrant, is looking at the gun in Gordy Truman's hand.

"You want *all* the money?" says Claver Hakizimana.

"That's right," says Gordy Truman. "Just give it an' let's be done."

"All the money . . ." says Claver Hakizimana.

There is tension. (Gordy Truman will later tell brother Butch he could almost *see* it in the air, just like described in books.) But this tension is not the normal prescribed tension that's part and parcel when you pull a gun on someone; this tension is something different, more palpable, Claver Hakizimana reaching into the till. Gordy Truman watches, sees bills in the store clerk's hand.

"Now look see . . ." says Claver Hakizimana. "I now have all the money in my hand. And you know how much money this is in my hand? It is fuck-all money in my hand because *we keep fuck-all money here just in case of fuckheads like you and now you want to take it?*—"

"Look, asshole—" says Gordy Truman.

"*And now,*" says Claver Hakizimana, "*I have this money in this hand and in this hand—*"

The machete appears already raised, slicing down across the

Plexiglass countertop. A jagged crack appears across the faces of assorted scratch-and-wins displayed underneath it, Gordy Truman stepping back, extending his arm full length and aiming the gun.

"I'll blow your fucking head off!"

"AND I," screams the store clerk, "WILL CUT YOURS FUCKING OFF, YOU FUCKING ASSHOLE . . ."

A pause here in the proceedings, the two angry men facing each other across the counter, an imposing display of red veins pulsing along necks, purple ones rippling across foreheads.

Gordy Truman: *"Look, just give me the fucking money!"*

Claver Hakizimana: *"I have seen the blood of my people soak the water reeds along the fucking Rurubu River! What have you seen, you fucking ass-punk?"*

Gordy Truman at a loss for a reply, the gun still pointing. Claver Hakizimana staring now not at the gun barrel but at Gordy Truman. The gun trembling, a methodic *tick-tick* from the hot-dog rotisserie turning slowly on the counter. The Slurpee machine gurgles from the back wall. Gordy Truman sees the store clerk's shoulders slump, just a bit. Muscles begin to relax, the dark eyes soften.

"Look," says Claver Hakizimana, "we are both reasonable if unhappy men. Believe me, a bullet in the head would not be the worst thing that could happen to me right now. And I can easily see that you, yourself, are leading an equally unrewarding existence irrespective of the advantages you may have had and obviously ignored. I have thought this through, and this is what is going to happen, my sorry friend. I have two hundred and thirteen dollars only in my hand. I am going to give you only sixty-five, no, *sixty* fucking dollars, and I am going to keep the rest and blame the whole robbery of the two hundred and thirteen dollars on you. The fucking cameras are not working, so that will not be a problem. I will give an accurate description of yourself to the police, but I may lie about the make of your car, which I assume is the one sitting out there with the engine running with another asshole at the wheel. You will leave Wetaskiwin and be grateful for small mercies. You may be a little disappointed by this outcome, but disappointment,

I believe, is not something new in your miserable life. This experience has given me an idea whereby I may make some improvements in my own wretched existence and for that I may even thank you, some day. Here is your sixty, no, *fifty* fucking dollars . . . Now fuck off."

BUTCH TRUMAN SEES brother Gordy coming out of the store, not running, not frantic, Gordy Truman opening the passenger side door and sliding into the passenger seat. Some bills visible in one hand, a bag of potato chips in the other.

"The guy gave us these," says Gordy Truman handing over the potato chips.

Butch Truman taking the bag and crinkling the cellophane, crinkle, crinkle, but doesn't drive.

"Gordy?"

Gordy Truman looking straight ahead. "Some people are just fucking crazy. Let's get out of here . . ."

Butch Truman releasing the brake, easing the car out onto the highway.

"What'd we get?"

"Fifty bucks," says Gordy Truman.

"Fifty bucks?"

But Gordy Truman is done talking and remains so. And leaving the town limits, a hint of dawn low on the prairie sky as the Truman brothers roll out past the gold-skimmed farmlands, fields of wheat, canola, barley. Sugar beets, dairy cattle, hogs, and cotton-batten bundles of sheep, the rich warm colour imparted freely by the rising sun and painting all in the weave of a perfect picture postcard of abundance, beauty, and prosperity. On the seat between them, a brochure, Wetaskiwin's Dan Simpa Used & Collectible Auto Mart, a small blurb printed along the top on the meaning of the word *Wetaskiwin*, from the Cree meaning "the hills where peace was made," this peace made long ago between the Cree and the Blackfoot goes the story, and now for all intents and purposes appearing to repeat itself in the small encounter between two simple and angry men, two simple and angry men who, too, are but the random products of two mismatched tribes . . .

5.

Of Soil, Seeds, and Fertilizer

AUNT INGA PARKS the car at her dead sister's townhouse. Visible in the small carport, a well-kept, compact, powder-blue Toyota Matrix. On a holder on the wall, a green garden hose coiled neatly next to two blue garbage bins, the kind you can wheel to the curb. Against another wall, assorted flowerpots and what appear to be bags of soil, seeds, and fertilizer propped in a corner; a battered and much-used bamboo rake, some tines missing; and a small spade and mud-caked wheelbarrow.

"Well, here you are, Louella, and I understand fully. You've had a week with us and probably need some time alone."

"No, Aunt Inga. It's not that. You and Horst have been great. Everything's just so . . ."

"Hmm . . . weird?"

"Yes. Weird."

"Well, it can only get weirder, I'm afraid, for a while anyway. Take your time, though, my dear. See how you feel. I'm a phone call away, love. My life's not that fixed, you know."

Louella left standing alone at dead Momma's townhouse door, watching Aunt Inga drive away, the feel of Aunt Inga's hug lingering, the key to the Toyota and the key to the townhouse in hand. Dead Momma's Toyota and dead Momma's townhouse in Deep Cove, North Vancouver. And now both belonging to Louella Debra Poule, dead Momma's only child, the townhouse situated at the end of a cul-de-sac under tall, dark trees. It's an end unit of the complex, and spied through the lattice along the top of the cedar fence on her left where the property ends is an older model, ranch-style bungalow just visible through the trees on the lot next door.

Louella turning back, to face the townhouse. To face the job at hand. And inserting key into lock, the townhouse door unlatched and pushed inward. Just inside the door, her bag placed on the floor, not dropped. And a smell, discernible but not quite identifiable. Have been to Momma's townhouse only a few times, stoned or drug-sick and only to try to score money. Of all the sense organs, it's the nostrils that seem to be the first that are assaulted when getting out of stir, accustomed as they have become to the bland, killing odour of institution walls, institution food, and institution people.

"Freedom," Aunt Inga had said when Louella kept commenting on different smells she was experiencing the first few days at Aunt Inga's. "That's all it is."

Louella had looked cynical.

"I'm not a poet, god forbid," said Aunt Inga. "But what else could it be, dear? I've smelled it myself at some time, I'm sure."

Now inside dead Momma's townhouse, one is suddenly aware one's toes are aching, and realizing they've been gripping the welcome mat through the thin soles of one's sandals like an eagle talons its prey. Louella releasing her toes, stretching them out—relax—relax—and advancing slowly into the smell.

What is it? Furniture? Carpets? Momma? And down this short hallway and into the salmon-coloured kitchen, bright with large windows. And where one has a few times in the past sprawled across that circular white kitchen table, eyes glassy and drug-pinned and ass sliding off those black-lacquered, steel-frame kitchen chairs while asking Mom for money, for a break—*aw, please, c'mon*—and Momma not giving in, and one finally forced to head for the door cursing her and all mothers and keeping it up all the way down the hill into the Cove where one could catch a bus back along that achingly long motherfucking ride over the Ironworkers-fucking-Bridge, back downtown to score somehow and forget you ever went out to Momma's to try to bum some money for drugs and grovelled like a shithead in her brightly lit, salmon-coloured kitchen. It's probably a good thing to keep in mind that Aunt Inga has mentioned that moving into Momma's townhouse so soon after, well, everything, might cause some unpleasant sensations to surface, might even prove unhealthy overall.

A note spied tacked to a small bulletin board next to the fridge: *Meet Mona—cards Tues.—bring wine*—and a thought: "Does this Mona know? Was she there midst the headstones with Momma being lowered into the ground? Did the dew sparkle on her shoes, too?"

Louella at the fridge, peering in. Some newly bought heat-and-serve pasta dishes. Yogurt cups and a bagged salad. Milk, cream, cheese, and a container of fat Greek olives. Aunt Inga must have stocked it; at least someone is thinking ahead. A small army of plants hangs from the ceiling and more drape the sills and counters, Louella finding crackers, bread, and cereal. And high in a cupboard a half-full bottle of vodka, an empty glass plucked from another cupboard next to the pink lace curtains fronting the window over the sink, and Louella soon blowing smoke from a cigarette through the now-open window toward the tops of the other townhouses visible through the part in the kitchen curtains, and a voice saying, "Watch it with the drinking, dummy. You're clean now."

A faint exchange of voices can be heard from the other side of the lattice-topped cedar fence enclosing the small backyard, the words indiscernible. A low stone wall running parallel below the fence holding back a flower bed thick with a variety of flowering and non-flowering plants.

You're gone, Momma, but things go on.

And turning back to the circular white kitchen table, one of the black-lacquered, steel-frame chairs pulled out and a seat taken under a low-slung knock-off Tiffany. A book open on the table top, *The Complete Home Gardener.* Birds heard chirping outside, wind scraping the tops of trees. Kid's voices raised somewhere out there in the maze of lattice-topped cedar fences, adult voices, and, *good god—neighbours—it's the sounds of neighbours*—and one will surely, at some time, have to meet them, talk to them—*socialize.*

Too mind-numbing to even think about, all these unknowns, Louella once more on the move, toes scrunching up again while treading the russet carpet of the living room. More plants here, much larger and appearing well kept and embracing the room. Aunt Inga must be watering them. Or Mona. And tucked behind some large dark leaves, an unlit aquarium where float two dead fish, their once-bright colours faded to a dull whitish grey. It can't be Aunt Inga who's been coming over; she would never let them die. And supporting a blue-stained softwood lamp next to the aquarium, a black iron nesting table with some photographs standing in thin silver and gold frames. Momma in a yellow bathing suit, smiling and holding a fat baby girl in her arms, a sliver of lakeshore visible over her left shoulder. In another, a man, poised over the same fat baby girl and wearing a red straw hat, Poppa, his upper face shaded, his smile lit by the sun. And moving farther on around the room, Louella silent and taking it in.

Have been here before, but never really looked at anything; always on the take; just give me something, Momma, so I can leave and go score. But now, Jeez Louise, a six-seater corner sofa of dark blue leather noticed snaking two walls and abutting on one end to a ceiling-high front window edged by large green-leafed plants. Facing it, a low coffee table of tempered safety glass inset in lacquered dark wood, and a swivel reclining armchair on a wooden base of the same sofa dark blue leather, where one sits, turning slowly. A small wine rack holding four bottles slouched next to a combination wall unit of clear-lacquered beechwood covering the opposite wall that wasn't there before. High definition TV and CD player supported there. Jesus, what a setup, Momma. Contemporary stuff—what is that fucker, a fifty-seven incher?

Louella shocked, because one is crying now in the reclining swivel chair. And because, well, Momma, you really did all right. You were always sort of younger than your age, if that makes any sense. That's one of the things Poppa couldn't get used to, I guess; you always trying new things. The yoga phase. Meditation. Native art and mythological studies. God, how poor Dad seemed so lost when you were talking about that, Poppa pouring another whisky, no ice, and asking, "What you want to learn that stuff for, damn it?"

And you saying, "It's interesting." And Dad saying, "Like knowing what an eagle flying over your head three times means to a bunch of yahoos in a war canoe?"

Yes, Momma, I agree, he wasn't very sympathetic to anything that wasn't scientific. He was very smart and very dumb. And he drank too much. And, yes, I agree, he was my dad and I did love him anyway.

A jolt now, the phone ringing from the kitchen, Louella bolt upright in the reclining swivel chair, sniffling back tears. And who could that be. Mona? Momma's friend, calling about the card game and a reminder to bring the wine. But this Mona-lady knows, she must know Momma's dead. She was at the service, must have been, everyone was. Maybe it's Aunt Inga calling, but she only just left a while ago; Louella with ear cocked, hearing the answering machine switch on. Her mother's voice, "Sorry, unable to come to the phone right now." My god, dead Momma's voice, talking, here but not here. And noticing some of her old CDs mixed in with her mother's, shelved in the combination wall unit. This is strangely touching (is that the word?), makes one want to cry all over again, and the answering machine has clicked off, no message, thank Christ. And tip one's head back once again in the dark blue leather swivel chair, eyes to the ceiling and turning slowly, a welling up of feelings—grief—sorrow—pain—confusion—this ball (yes, it feels like a huge ball) of emotion, so big, so heavy and scary, it seems a small planet of its own and impossible to isolate any one source for it, any single target for regret or sadness. It just *is*. And one may not really be ready yet to find out how one's Momma lived, who and what she really had in her life. Who she was.

6.

Of Pushers and Great Schizoid Beasts

AS LOUELLA DEBRA POULE revolves slowly in her dead Momma's blue leather swivel recliner and finds it difficult to come to terms with all she doesn't know about her own mother's life, Constable Dusty Yorke of the North Vancouver RCMP struggles with her own mini-quandary of what she may not yet know about certain aspects of her own life, the professional part, not the personal.

"And so what's all this," she's saying to the desk sergeant, a finger flicking a piece of paper she holds in her hand. "Parking violations on Keith Road. 'Questionable persons' seen hanging around the SeaBus terminal—is there ever anyone hanging around the SeaBus terminal who isn't 'questionable'?"

"So, your point?" says the desk sergeant.

"My point is," says Dusty Yorke, "would we not be of more use to the general public if we were getting out and dealing with a little real crime now and then, like raiding the odd crack house or taking down some pushers . . ."

"Taking down? Pushers?" says the desk sergeant. "You mean *dealers*, maybe? This ain't the eighties, constable."

A dark look here from Constable Dusty Yorke, because, oh, but it *is* the eighties, so to speak, at least for rookie Constable Yorke. Rookie Constable Dusty Yorke, of a face reflecting the generic good looks that run compatible with society's accepted norms: the straight nose, the evenly aligned eyes, lips not too thin not too full, a face twenty-four years old that's been protected for the most part from the harsher elements of standard growing-up-ness and experience by her enthusiastic young parents *of* the eighties, for god's sake, well, until she turned eleven, when, of course, it all turned to the nineties. But to all who know her, it's definitely the influence of the eighties that has seemed to stick, or get stuck, in rookie Constable Dusty Yorke's impressionable psyche. Constable Yorke still liked much of the cultural detritus left over from the eighties— disco tunes, simplistic family sitcoms, and bebopping to the obscure pop sounds of bands like Fairground Attraction and The Bangles. She is often the victim of her own somewhat outdated jargon, saying things like "Let's get it on" or "Let's do our thing," when getting out of the car to serve a traffic citation. Her much-older partner and department-appointed mentor, Marv Klep, tolerates the younger Yorke's idiosyncrasies, having cultivated a broader scope of just general acceptance glommed from years of serving the great schizoid beast called *the public* as a law enforcement officer and having from simple necessity been forced to modify and expand his general tolerance level of human behaviour in almost every category barring that which would be considered intrinsically dangerous or exploitive to women and children. No, if anything, Marv Klep would describe his younger partner's temperament as *evolving*, albeit a bit of the *hair-trigger type*, a term in itself more akin to the 1880s than the 1980s. Easily excitable and leaning more toward the masculine than feminine in some areas, that would be Officer Kleb's temporary assessment of said subject, having often witnessed the somewhat overly stern, by-the-book reprimand to offenders of the law by the young Constable Yorke when writing out no more than a simple speeding ticket, one watching as the victimized driver's eyes begin to glaze over, head nodding absently, a driver who is no doubt thinking silent thoughts like: *"Please, God, give me the strength to not say something inappropriate to this dickhead lady police officer so I can just be on my way."*

Marv Klep is also aware that one might easily enough jump to the conclusion that his youthful partner's tendency to excitability could be a liability in certain high-risk law enforcement situations, but he has managed (after much serious consideration) to reconcile himself to the belief that it is simply a stab at self-esteem, however superficial, that may even be conducive to helping keep his younger partner on an even, if not somewhat militaristic, keel. It was with a gung-ho Constable Dusty Yorke fresh from the academy and just newly assigned that this belief was (in Officer Klep's mind at any rate) corroborated when they had been on routine patrol and found themselves in a situation where they were forced to draw their weapons and issue a warning to a couple of B&E suspects, an eager Dusty Yorke springing into action and hollering, simply, *"Freeze, scumbags, or I'll blow your fucking blaines out!"* The scumbags did indeed "freeze" as directed and were taken into custody without incident.

It was only later, while debriefing over coffee, that Marv pointed out the only telltale sign that Dusty Yorke had been highly excited during the incident, mentioning to his partner her reference to *blaines* in the heat of the moment.

"I didn't say that," Dusty Yorke had replied.

"Yes, you did," said Marv Klep. "It's not a big thing."

"It's not a big thing because I didn't say it," says Dusty Yorke.

"Well, you did."

"Did not."

And, as Marv Klep soon learns, this is to become the standard closing exchange that signals the end of many of their conversations. He is also aware that he can accept the chronic verbal denial from the young constable as long as his suggestions are attended to and mistakes are corrected, however grudgingly. He also feels that the fact that Constable Yorke is female explains a lot, as it's been his experience (twenty-three years married and well primed with his own bias) that women in general aspire, in most situations, to have the last word, and, as if needing any proof of the pudding, in the North Vancouver RCMP station that morning Constable Dusty Yorke taps a painted fingernail on the missive advising assignments pertaining to parking violations and questionable persons hanging about at the SeaBus terminal as Marv Klep gulps the rest of his coffee and heads for the door.

"Well, let's go, Dusty. And don't forget to gear up, like happened yesterday."

"I did gear up," says Dusty Yorke.

"Well, there were a few things . . ." says Marv Klep.

"There was not," says Dusty Yorke.

"Well, there was. No big deal."

"Nope."

"Yup."

"Wasn't," says Dusty Yorke.

7.

Headlong Impacts

AS THE TWO North Vancouver RCMP police officers begin their day and close out another of their conversations in familiar agonistic fashion, Vancouver Police Department plainclothes officers Ruben Gerald McFadden (a.k.a. the Mick) and Peter Manfred Rourke (a.k.a. the Cuban) begin theirs by stealing perhaps a little musical tradition from the Scots as opposed to their own Irish folk, as one, so to speak, takes the high road and the other takes the low in a foot pursuit through the upper east side of Vancouver.

As things have happened, Jimmy Flood has taken flight on foot up the alley from the house on St. Catherines Street, heading west toward Fraser Street as fast as his strung-out junkie legs can carry him. The Cuban has taken to East Eighth Avenue to try to head him off, the high road just south of the alley, while the Mick has taken East Seventh Avenue, the low road north of the alley, with the same aim in mind. A third plainclothes narc, Garth Barnes (of obscure Swedish descent, it's said, and some twelfth- or thirteenth-generation tie to a tribe of Vikings whose only claim to somewhat modest notoriety, ironically enough, was the pillaging of the actual Irish some seven hundred years ago), has taken up the position of rearguard, pursuing the fleeing Jimmy Flood directly up the alley, trying to keep him in sight.

And as all four hoof it west by separate routes and at slightly different speeds, back at the house on St. Catherines Street, Blacky Harbottle is leaving by his own preferred route and speed by the back door, bounding through the mile-high grass of the never-tended back lawn and luckily (once again) unnoticed or just plain forgotten by the three plainclothes cops who were just there banging at the front door and trying to kick the fucker down, and just there when Jimmy

Flood, as Jimmy Flood so often did when this situation presented itself, panicked and leapt out the side living room window into the alley and took it on the lam, attracting the three cops' attention and causing them to give chase. This distraction allows Blacky to grab his stash of drugs from the temporary hiding place in his backyard and hightail it out the back gate in the opposite direction, as he does, intent only on reaching the abandoned garage a few doors down where he keeps his permanent stash.

One of the secrets of fleeing the house on St. Catherines Street, he knows from having had to flee the premises many times, is to never flee in a northeasterly direction toward the corner of Seventh and St. Catherines, as one's instincts may lead one to do, the impulse being to make for the park situated there because it's all downhill and would seem an easier getaway. But this park, he knows, affords little to no cover, open space with but a few aging trees spaced here and there, and the beginning of the park is no more than a steeply pitched grassy hill that leads down to playing fields below, a slick, steeply pitched grassy slope where one can only gain momentum and end up invariably sprawled on one's face at the bottom. Many an unfortunate cohort has taken this path only to be busted anyway, face scraped raw along the stony and barren grasses at the bottom of the hill, the subject generally spread-eagled and semi-conscious from the sheer violence of the inevitable headlong impact.

So, while Blacky Harbottle trots the few doors east, Jimmy Flood gains Prince Albert Street to the west, crosses in a full sprint, and continues his romp up the alley. Moments later the Cuban crosses Prince Albert to the south, and the Mick can be seen in a dead heat with him crossing Prince Albert to the north. A slower but equally game Officer Barnes maintains a dogged pursuit up the alley, their quarry still in his sight. Jimmy Flood knows he's got three blocks to make a decision whereupon by the end of those three blocks he will have reached another park, Guelph Park, and like the park at the corner of Seventh and St. Catherines, Guelph Park affords little cover, sporting a lot of open ground.

His sneakers slap their way across Fraser Street, then Carolina, a quick look back and seeing the single plainclothes cop toiling some distance behind down the alley. St. George Street coming up, now's the time to make a move. And over a fence into a thickly tangled backyard where he knows there's a crawl space, there, between the side fence and small gardening shed. Can sit tight and stash the small amount of cocaine he has on him, wait for the cop in the alley to pass by. All three cops should then meet on St. George Street, realize they've lost him, and double back. One has only a short high-risk time to have to lay low, then one can stick to the cover of the backyards and begin heading west again, avoiding the park, and surfacing safely several blocks farther west.

As predicted, the Cuban, the Mick, and Officer Barnes do all meet on St. George Street, stopping to get a breath, bending over and supporting themselves with their hands propped on their knees.

"Lost him," says Officer Barnes.

"Maybe, maybe not," gasps the Mick.

"By all the dead and sufferin' saints, as my dear mother would say," says the Cuban. "But I don't see the little bastard."

"Look around?" says the Mick.

The Cuban straightens, rotates his head left, then right.

"Forget it. Our little Jimmy the blow job seems to be once more in the wind," says the Cuban. "But he'll be served up again in no time soon, mind ya. I'm sure of that. Like death and taxes is our dear little Jimmy."

Garth Barnes keeps silent, unable to speak anyway and trying to catch his breath. He has been privy to the scuttlebutt around the station that this chase scenario between the two narcs and one Jimmy Flood has been enacted countless times before and will no doubt be enacted countless times again. There is a strong consensus among his fellow officers that the obsession of the two narcs with Mr. Flood makes no practical sense to anyone except perhaps the two of them, Jimmy Flood being thought of, in a criminal sense, as a person of little or no real consequence.

"Let's get some breakfast," says the Cuban.

"Breakfast?" says Garth Barnes (it's two thirty in the afternoon).

"What, you ain't been up all night, Barnes?" says the Cuban. "What fuckin' kinda plainclothes shift you used to workin', huh?"

"That little pecker can sure run when the fear of God's in 'im," says the Mick.

"That's fer sure, Mr. McFadden," says the Cuban.

They turn and head back along the alleyway.

The Mick breaks into song.

He sings:

"*Casey wore his brand new hat to Murphy's wake last night.*
Someone stole his hat and, lo, it started up a fight . . ."

"*Heyho!*" adds the Cuban.

8.

Of Smiles and Introductions

LOUELLA DEBRA POULE sits at dead Momma's circular white kitchen table. Open in front of her, dead Momma's book, *The Complete Home Gardener.*

She reads:

1) Air Needs of Plants—Plants, like all living things, make certain demands on their surroundings . . .

SHE HAS SURVIVED a week, a week alone in dead Momma's townhouse. A week of solitude for the most part, although she did, on the third day, brave a walk over the bluff and down into the small village complex that forms the Cove. She had scouted the directory and found an evening 12-step meeting in the Cove, a small realtor's office above a store that one of the attendees makes available for a meeting once a week. Just inside the office door a small group of people. And greeting her with smiles and introductions, her nerves somewhat assuaged when told she would not be asked to share at the meeting if she didn't wish to. She did decline to speak during the meeting but mingled a little nervously with the group for a coffee following, figuring in all honesty she had no place better to go. Although she has been clean of drugs (barring the odd hit of Momma's discovered vodka) for close to eight months now (she had managed to get and stay clean during her stint in jail and had attended 12-step meetings while inside), prison counsellor Jane had recommended she continue attending 12-step meetings when she got out as part of a healthy, proactive routine, and, although she didn't usually want to go to meetings in the first place, she always felt surprisingly good after them. And it will forever strike her as completely nonsensical but so typical of the general craziness of addiction that, when one is on the street, one feels perfectly at ease entering the downtown bars, sleazebag hotels, and countless unlit alleyways to associate with people who would probably prefer to rob you or even kill you more than anything else, while, at the opposite end, one can conjure up such anxiety and fear over attending a gathering of well-meaning individuals whose only agenda is to wish one happiness and success.

In fact, Louella feels so good after this first little meeting in the Cove, the following day she ventures out with no intention of actually going anywhere, but just going. A childlike tingling of discovery as she follows a narrow path that leads over a small wooden bridge at the south edge of a large grassy playing field just down the road from Momma's townhouse. The path winding into the woods, past wide-leafed ferns, through thick mats of moss and lichen of the most intense greens she's ever seen. The path then widening again, the undergrowth thinning and gnarled mounds of fungus hanging white off the trunks of trees.

And now treading past more fans of green, damp and dripping from an early morning shower, nondescript bundles of sharp, pointed leaves tugging for the light on long and tangled vines, the forest floor a dark brown, soft underfoot, amass with dead and dying leaves, seeds, pine needles, and whatnot, and everything would have a name, she thinks, a history, plant or not, but she's also aware that it doesn't really matter what anything's called as she would know none of the names of these things anyway, none of the histories. A sudden feeling of ignorance, *dummyness*, under the tall trees, a person misplaced, trespassing. It seems one has never bothered to really look at things, never been interested.

The trail winds left, undulates over thick earthbound roots that channel their way outward from the bases of these wide-girthed trees, pines maybe, firs and cedars, and, again, whatnot. One is not sure of the names, one has no idea of the names but Momma would've known. Momma would have known what these small yellow flowers that are clumped over and around a rotten stump are called. Maybe they're weeds, maybe not. And do "weeds" exist in the wild, thinks Louella, like, in the natural habitat, or is the concept of weeds, the unwanted, only pertinent in the context of "gardens," the picking and choosing of what grows where, keeping everything under control? And, Christ, what thoughts arising from nowhere while one just takes a simple walk through the woods. Does this happen to everybody?

A dip, the pathway curling down, washboard effect of gnarly underground roots zigging their way across the forest floor to disappear under thick clumps of more green leaves and stuff. Bushes? Or thickets? They, too, will have a name, and pervading everything— the smell. Sweet. Acrid. Of what? Growth? Decay? Doesn't matter, really, and wander on along this path, and veering suddenly upward and to the right. A stumble over an unseen root while staring upward at the high shadowed undersides of trees. A bird screeching, can't be seen but sounds like a crow. Or a jay, maybe—my god—how does one learn the names of all these things?

The path climbing steeply out from cool, moist air into sunlight, the roadway suddenly there, black pavement that one crosses to stand on a small spit of land, swamp grass reaching up to one's thigh tops, and waving wildly in the breeze, and one stands a moment as the water of the inlet shimmers, wind blowing ocean smell—salt, shell, fish scales, and seaweed rot—and how far that short fucking path seems to have taken one away from, well, everything.

"It's all so, well, weird," she will tell Alcina over the phone.

"It's all so, well, normal," says Alcina. "It's what they call *normal*. I'm coming out."

"Don't bring any dope."

"Honey, please. I'm not fucking stupid."

"Don't tell anyone where I am."

"Don't you be stupid."

"I mean it, Alcina."

"So fucking do I, honey."

9.

Petersville Slugger

LOUELLA PREPARES TO ANSWER the front door. The question arises, even to Louella: "What sort of 'preparation' could possibly be needed to answer a freaking door?" And there seems no succinct, clear answer to this question, no rational explanation. It depends on many variables, the foremost being, of what is the past and present state of the answerer, in this case one who has been out of touch with performing the commonplace for so long that most actions are no longer customary, let alone spontaneous; no longer in tune with any conventional demands that may be imposed by the most obvious and simple of social stimulus.

So, in this case, the "preparation" begins with a hurried look into dead Momma's front-hallway walk-in closet with folding mirrored doors, the doors open, and who can know what makes one take this moment of all moments for a look-see. Inside the closet this string of dead Momma's coats and some outdoor sweaters dangling from a chrome tube rack, a small sticker on the chrome tubing at eye level as one leans close to read: "Strong, durable, lightweight ABS plastic brackets, CMHC-approved and consumer-tested for more than 5 years; Modular design to fit every new and existing closet . . ." and one is strangely reassured that if this much fuss and attention goes into the making of closet racks, maybe the world is a safer place than one has been believing. And there, below on the closet floor, a thousand shoes and a couple of pairs of boots, high-cut and low-cut. And here, propped in the back corner deep in shadow under the coats, a baseball bat. Momma was careful, and by the heft of this bat, she meant business.

Louella now, fingers of one hand opening the thin iron grate covering the peephole in the front door, fingers of the other hand curled around the reassuring shaft of this Petersville Slugger (what the label on the baseball bat says). And looking through a fish-eye lens effect that presents the outside world in a full circle of itself, at the bottom of the circle, barely visible, the top of a straw hat.

"Who is it?"

Louella controlling her voice, keeping it light, unassuming (she hopes), her own rendition of what someone might sound like who lives in this area and deserves to live here. And images of Jimmy Flood, Blacky Harbottle, Ginger Baumgartner, or any of the five hundred or so other junkie fucking nutcases that one has been hanging around with for the last ten years. And how the hell would they know where one has wound up after one's Momma's died and left everything in her only daughter's name, and is this straw hat, in fact, sitting on the fucked-up head of someone who's strung out and drug-sick and real mad and real dangerous, someone that one has ripped off some forgotten time ago and who's tracked her down and now wants to collect? And just who does one know from the street who would actually wear a straw hat as one tightens one's grip on this baseball bat and will unlatch nothing until identity and intent have been determined.

A voice: "It's okay. It's me, Mona Rose . . . live next door and a friend of your mother's."

Mona, Mona of the note on the fridge, possible dew on her shoes, "*Bring the wine . . .*" Mona, who was or wasn't at Momma's funeral, and Louella unlatching the latch, drawing the bolt. The door opening, and one can't help but feel a little embarrassed by what must appear to be one's obvious highly paranoid state.

"Hi."

"Louella, how are you?" the straw hat entering the hallway, moving by. An impression of sunglasses, pink or orange tint. And white jogging pants on a slim frame.

"How are you making out? Sorry I haven't been over sooner but I've been out of town. My own mother is in a home in Kelowna, of all places, and I was obliged to tool up there last week to take care of some legal problems. I've got a brother who lives there but he's quite useless and mother refuses to move here, so . . . Well, family's family and all that."

And one Mona Rose moves on into the kitchen, casserole dish with blue and green fish painted on its sides set down on dead Momma's circular white table, Louella following along, unsure as to expected protocol. While serving her time, manners were a hindrance if anything. And before that, with the crowd she ran with, they were practically non-existent. She makes for the counter.

"Coffee?" she says.

Mona with a warm smile, shaking her head.

"No, thanks. I'm pretty buzzed as it is. I'll just stay a minute."

They sit at the circular white table. Outside, evening settles, a dull pink glow in the sky.

"Your mother and I spent a lot of nights like this, sitting here. We were akin to many things. She didn't smoke, though. You know that, but she never minded I did. You smoke? Great, have one of mine."

Louella lighting a cigarette, looking at the casserole dish.

"Chipotle chicken and pintos with Spanish rice. Hope you like spicy."

Louella nodding, "I do. Thanks."

"Should be enough there for two, maybe three meals. I know that you're probably not much for cooking at a time like this. But you got to eat, even if it doesn't really matter what, eh? Rest and digest. When my father passed that's all I did for three weeks. One-dish meals and sleeping in-between. I alternated between Hungarian goulash served over spaetzles and straight in-your-face chuckwagon stew."

Mona Rose leaning back, a creak from the black-lacquered, steel-frame chair. The fridge hums. Mona looks around the kitchen.

"I've always liked your mother's taste, Louella, especially the plants. I love plants. Herd, my husband, he doesn't like plants in the house. He says they 'affect' him. Herd is very vague. Things 'affect' him. Me being over here right now is probably 'affecting' him. Well, what can you do. Can't just haul out a gun and shoot them every time they're annoying. That was something your mom and I had in common. What you might call 'man troubles.' But 'troubles' sounded too much like something we couldn't, or weren't supposed to be able to, handle. So we just called it 'stuff.' Oh, yes, she had her share of 'stuff,' your mom. You don't mind me talking about her? Sometimes I don't think, put my foot in it, don't you know. Yes, I felt bad for your mother, all she had going for her, but not lucky in her men friends. Not that there were many, but those there were all seemed to be pretty much the same . . . nice as pie for a while, then *kapowie*, jigs up, and, 'I am now going to turn into an asshole and slap you upside the head a few times. I will then drink a fishbowl of whisky and refuse to leave without a long drawn-out scene which will invariably end in me crying and blubbering and saying something like, 'I love you, you bitch, and the next time I see you I hope you've suffered like you're making me suffer and I hope you die before I do.'"

Louella laughs, surprising herself.

Mona looks pleased.

"Jeez, but I do go on," says Mona. "But plenty of time for that later. I'll be around and let me know if you need anything. You're okay?"

And Louella is okay, or feeling better anyway. And this, too, surprises her.

Mona leaves, back to her husband who is "affected" by things. And one believes that Mona mentioned she has a son, too, a Herd Junior, one supposes, aged somewhere in the early teens. And the whole thing wasn't half bad, the impromptu visit, hearing things about Momma. Yes, that was okay. Adjustment. This must be what adjustment is, what prison counsellor Jane always talked about. Making Adjustments. Change. Doing Things Differently. And hearing things about Momma, Mona could do that. She could fill in the gaps, of which there appear to be many.

Louella Poule back at dead Momma's kitchen table, lighting another cigarette. Momma's book is still open on the table.

She reads:

2) Bottle Gardens—Once established, a bottle garden needs little more than warmth, light, and periodic inspection to see that all is well.

10

Black Hooker-Man-Freaking-Women

IT'S LOUELLA DEBRA POULE sunning herself, body stretched along one of dead Momma's folding lounge chairs on the small stone patio out back the day Alcina comes out. It's hot, but a light breeze does manage itself over the lattice-topped fence. She is not completely comfortable, however; this is not something one is used to doing, having run the streets for so many years. But one has noticed in the past week or so that tans seem the norm in the Cove. Brown faces and the pervasive scent of suntan oil accost one on visits down to the Cove. One should attempt to have some colour, anyway, to at least blend in.

One sports a two-piece bathing suit, red, found among dead Momma's things, one's pasty, white body liberally coated with sunscreen, eyes closed behind a pair of large dark sunglasses. It's quiet, a weekday, so there's none of the usual clamour of the weekend rituals of lawn mowers, power tools, and screaming kids. Instead, birds can be heard chirping, insects buzzing. The languid drone of an airplane from somewhere over the inlet. And another sound, felt more than heard. Subtle, a slight creaking of wood, perhaps. A faint scrape, a short brush of something against something. Then silence, one's eyes open but obscured behind the sunglasses. And peering down the length of one's body to focus between one's toes. A short, green hedge spied running along the base of Momma's lattice-topped cedar fence. And above the hedge, there through a tiny gap in the slats of the fence, one beady eyeball. *Jesus-H-Christ*, can only be the roly-poly eyeball of roly-poly Herd Rose Junior, who goes by the unhappy name of Shamus. And staring right up one's crotch.

She doesn't move.

What to do? The poor kid is the son of Herd Rose Senior, and from what she's heard about Herd Rose, it must surely allow for a certain level of understanding and tolerance for poor Shamus just for being raised by the guy. But he's also a young, overweight teenager and probably not all that popular and because of these conditions he's bound to do plenty of idiotic things that aren't even the fault of being raised by Herd Rose. All the same, knowing that a beady little eyeball is focused where it's focused is unnerving if not downright grunge-feeling, the suntanning gig taking on a sordid aura. Best to nip it in the bud, maybe.

"Hey, Shamus! Get your fat ass away from here! Spy on me again and I tell your mother. Got it?"

A shuffling sound. Then silence. The beady eyeball gone and Louella once again ready to do the suntanning thing, eyes momentarily raised behind the sunglasses to a window above in Rose's townhouse next door, and there behind an upper window-pane, the shadowy, bald dome of Herd Rose seen darting out of sight. And, oh, lord—girl, close your legs, the joke's over. Like father, like son. Christ, a feeding frenzy of dink-asses, old and young. One may forgive Shamus the younger, poor goofy kid, but will cultivate a wary dislike of Herd the older, degenerate. And one has found at least a baseball bat in dead Momma's front-hall walk-in closet with folding mirrored doors, and one no longer has to wonder what it was for. Momma was careful. "Man stuff," Mona had said. And Poppa himself would have been part of that "stuff," still clear childhood memories of those arguments, sometimes furniture toppled, shards of a ceramic lamp with a pale grey base scattered along a dark green living room carpet. Then a rough hand pushing one out of the room and a door slamming shut that you stay behind hugging your dolls and whimpering cuz the box you're in feels like it's sinking through the floor and right into the ground while small fingers tug on the ear of a tear-wetted teddy bear cuz you can't figure out why anybody had you in the first place.

"You might think of a hobby when you get out," counsellor Jane had said. "Something enjoyable to occupy your time, and I stress the term *enjoyable*."

And so pertaining to enjoyable "things to do," it would seem that building up a decent supply of fatty foods in your dead Momma's fridge would be one. And don't phone anyone from the past if you want to make a change, and do not remove the four bottles of wine in the small wine rack in the living room as one doesn't yet know if they will be needed. The list of dos and don'ts goes on and on; nobody said it was going to be easy. And poor Mona next door with her husband, Herd, and wayward son, Shamus, to contend with, has visited almost every day for the last two weeks, bringing with her doughnuts and potato chips and various flavoured spring waters, at least providing some kind of window on the normal life, one guesses. Mona's bright orange nails tapping the circular white kitchen tabletop, and her voice describing a woman you never knew whose place you're now living in, a woman called your mother whose image flies by with the unpredictable, almost suicidal, flit of a barn swallow that swoops down from the shelter of trees and rooftops to skim the heads of short-cut grasses without touching them, always in flight and just an ill-defined blur to the naked eye.

ALCINA OMOJOLADE AJUNWA is black, transsexual, six feet and one-half inches tall, and has had her (his) boobs done but cannot yet afford the "full lower monty" for a sex-change operation. She arrives by cab wearing tight white pants, a white halter top, and gold-braided stiletto sandals with her arms bearing flowers, chocolates, and heartfelt condolences. Of Nigerian descent, he (well, she) has lived in Canada all his/her life. Born male but realizing in his late teens there had been a mistake (namely, he was a she, or wanted to be, the die was cast), and he has ever since pursued the necessary changes needed to make his transformation to "womanness" complete. His parents, at first shocked, outraged, frightened, and homicidal, gradually calmed down over time and have, apparently, accepted what God has given them, even allowing "Alan" to change his name, hence, "Alcina." They did insist, however, he keep a true Nigerian name from the Yoruba tribe (the tribe of their own families), and so his/her original middle name of *Shoyebi*, a male's name meaning "wizard ward off evil," became *Omojolade*, a female name meaning "child favoured by the king," a name that even Alcina felt did her justice.

And now a high-end hooker following a career launched on the streets of Toronto at the age of eighteen and then furthered on the streets of San Francisco and at present culminating as a respectable "escort" working the higher-end streets of Vancouver. Her parents may have accepted the change of gender but have not, and never will, accept the chosen lifestyle. And, as Alcina is often heard to remark, she maybe should have kept her original Yoruba name as one seldom seems to feel favoured but often enough does feel like one who is constantly having to ward off evil.

Stiletto heels click on Momma's kitchen tile.

"Good grief, but your mother appears to have gone ultra yuppy cool in her later years."

"Yes," says Louella. "I was a little surprised."

"There's a certain *o' de catalogue* feel about the place, but I like it. Are you drinking?"

"Booze, you mean?"

"Yes, love. You said no drugs but did that include liquor? I brought some Southern Cee. I hope that's okay."

"Well, Jesus. I don't know, really."

"We don't have to."

"Screw it. Let's have a drink. That'd be nice."

A bottle appearing from Alcina's shoulder bag, Louella reaching into the cupboard for glasses. With drinks poured they sit at dead Momma's circular white kitchen table, Alcina acknowledging the array of plants.

"Your mother had a green thumb?"

"I suppose so. Looks like she got into it in a big way. There are more in the living room. How's things with you?"

"Not too bad, actually. I feel like Valentina Tereshkova, I've been flying today. Business has been good of late. As proof I did take a cab out here, for god's sake. Who, who isn't filthy rich, can afford that? I escorted two quite fine gentlemen last night, both of whom paid a bundle for their pleasures, and there appear countless options for repeat performances. I think I'm experiencing job security of all things. Make hay while the sun shines, as the hard-working farmers say. Do farmers really say that, you think? I daresay one of these guys even offered me a job. I mean a *job,* job."

"Good, lord. Doing what?" says Louella.

"Some secretarial thing, I think. I declined, graciously. The poor boy. It just wouldn't work, you know. I'm just not 'fashioned' for that kind of shit, you think?"

"Yes, I think, Alcina."

While touring the upstairs, Alcina strikes a seductive pose on dead Momma's queen-sized bed in the master bedroom.

"It's a nice bed, but you do not sleep here, darling. The massive leather couch in the living room below, I suppose."

"How did you know?"

"Oh, old habits, love. I've done time, too, remember. I slept on the floor fully dressed for months when I got out. Gotta be ready for anything, you know. Although what that anything is, I never did figure out. Waiting for some kind of disaster at all times."

"I'm still trying to adjust to it all, I guess," says Louella.

"Yes," says Alcina. "Adjustment. I do know about that, dear heart. Have I recounted my return from hospital after getting my boobs done?"

"A hundred fucking times."

"And it never gets boring, does it? Ah, you laugh. That's good. Please don't talk to me about 'adjustment,' dearie. I'm doing it 24-7."

In the living room, Alcina reaches behind dark green leaves into the aquarium, scooping out the two dead, grey-white fish and depositing them into the base of a large potted plant.

"Excellent fertilizer, fish is. From death comes life, missy. You should get some more. Fish are very soothing to watch, but, alas, only when *alive*, honey."

Alcina spends the night as arranged.

"I'll make you some *obe ata*," says Alcina. "Pepper soup. I notice your mother has a well-stocked spice cupboard and even palm oil."

They camp out in the living room watching movies. Alcina makes popcorn while Louella hauls in more blankets and pillows. At one point Louella says, "I shouldn't be drinking, I don't think."

"Then don't, dear stupid," says Alcina.

They stay awake until dawn. They then sleep until noon when Alcina makes lunch: bacon and eggs, toast, orange juice, and coffee. A new note has appeared beside the Mona note on Momma's bulletin board in Alcina's handwriting:

Valentina Tereshkova—first woman to enter outer space.

Alcina stands at the kitchen sink in one of Louella's dead mother's robes, rinsing her plate and looking out the window.

"I spy with my little eye something that is bald."

"Oh, the husband of my neighbour I was telling you about."

"Ah. That's the one. Felt he undressed me twenty times while I came up the walk yesterday. And I still see him looking over here. If he only knew the truth, eh?"

Louella munching soft egg on toast.

"Like what?"

"Like what? Like who, or what, I really am, my sweet."

"And who, or what, would that be, my love?"

"You know what I mean. I remember a john a couple'a years ago, you know, just after my boob job. You knew me then. I was a lady in my mind but still with the guy paraphernalia, you know? And a lot of guys don't particularly like it when they find out, and some can become quite pissed, although what the big surprise is I've never quite figured out. I mean, surely it's obvious that at the very least I'm a guy in drag. Anyway, this one guy, well, he gets 'down there' and freaks completely out, starts shouting and crapping around, and Gerry comes in the door, you know, to deal with this guy, and the guy yells, 'Godfuckingzooks, man, get this black hooker-man-freaking-woman the fuck out of here! Now!'"

"He didn't say 'godfuckingzooks,' did he?"

"I believe he actually did, hon. I think the correct term is *gad*fuckingzooks, but this guy was highly stressed. Anyway, Gerry threw him out, calling the guy something that had the words *white*, *mother*, and *dickless* in it, I believe. Or something like that."

"Sounds like a *chawming* evening."

"Ummm, it was ripe with creative expression, at any rate. But the weird part of it all was that *I* felt bad! My feelings were actually hurt by that jerk-off. It was so stupid, feeling ashamed like I let this poor dickhead down or something. A john, for god's sake. Anyway, this guy, Herd's his name? He reminds me a bit of this guy, same build, same face, same slimeball *esthétique*. He may one day warrant a kick in the balls if this behaviour keeps up."

Louella wiping egg from her chin, nibbling the last piece of bacon.

"So, I take it today's not the day, then . . ."

"Darling, I hardly know the man. And I've just shocked myself. Sometimes my man side gets the better of me. This is no way for a lady to be talking—*You bitch! That the last of the bacon?*"

IT'S LATER THAT day Louella shoulders Alcina's bag as Alcina's heels click along the road over the bluff. They have decided to walk down into the Cove for a coffee and Alcina will take the bus from there. She refuses a ride back to Vancouver from Louella and the notion of taking a cab again with the claim that occasionally riding the buses keeps her honest and in touch with her working-class roots.

"*My daddy was a bushman . . .*" she sings.

Louella laughs.

The air is warm and heavy with the scent of spruce and pine.

"I love that smell," says Alcina. "And I repeat, I want you to know I'm here, sweetie. I'd stay on a bit, but I've got to get back to work. I should warn you, though, Jimmy's looking for you. That's something you probably don't need. But I'll call, will come out again. Make you more Nigerian food, some *chidis' igbo* stew. It's nice out here, bit boring, maybe, but that might be a good thing. I, myself, seek creative boredom, if there is such a thing. And masturbation is always allowed to relieve the humdrum. Ah, you laugh. That's good. Good neighbours true, that's what we be, love."

Once back in dead Momma's kitchen, Louella notices another note in Alcina's handwriting tacked to Momma's bulletin board:

1917—Women textile workers start the Russian Revolution.

LOUELLA WOULD HAVE preferred not hearing anything about Jimmy Flood and she told Aunt Inga so.

"I don't pretend to know a lot of what's been going on with you, Louella," says Aunt Inga. "Your mother only told me so much. I suppose she talked to someone about it all, and even though she was my sister, we didn't share a lot of intimate things. And, of course, she could never talk to your father when he was around. And I will say, dear, that I haven't approved of a lot of your choices over the last years, not the least being some of the people you've hung around with. But, then again, who would? Would you, even, if you stood away and watched the tableau? Look where you ended up. As for mistakes, good lord, we all make them, so who am I to talk. Look at my relationship with your late uncle Bobby. We were always incompatible and he always so loved his old boys' clubs."

"And little girls," says Louella.

"Yes, that was a terrible thing, Louella, terrible. And I never forgave him for that, you know. It took real courage for you to tell us what he was trying to do with you."

"Well, you stayed with him," says Louella.

"Yes, I did, and maybe I should have had my head examined. And there was the money, I won't deny that. I wanted to take him for every penny, love. He owed you, me, and the whole family that much."

"Well, it doesn't matter now," says Louella.

"Oh, but it does matter, Louella," Aunt Inga says back. "It matters a great deal. These kinds of things always matter. The only problem is what to do about them. And I want you to know that, as far as you're concerned, I've never judged you, even after you went to jail. Like I say, who am I to say anything about anybody. I will say, though, I don't think you should see this Jimmy person or any other people from that part of your life. You have a chance to change all that now."

"Yes, I know."

"Do you know what happened to your uncle Bobby after he tried that with you, by the way?"

"Well, he died soon after," says Louella. "And that seemed to be the end of it."

"I swore your mother to secrecy, when she began talking to me again. I considered filing charges myself, you know, against your uncle, but my attorney said it would be extremely difficult to prove anything under the circumstances, and it would be even worse for you to go through as a little girl like that. So, I then began to think of something physical, you know, hire someone to break Bobby's legs or throw acid in his face. I believe I went a little crazy, and I remember thinking, 'Good, god, Inga girl, have there ever been gangsters in the family tree because you're sure thinking like one.' I was drinking a lot, too, then. Took sedatives, pulled my hair out very dramatically, and while very drunk I *think* I *did* call someone to do something nasty to your uncle Bobby . . ."

"You think? *Something*?"

"Like I say, I was drinking a lot, very upset about the whole thing. Anyway, whether I did anything or not, none of us will ever really know. I do know there was a sizable cash withdrawal taken out by me from my account around that time and I've never been able to track down what I did with it. All that anyone knows for sure is that Uncle Bobby died of undetermined medical complications following a somewhat semi-suspicious tumble down the stone steps on the breakwater."

"Thank you, Aunt Inga," says Louella.

Aunt Inga cries a little. Louella waits.

"You're welcome, dear," says Aunt Inga.

II.

Of Middle-Class Facades

CONSTABLE DUSTY YORKE sits in her police car by the side of the road on the bluff above the Cove. A thick mantle of cloud rolls slowly down from Seymour Mountain. Soon it will engulf the bluff, engulf the Cove. A slight drizzle glistens off the windshield.

Constable Dusty Yorke will often sit in her police car by the side of a road in the Cove, changing location with each sitting, recon-noitring. A sense of excitement is apparent, an anxious vigilance, although it may appear to anyone passing by that nothing remark-able is going on. But for Constable Dusty Yorke, there runs a deep-seated conviction that beneath the Cove's outwardly pristine, middle-class facade, a darker world endures, a darker world bound to illegal drug trade and taking the form of high-end crack houses and, even more sinister, meth labs. And although her suspicions seem for the most part unfounded to most of her law enforcement colleagues, it has become somewhat of an obsession, the presence of a clandestine drug industry thriving in the Cove. This obsession, although fuelled by a genuine desire to do good for the community (why else make the leap into law enforcement?), is also fuelled by a genuine desire, want, need, to simply do something substantial as opposed to busting small-time criminals stealing bicycles or even the occasional grow op. (These babies, she has found, are a dime a dozen all over the Lower Mainland.)

Yes, bringing down a real hard-core drug ring would be quite a fine thing, the cat's freaking meow; an actual meth lab, complete with booby traps, would be the ultimate. An operation that would lead to the downfall, like a row of dominoes, of an international (or one would even settle for a national) trafficking network. And the Cove is the ideal area to set one up, oh yeah, with its hidden drives and forested pathways and the general wiggly-piggly layout of the place that makes any serious attempts at surveillance pretty well impossible. The roads follow the craggy, rough shoreline landscape they're built on, snaking their way up, down, and all around granite outcroppings, sides of cliffs, thicket-choked ravines, and lichen-shrouded stone bluffs, with driveways climbing steeply off the main road and meandering upward through dark forest to disappear somewhere at a residence perched high and unseen through the trees and virtually impossible to survey from any decent vantage point. Anything could be going on in these places.

The cloud has now rolled down and around and off the bluff. Constable Dusty Yorke is able to make out only vague grey shapes through the front windshield. A dog shape trotting out of a clump of bush on one side of the road and moving with nose to the ground to disappear somewhere on the other. A grey car passing, brake lights coming on as it stops for someone to cross the road ahead, the dark silhouette of the pedestrian waving the car on, then crossing and following the road over the bluff down toward the Cove. A female, one can tell by the walk, with a slight build but fairly tall. Shoulder-length hair, dark, can tell even in this fog, Constable Dusty Yorke honing her senses of observation, one never knows on this job when the memory of seemingly unimportant details can make or break an investigation. Who knows, maybe this chick is heading to a crack house right now. Maybe she's heading home to her very own meth lab, cool as a cucumber at the sight of the police car. (Oh, she noticed, you can bet on that.) Then again, maybe not. But a helluva night for a stroll, one would think . . .

SO, HOW IT WORKS: The truth is Louella has noticed the police car. She sees it parked by the side of the road as she waves the other car by and crosses the road herself. And she does have a reaction, although Constable Yorke is mistaken about the "cucumber" thing. Quite the contrary, Louella Debra Poule is immediately awash in a wave of paranoia, a tingle of fear spiralling up from her feet and seeming to spin off through the top of her scalp. Logic says she has nothing to fear, it's not about her. Old habit says, Why the fuck me and what have I done now? *Oh, god, oh, lord, shit and destruction.* She is doing nothing, nothing wrong that is, just heading to a 12-step meeting down in the Cove, hardly a fucking crime (she tells herself).

She walks on, the shadow of the police car temporarily disappearing behind her in the low-lying cloud.

SO, HOW IT WORKS: Constable Dusty Yorke has no idea there's anything like a 12-step meeting in the Cove. The fairly tall, slightly built silhouette with dark hair who has disappeared up the road into the mist may or may not be intent on criminal undertakings. Experience-wise, Constable Dusty Yorke has not that much to draw on, hence, the supposition that most often comes to the fore is that anyone appearing even a little out of the ordinary is most likely somehow up to no good, so eagerly does one dream the rookie dream of that big bust in the sky.

She puts the car in gear, white plumes of fog curling around the headlight beams. Christ, that cloud's really moved in, visibility must be no more than ten feet max. And letting the car roll slowly on to where the road right-angles and narrows to one lane, blacktop cracked with rough fissures and dropping steeply, gnarled and bowed more like the bottom of a high mountain ravine than a road. And ahead, appearing out of the fog-bound furls reflecting off the headlights, that slim frame in silhouette with dark hair walking, jeans and a leather jacket and a quick glance over its shoulder at the coming lights, squeezing over to the edge of the road to let the car go by. Constable Dusty Yorke stopping the car, window rolling down, and damp night air felt against her cheek.

"ID, please?"

The tall but slight frame bending forward, Louella reaching into her jacket pocket. ID produced and handed over, Constable Dusty Yorke taking a look . . .

Louella Debra Poule, DOB 02/10/78.

"That your real name?"

"Huh?" says Louella.

"This your real name?"

"Um. Yeah. I—"

"Where you off to?"

"Down to the Cove."

"Cove, huh?"

"Is there a problem, officer?"

"No, not really. Routine check. Been some . . . things going on."

"Oh . . ."

"Yeah. Things. Not important. You live around here?"

"Um, yes . . ."

And there it was, the question, wham, coming right out of the evening fog. A common-enough question asked by cops doing routine checks; one must have been asked it a thousand times over the last few years. But this time it's different, she hasn't paid any attention to if she is actually *living* in the Cove, in dead Momma's townhouse. *Crashing* has been the terminology to describe one's living situation until now, a month here, a few months there. Nobody, except maybe Blacky Harbottle, who through some inheritance thing actually owns and lives in the house on St. Catherines Street, but no one she's hung with could actually be said to *live* anywhere. A place of residence? No, the scenario's always been something more like: "You live here or just crashing?" "Just crashing—*you think I'd fucking live here?*"

And an impromptu slide show commencing in Louella's mind and burrowing out through the night fog of the Cove, image after image of rooms: green ones, beige ones, maroon and burnt umber ones, piss-coloured ones, ones with windows and ones not with windows, pigeon-shit-streamed glass, black grime along sills and ledges and crushed and misshapen couches, settees, and divans, sometimes an actual bed but mostly just mattresses flattened on sticky, paint-peeled floors, wood slivers picked up just under the skin from lying along unfinished boards, lacquer worn thin by the endless traffic of gummy feet, and piss-coloured sinks and toilets,

piss-coloured curtains, dishes, lampshades, and piss-coloured cig-
arette-burned wash towels and underwear and piss-coloured bugs
and piss-coloured fleabag hotel night clerks—

"Okay . . . have a good night."

The female cop handing back her ID, Louella watching the police
car disappear into the fog, tail lights bouncing to the uneven rolls
of the road. And she is here, night falling by the side of the road in
Deep Cove. Deep Cove, it's here where she lives—*resides.*

Home? Well, she ain't crashing, but dead Momma's townhouse
with no piss-coloured anything in it, come and go as you please,
no matter what happens, dead Momma's place is there. It's where
you live, baby, one's abode, one's Place of Residence.

And one's feet are moving again, each step feeling a little more
rooted to the ground, a little more rooted to this narrow road
leading down to the Cove. And going to a meeting, yes, ma'am,
thick mother fog and the meeting's down *there,* and one lives *back
there,* by golly. No immediate change of address, an address one
might even want to commit to memory. Home may just be a place
where the dink-asses aren't, one guesses. No surprises when
opening the door, no one asking to crash, hide out, get a fix or a
loan. And things just might turn out okay, just might. And speaking
of "things," just what "things going on" could that lady cop have
been talking about, one supposes. Bad things? In the Cove? Cove
Crime, what would that look like? Computer fraud. Pirating cable,
maybe. Can see the occasional family murder-suicide of a bankrupt
retired couple or a bankrupt up-and-coming couple. But real bad
things, hard-core criminal things, that's hard to imagine. And one
senses that a part of one is already starting to take an *interest* in
"things going on," things going on in one's *own* neighbourhood. A
concerned *homeowner,* and what the fuck is that feeling?
Gratitude? Relief? A feeling of reassurance knowing the authorities
are out and about, checking up on strangers wandering the
neighbourhood, keeping an eye on things, keeping an eye on *you,*
not to bust your ass but for your safety and well-being and the well-
being of your *property.*

And Louella Debra Poule walking the road down into the Cove, the fog since lifting but one's eyes are blurry anyway, tears coming at the thought of dead Momma and the lack of anything ever given her in return for, well, just being there. For just being a mother, and out of this feeling of loss comes...what? Gain? A chance? And blubbering her way on down the hill, scared, distraught, so stupid talking to one's dead Momma, saying, "Sorry, Momma. Sorry, sorry, sorry. And one can't be a citizen. One can't be a homeowner. Dear *Matilda Goomba*, one doesn't know how..."

12

Matilda Goomba

THREE-YEAR-OLD LOUELLA DEBRA POULE sits at the old Formica kitchen table, small forearms resting on the shiny, speckled orange surface, tiny chin resting on the backs of her hands, and her foot absently kicking one of the metal legs. She stares ahead at a plastic bottle of Mrs. Butterworth's syrup, the bottle moulded in the form of a portly grandma-type lady. A plate, now devoid of toast and with a bright red-and-yellow rooster painted on it, is pushed aside.

"Matilda," says three-year-old Louella Debra Poule, staring at the plastic bottle.

"Is that her name?" says Momma.

"Yes," says three-year-old Louella.

"When the honey's gone, do you want the bottle?" says Momma.

"Yes," says Louella Debra.

Three weeks later and after her fourth birthday, four-year-old Louella Debra Poule sits strapped in her car seat in the back seat of the family car. Poppa, who's been drinking, is driving.

Poppa swerves the car, hollers out the window—"Hey, Goomba! What the hell you doing?"

Louella likes that word.

Four-year-old Louella Debra Poule sits at the old Formica kitchen table, small forearms resting on the shiny, speckled orange surface, her tiny chin resting on the backs of her hands, and her foot absently kicking one of the metal legs. She stares ahead at a plastic bottle of Mrs. Butterworth's syrup, the bottle moulded in the form of a portly grandma-type lady and now almost empty.

"Matilda Goomba," says Louella.

"Oh, is that her name now?" says Momma.

"Yes," says Louella.

"That's a funny name," says Momma.

"Yes," giggles Louella.

Fifteen-year-old Louella Debra Poule sits stoned on LSD in the basement of a friend's house. It's her first "trip" and not much is happening. Then, sometime after thinking this, everything is happening. The carpet becomes water, the walls gelatin. The people in the room become deformed, the room itself a rubbery car on a roller coaster. Louella starts anxious, becomes terrified. Can't turn it off, and sinking back into the couch with toes curling, fists clenching. One can feel the appropriated arrogance and self-confidence of adolescence disintegrating like everything else. One feels the years slip away, and one is once again no more than a frightened little girl who cries and finds herself saying: "Matilda . . . Matilda Goomba . . . help . . ." And lo and behold, Matilda Goomba *does* help, or the mention of her name does, the room and its occupants returning almost to normal with just the odd filmy ripple occasionally making everyone look like they're under water, like dancing flames. It's a miracle, really, her anxiety completely gone, and she will find that whenever anxiety and panic threaten to overwhelm, a simple incantation to Matilda will usually send them packing.

For Louella Debra Poule, and not unlike so many countless others, the personification of a "God," or a Greater Power of sorts, is a personal condition and is sadly perhaps only brought into play when all human effort at last fails and all appears bleak and hopeless. From this day on, for Louella Debra Poule, this power will go by the name of *Matilda Goomba*. There is no rationale, no logic. Years later when deep into her heroin addiction Louella will often find it necessary to pray to something or someone to alleviate the pain and misery she's putting herself through, Matilda Goomba will be that someone or something, calming her soul, so to speak, easing anxiety and portents of doom, if only for a short time at least. And, although Louella keeps Matilda to herself, she does feel secure in her choice of guardian angel, for who can argue that the smiling image of a portly grandma-like lady, who's also shiny and the colour of honey, can be anything but a good thing for you?

13

Of Pink Cadillacs and Conditions of Residency

UNBEKNOWNST TO LOUELLA DEBRA POULE while incarcerated, ex-boyfriend Jimmy Flood becomes for a second time a resident at the house on St. Catherines Street in the upper east side of Vancouver, having worked some vague arrangement with Blacky Harbottle. When a couple, Louella and Jimmy had both resided for a time at the house on St. Catherines. The irony of the district's name, Mount Pleasant, was not lost on Louella even then; things were anything but, and she and Jimmy had been homeless for two weeks before negotiating an agreement of temporary tenancy with Blacky Harbottle. Blacky's hospitality had its limitations as they were to find, this hospitality being subject to Blacky's own set of house rules that could be made, or unmade, at any time.

These "Conditions of Residency," as Blacky Harbottle insisted on calling them with great solemnity, possibly to lend a more legal and formal tone to the arrangement, included, above all, the sharing of any drugs brought into the premises with the host himself, but not necessarily with any other guests who might be present at the time. (Drugs were not, under any circumstance, to be stashed in the house but were to be hidden outside somewhere, buried in the ground or hung in trees, Blacky Harbottle didn't care; just not *in* the house.) Also, none of the host's modest food supply was to be at any time consumed by guests or tenants; all were to supply their own sustenance. As for other necessities, like toilet paper, toothpaste, soap and/or shampoo, and so on (as Blacky so wistfully put it, "depending on how much of a pig you are"), it was for all individuals to supply their own.

"Simply put," Blacky Harbottle was to say in summing up, "expect nothing from me, take nothing from me, and give me ninety dollars a month. *Each.* Should all these conditions be met, it should be mutually beneficial to all."

"And give you all our drugs," said Jimmy Flood.

"*Share* with me all your drugs, if you're going to use here, that is," said Blacky Harbottle.

"Sounds okay to me," said Louella Poule.

"Sounds like bullshit to me," said Jimmy Flood.

"Sounds like a deal to me," said Blacky Harbottle, extending his hand, not to shake on the deal, but to begin the sharing of any drugs to be used on the premises, having noticed a flap of what could be cocaine or heroin hidden from view in Jimmy Flood's fist.

SO, HOW IT WORKS: In keeping with the fickleness and general ongoing chaos that accompanies a life subject to chronic drug use, while Louella Debra Poule does her time and then gets out and Jimmy Flood begs and receives shelter from Blacky Harbottle, enter unannounced and unexpected the Truman brothers, Butch and Gordy from Edmonton, Alberta, along with their girlfriends. The two brothers arrive at the house on St. Catherines on a bright, sunny day, replete in a 1959 bright pink (yes, pink) Cadillac convertible Coupe de Ville.

In the world of Blacky Harbottle, there are few friends but many associates. These associates can and will show up at any time, for any reason. It's a fact, though, that few in Blacky Harbottle's world take "trips." Any physical movement to other climes is generally motivated by things becoming uncomfortable where one is at the time (warrants, evictions, death threats), resulting in a need or simple desire to leave that particular place for one that is less uncomfortable. One exception to this rule may in fact be Butch Truman, who, it's been said, has often been motivated to change location solely on the advice provided him by self-interpretation of none other than his very own dreams, of which, it's been said, are many and totally incomprehensible to everyone but Butch Truman himself.

"What the fuck is this?" Blacky Harbottle is to say upon their arrival and eyeing the Cadillac. "A Hollywood movie?"

Gordy Truman, the older of the two brothers and the only one to have done time, two years in Kingston Pen in Ontario, wades through the high grass of the backyard of the house on St. Catherines Street to take a seat on the back steps.

"I've got fuck all to say at this point about any of this," says Gordy Truman, "except that it's always been Butch's dream to drive a pink Caddy to the West Coast with a blond by his side. And the miracle is, he's finally done it . . ."

And Butch's girlfriend is indeed blond, notices Blacky Harbottle, real name Tina Blout, but referred to by Butch as *Baby*. Butch, in turn, is referred to by Baby as *Daddy*, this exchange of personal endearments being immediately sickening and invidious to Blacky Harbottle, who can only commiserate with a sympathetic glance to Gordy Truman who's had to listen to it all the way from Edmonton. But for all that shit aside, for Blacky Harbottle and Jimmy Flood the sudden presence of Gordy Truman and his brother on the scene is not likely to make things any better or even just slightly worse, but most likely will manifest a playbook all its own that could well bring everyone's world tumbling down. And as living proof of Blacky Harbottle's and Jimmy Flood's possible cognizant abilities, it takes only two days in town for the tumbling to begin, tension between the two brothers coming to a head one evening when Gordy Truman ventures out from the motel room where the four of them have been staying to get something from the trunk of the Caddy, and there, taped in one-inch-wide blue trimming tape across the rear of the car are the words:

"We have to rent our own car," Gordy Truman says to Blacky Harbottle, his eyes conveying the message that there is no other option. "The fucking Caddy was a heat score in the first place but now it's just too much. You have ID, and I'll give you the deposit, and, of course, pay the tab. You have to help us out here, buddy. Sherry and me got to separate ourselves from those two."

Hesitant, but realizing that he himself wouldn't be caught dead riding around in a vintage pink Cadillac with Alberta licence plates, and especially when engaging in what are bound to be criminal activities like buying and selling dope, Blacky Harbottle agrees, arranging the rental of an innocuous dull silver Volkswagen Cabriolet.

"Perfect," says Gordy Truman. "We'll look like commuters."

"Thank Christ," says Sherry Kinsella, Gordy's girlfriend, who met Gordy at Kingston Pen while Gordy was doing time and she was working there as a nurse, and, just as fresh vegetation and life can spring up from the most desolate areas of the planet, then why, too, cannot true love blossom up from the tired desolation of an Ontario prison? So may say Sherry Kinsella in her own defence, and who after Gordy's release quits her job, gets hooked on heroin, then crack, and accompanies Gordy on a romantic journey across the country to Edmonton and now farther to the West Coast where they will spend every waking hour hustling around town in an effort to support both their hard-core drug habits.

"Just keep up the payments," says Blacky Harbottle.

"Not a problem," says Gordy Truman.

"It's better for everybody we ditch Butch and the bimbo," says Sherry Kinsella. "Better than ending up murdering them both."

"Let's hope so," says Blacky Harbottle, not fully convinced.

14.

Meagre Deerstone

LOUELLA PREPARES ONCE AGAIN to answer the door ("These peepholes in the door with the tiny iron grates are the greatest fucking invention in the world!"), and although one's paranoia of this new world one is now attempting to inhabit has somewhat lessened over the last few weeks, it's still strong enough to warrant at least some level of caution when greeting people on one's own doorstep. The only complaint may be that this peephole is set a bit too high. Again, one can only see the top of a head waiting outside. Not Mona's, no hat and the hair's darker, jet black but with a few streaks of grey. And standing close. A kid on a bike can be seen gliding by on the road behind.

Always ask: "Who is it?"

"It's Meagre."

And never allow one's self to feel like a complete cowardly idiot to ask the question again if in the slightest way one is not sure.

"Who?"

"Meagre, Meagre Deerstone. From the meeting. Friend of your mother."

And, oh, yeah. One remembers. Small native woman, attends the weekly 12-step meeting down in the Cove. Had stayed for coffee on the small office balcony after the last one. Didn't talk too much, lives close by, though. In the same complex, think that was it.

And then Meagre Deerstone, standing in the open doorway. Does not come in. Waits, something packaged in her hand.

"You like smoked salmon?"

Apparently Louella must have said yes, because Meagre Deerstone is now following her along the short hallway into the kitchen, Louella carrying the wrapped package, Meagre Deerstone sitting herself at dead Momma's circular white kitchen table and exuding a certain familiarity with the place apparent from her lack of hesitation. Louella over at the counter to make the coffee and misjudging the scoop over the filter, ground coffee spilling onto the counter and some on the floor. Meagre Deerstone smiling from dead Momma's circular white table, round brown face, black eyes. And watching Louella. She speaks softly.

"Not now. Later, maybe."

Louella turning, coffee grounds grinding under her bare toes.

"Pardon?" says Louella.

"Sorry. Was talking to my grandfather. It happens sometimes."

Louella looking for a cellphone, but Meagre Deerstone's hands are clasped in front of her on dead Momma's table.

"He's dead," says Meagre Deerstone. "But we still talk. Yes, I would like some coffee, thanks."

The black eyes of Meagre Deerstone, her hands moving now and leaving the top of dead Momma's white kitchen table and reaching down into a shoulder bag. Louella watching the bag.

"Mountain goat," says Meagre Deerstone. "Nice wool, eh?"

And Meagre's hands bringing forth from the folds of the bag a stone bowl and some small branches. Then setting the branches in the stone bowl, a cigarette lighter appearing, flame flickering and the branches lit. White smoke rising from the bowl over dead Momma's circular white kitchen table, Meagre Deerstone motioning to come sit, to come sit with the smoke.

"Used to do this with your mom quite often. You know she was interested in this stuff? Native stuff?"

Always be prepared to say "um" at any time when unsure of the answer.

"Um . . ." says Louella.

And now sitting herself on one of dead Momma's black tubular chairs, Meagre Deerstone pulling the smoke toward her chest with a cupped hand. And pushing the stone bowl across to Louella, dark eyes smiling, Louella uneasy, what the fuck was Momma getting into, but cupping her hand and doing what Meagre Deerstone had done, be polite, waving the white smoke toward her, the white smoke against her chest, rising under her chin and over her face, her hair, not acrid but a sweet smell, and white smoke curling up and along dead Momma's ceiling and around the hanging plants and furling above the kitchen sink and the lace curtains hung at the window.

"It's just a cleansing," says Meagre Deerstone. "Your mother said it brought her a peace of some kind. She liked doing it."

Louella nodding, Meagre Deerstone's hand once again fanning the smoke. No, not fanning, more like pulling. And one does feel a certain calm, a certain *solemninity*, if that's even a word. And can see Momma doing this, yeah, somehow a clear image of Momma, eyes closed under the hanging plants, sitting in the smoke at her circular white kitchen table.

"How you doing?"

Louella quick to answer, "I'm fine, actually. Fine."

Meagre Deerstone humming, or something. Not a tune, sounds like a chant of some kind. And setting the smouldering bowl aside.

"Um. What you like in your coffee?" says Louella.

"Black. Just black."

And Louella pushing back her chair, on her feet and moving to the counter. Toe prints in dark coffee grounds on the floor, animal tracks. And opening the cupboard door above the counter, two cups procured and two coffees poured and placed on the table. The prolonged silences she's noticed don't feel awkward. Weird, maybe, but not awkward, Louella feeling that it's her silence, too; it's her turn to break it if she wants but there's no rush.

She waits. Sips once, twice. Three times.

"So, you live close by, you said," says Louella.

"Yes," says Meagre Deerstone, "just three doors down, actually. Or as your mother used to like to call it, 'Three Peaks' down."

"Three Peaks down?"

"She liked to name things what she called the 'native way,'" says Meagre Deerstone. "Made me laugh. Your mother didn't like the way the white man names things. She was always asking me the 'right' name for a place. Like a mountain. Or a river. She'd say, 'You guys always name a river or a mountain or a spot after *it*self, while we always name them after *our*selves.' She always wanted to know the 'native' name for things, like, what the 'real' name of the Fraser River was. Or the 'real' name for Mount Seymour. And I didn't know the 'real' names either half the time, and she'd say, "That's a terrible thing, Meagre. You're the fucking First People here!' And you know, she was right about that. 'Your people's names for things are so much more true,' she'd say. 'Like, if a mountain looks like a billy goat you call it Billy Goat Mountain or the Great Billy Goat Mountain. We look at the same mountain and if my name's Shirley Fuckbucket, then we'll name it Shirley Fuckbucket Mountain.' She'd get real worked up. Was funny. Bothered her more than it bothered me. My grandfather would joke with me sometimes about it."

Louella watches Meagre Deerstone, their coffee cups now empty, Meagre Deerstone of a face like smooth leather, laugh lines, dark eyes with reflections of eagle roosts, deep channels of fish, rivers and deep forests, wood smoke and bears, wolves and elk, of a breathing with and of land, life's pleasures and sad losses and pain sunk deep into the earth under green layers of coastal moss and wood rot and a stillness like an animal, a stillness like *being* an animal.

Meagre Deerstone putting the stone bowl back in her bag, getting ready to leave. And Louella asking: "Your grandfather, did he joke with you about it before or after he died?"

"Oh, this is after, a lot after. He died twenty-five years ago."

"Um . . ."

"You like the smudging?"

"The what?"

"The smoke thing."

"Oh, yeah. Yes, I did, actually."

"Good. We'll do it again."

"Does it work? I mean, does it really 'cleanse,' um, stuff?"

Meagre Deerstone smiling from across dead Momma's white kitchen table.

"Oh, yeah. Cleanses all sorts of stuff."

AFTER MEAGRE DEERSTONE leaves, Louella is on the phone to Aunt Inga, asking: "Did you know about Momma's 'native' thing?"

"Of course, I did," says Aunt Inga. "Thought she was going to burn the place down one day. Came over and lit a small brush fire in one of my good china tureens. Waved smoke all over the place. I doused it with a just freshly made pot of Earl Grey. She got all nutty. Ruined my china tureen, of course. Native culture and plants. Those were your mother's passions near the end. Thought I'd see her taking to the bush wrapped in a blanket with feathers in her hair."

"Racist or what, Aunt Inga?"

"Oh, not at all, dear. There may well have been quite valid grounds for your mother's interests. You do know our side of the family does have a touch of the Micmac in us, don't you, dear?"

"Ah, no . . ."

"Well, we do. Oh, yes. Great-great-grandfathers, missionaries and the sons of missionaries, and ship building in the 1880s on Prince Edward Island, and men lost at sea and all that. Will tell you about it sometime."

"Really . . ."

"Yes, really. You sound well. I'm glad. Got to go. Heard a thump and a bang outside, and Horst is doing something that requires a ladder. Not a good thing. Bye, hon."

"Aunt Inga?"

"Yes, dear."

"Were Mom and Dad nuts?"

"What on earth do you mean?"

"I'm not sure, really."

"Well, to use a slightly watered-down version of the colloquial, crazier than outhouse rats, if you must know. But only while together. When apart, they were fine."

"Thanks, Aunt Inga."

"You're welcome, dear. Oh, and Louella, we have to go to the bank and sign some papers. Get you an account and all that. Apparently, your mother had a savings account set up for you, too, that you can access."

"A savings account? For me?" says Louella.

"Of course, dear. Now there's nothing crazy about that, is there?" says Aunt Inga.

15.

Of Perverts, Poison, and Foreign Lands

TWO MORNINGS LATER the air outside is heady with the scent of pine, damp grasses, and wet earth, following a heavy dew the night before. One sits at dead Momma's circular white kitchen table. Sips a coffee, exhales from a cigarette. And has to ask one's self: "When was the last fucking time you actually went shopping? For groceries? In a grocery store, not a corner store?"

And even though Louella is alone, the answer makes one feel embarrassed, inept: "Must be at least ten or more years now . . ."

And Mona Rose has invited her to do just that—go grocery shopping. They'll take Mona's car and, in Mona's words, "make a jaunt of it." Louella is asked to make a list and (again Mona's words) "be ready in twenty."

"You've been here a number of weeks now, and I have no idea what you've been eating," Mona had said. "I cleared a lot of perishables out after . . . you know . . . but you must need some new stuff by now. Some *nutritious* new stuff."

And Louella then with pen and tiny paper pad, standing in dead Momma's kitchen and turning a slow circle. It's obvious from the scattered debris that pizzas, submarine sandwiches, and Chinese food delivered to her door are all that have been keeping her alive. There's more to eating well, one does knows that. When Mona arrives to pick her up, she asks for her list. Louella's list looks like this:

bread
coffee
cream
toilet paper

Mona is supportive.

"Hmm, good. The toilet paper we can buy in bulk and split it. The bread, too, maybe. I've got a freezer for other stuff and we can always add to the list as we go. It's not rocket science, but it is a skill, of sorts. You'll get the hang of it."

And Louella feeling a bit resentful for a moment. What kind of moron must a grown person be who doesn't know how to buy her own groceries? You go in, get your food, and go home. Ain't that it?

No, it isn't rocket science . . .

The drive to the store is short, Louella left standing with her cart, the aisle marked Cereal, Cookies, Crackers. Mona has forged ahead with her cart and hollering back, "Check on you in a minute. I'll be in Produce!"

And Louella left alone facing this long wall of cereal boxes. These ones here at eye level look like the healthy ones, Mueslix, Blah Blah, and Blah Blah, pictures of nuts and raisins falling into bright red or yellow bowls. One with a wheat field stretching to a distant horizon; another with a spoon holding granola clumps (one guesses) with shaved almonds and some white matter that judging by the description must be vanilla yogurt chunks. And eyes roving up and along and down the stockpile of brightly coloured boxes— Jesus, what a selection, quite fucking insane—and does one even *like* cereal? And reach for something at least familiar, those good childhood years. Any box with a cartoon character on it will be safe enough, a box of Captain Crunch tumbling into the cart. Some Cocoa Krispies, screw the yogurt clusters and raisins and almond chips and granola combos. Too pricey, anyway, and the boxes look a helluva lot smaller. And one is aware that one's nerves feel a little raw, a little frayed even with this tiny bit of decision making. One is not comfortable in one's own skin as of yet; this is no longer a familiar world as once it was when younger and accompanying dead Momma.

Louella leaving the aisle of cereals, not bothering to check out the myriad crackers that would take one all day just to go through. And finding Mona in the produce section examining something large and red with spikes on it that appears totally uneatable, and following her along answering, "No, thanks," to any and all suggestions.

"Figs?"

"No, thanks."

"Apples?"

"No, thanks."

"Broccoli?"

"No, thanks."

And Mona Rose digging deep into a mound of oranges: "Never take the produce on top, Louella. That's where the perverts put the poison."

But then here, down this aisle and packaged and ready to go in sizable plastic bags, ready-made salads. "Produce" taken care of. And finding not far off ready-made meals, not frozen, just heat these suckers up and they all seem to be low on things that are probably not good for you. These items are at least fathomable. And on to the frozen foods section, Christ, one is just wearing shorts and it's cold enough in here to do some damage. Thank god, one is at least wearing long sleeves if only to hide one's track marks. And boxes at last piling high in her cart, making progress, more meals pre-assembled complete and unadorned, frozen this time but still ready for a simple zap in the microwave. And ice cream, a sweet luxury with a choice of a thousand freaking flavours, Mona standing beside her and staring into her cart at the checkout counter.

"You plan to *make* any meals?"

"These take some making. I'm not much on the cooking thing."

"No kidding. Well, we can change that."

And Louella then watching the items conveyed along the black moving belt, the cashier packing it all into bags and placing the bags into the cart. A strange feeling of accomplishment, and, yes, security, the cashier suspecting nothing strange or out of whack with this new customer, polite, smiling, and treating one as, well, normal, one guesses. Enough food here to eat for weeks, one's new bank card in one's hand, accompanied with a tinge of guilt knowing that dead

Momma's made it possible, possible that one has a place to live and food to eat. And one realizes that one is actually sweating, the sweat of the undeserving, the sweat of the unworthy.

Mona is not oblivious to Louella's state.

"We'll get coffee," says Mona. "You look like a deer in the head-lights, baby."

In the coffee shop Mona Rose gulping a huge double latte, at home in the world, telling stories of Herd and Shamus, other family members, and Cove gossip. Louella listening, nerves calming but still a feeling of alienation, a desire to get back to the relative safety of the townhouse. It's been a definite surprise that one can feel so much a foreigner in one's own land. Where has one been, one may ask? At some point something stopped, or changed direction, or just buried its head in the sand.

"You're stressed," says Mona.

"No, I'm okay. Well, maybe a bit. Yes, I am a little," says Louella.

"I know you've been away, Louella. And I know you had some differences with your mother. We all do, you know. We did talk about our families, her and I. You need anything just ask."

"Thanks, Mona."

Mona orders two more lattes, Louella taking a glance out the window toward the car.

"My frozen stuff," says Louella.

"Oh, that crap'll keep forever," says Mona.

16.

Shrieks All Around

FOR MANY, WHEN THE BIG CHANGES come, even the smallest deviation from the familiar (and no matter how horrible that familiar may be), might seem like the highest mountain to climb. And with that climb will always come some fear, fear of what isn't important, but the fear itself is. It must be faced. There need be no rational explanation for the fear; the person involved won't really care, anyway. Won't care if it's labelled deep-seated or mild or just plain *goomba*. But, however which way it's all presented, one *will* get on the phone to one's aunt, will get on the phone to one's aunt and say: "But, I don't want to go to a barbecue . . ."

And one's aunt will say back, "It's only a barbecue, dear. My god, what terrible thing do you think is going to happen?"

"It's not that," says Louella.

"What then?" says Aunt Inga. "You go to these things. They're *social*, you know, with people. You go and mingle in mutual fear and confusion like everybody else. That's how it's done, dear."

"I guess."

"Meet and greet your neighbours, Louella. It's great strategy when it comes time to borrow that emergency tool you don't have. For instance, do you have a toilet plunger?"

"I think I've seen one around somewhere."

"See what I mean? What if you don't? What if there's a problem? That's what neighbours are for, dear. No man, or woman, is an island."

"I've been reading Momma's gardening book," says Louella. "I've decided to learn the difference between a tub shrub and a herbaceous perennial . . ."

"That *is* good news, Louella," says Aunt Inga. "All creatures great and small, love. Bye."

HERD ROSE STANDS at a huge brick barbecue built into the garden wall, smoke billowing its way to the sky. Flames from oil lamps atop bamboo poles stand throughout the yard, the breeze-licked flames appearing to come dangerously close to passing hairdos. An intimidating mob of people spilling onto the small back lawn from Mona's back patio. Loud chatter mixed with occasional bursts of laughter, Mona Rose coming through the crowd and whisking Louella into the heart of the mob, firing off introductions, Louella pulled reluctantly along, nodding, smiling, trying to memorize names and faces. The Plummers, the Chapmans. The Van Beekums and the Cutbills. Ganczar-something and Adrian and Jennifer Thorsen. Or Thor*son*. Someone Maharjan, a doctor apparently. And the Dongnooks (sounds like). And a blur of elastic-waist cargo shorts, toe-thong sandals and PVC flip-flops, baseball caps, and annotated T-shirts: *Leaky Tiki Lava Lounge, Corona Beer, I Love Poodles.*

Louella on the defensive from the get-go; it's all psychological, of course. And if given the time to ponder and peruse, one would no doubt concede that there are no immediate threats present to one's being, but when in a state of general angst about what has for so long been unfamiliar, who has the time for sensible observation, pondering, and perusing? Instead, one manages with a simple "hello" here, a simple "hi" there. One keeps moving through the crowd, small children of various ages occasionally running past, dodging between legs, avoiding toes. And Louella snaring a burger from the grill, hoping to engage in some activity that might impede any chance of conversation. Mouth crammed full of burger, and Herd Rose no longer mans the barbecue. And passing by Dr. Maharjan, he glances over, "Caution is the word of the day, eh?" he confides. Louella smiling back, mouth full of burger (*say whaa*?) and unable to avoid a toe. "Sorry..." and Mona maintaining a maternal watch over her, appearing and disappearing by her side.

"Everything okay? Not too bored, I hope. Herd's gone to bed. It's all 'affecting' him too much."

And the evening wears on under the black, oily smoke of the

many and dangerous tiki torches, some of the guests taking their leave. The effects on those drinking heavily beginning to show, Jeannine Cutbill (mortgage broker) laughing loudly, it appears, all by herself in a dark corner of the yard. The first sound of a bottle or glass being dropped on the patio tiles, shrieks all around. And so begins the "performance" of the Manfreds, Neil and Roxanne, Neil a successful internet magnate and Roxanne his wife; Neil and Roxanne Manfred, who didn't really need an introduction as one has already heard of them through Mona, how they always arrive at social functions separately and commence to consume copious amounts of alcohol that culminates in a drunken exchange of endearments that succeeds in setting all who are still present on edge. Louella is almost thankful for the distraction, Roxanne Manfred in a georgette mid-calf ruffled skirt, cotton interlock-knit embroidered tunic and slingback sandals, Neil Manfred sporting the Leaky Tiki Lava Lounge T-shirt and facing Roxanne Manfred, a few inches shorter than his wife, Roxanne Manfred quite a beautiful woman albeit a little unkempt by this point in the evening, Neil Manfred with one foot on the patio, one foot on the lawn, unsteady and speech slurred.

"I'll stand by my suspicions . . ."

"You do that," says Roxanne Manfred.

"I suggest we no longer attend functions together..." says Neil Manfred.

"I was here first," says Roxanne Manfred.

"Arguing over the trivial is your mainstay..." says Neil Manfred.

"You're an imbecile," says Roxanne Manfred.

"Sweet mother of god, but I do hate you so... " says Neil Manfred.

"Sweet mother of whatever, the feeling's mutual..."

And Louella moving away, hopefully out of earshot and reminded of similar scenes between one's own parents at childhood barbecues, only those exchanges usually took place after all the guests were gone, forgotten burgers crisp and blackened left cold on the grill, the family's barbecue, a nondescript black metal affair with a wheel missing off one leg and the lid resting atop the grill at an awkward angle. And one silly memory triggers another and so on, like the family camping trip to a small lake north of Prince George in the interior, this particular lake a kid's dream devoid of the usual lake stones and lake grass that seem to encrust most lake bottoms, that weedy lake growth that lies secreted under the surface to tangle in uncomfortable freaky-feeling knots around one's tiny toes and ankles, like the lake itself is trying to hold onto you. No, this lake had a sandy bottom, the sand rippled into a firm washboard pattern by small wind-whipped waves, the ridges of sand messaging the soles of one's feet, allowing one to walk far out into the shallows and out of earshot of the sound of one's parents arguing on shore.

And another lake, another vacation, this one in Manitoba somewhere and visiting Grandpa and Grandma, a cabin right on the water and Grandpa says it's okay by him if one wants to use the old wooden kayak, circa 1940, use it to paddle around in, Momma's objections heard from the small dock as one paddles the unwieldy thing around the point and once again out of earshot. One is fourteen now, the old kayak drifting through tall reeds that wave high above one's head, and one is unable to know exactly where one is heading, marsh birds calling out, plop of a fish jumping, and a family of ducks gliding out of the curtain of reeds only to disappear again across the prow of the boat into more reeds as one sits hidden from the world at the end of the lake, the surrounding shoreline and sky reflected upside down in the water below. And wondering how long one can stay floating on the sky without getting into too much trouble, until someone sends the alarm out.

"I see Neil and Roxanne have not disappointed," says Mona appearing suddenly. "Right on cue, the lambs."

"Mona!" says a large, red-faced woman. "I seem to have misplaced my purse . . ."

And Mona disappearing again, Louella squeezing through the patio doors into the living room and back out again, far too claustrophobic inside, and passing Neil and Roxanne Manfred—"You are, as usual, wrong, my dear . . ." "Oh, kiss my ass"—and one makes for the far corner of the yard, some breathing space, the sky black against the lattice-topped fence, the darkness carrying a sweet smell, the sweet smell of pine sap, shaggy moss and dew, forest rot and salt-sea air, and the smell of newborn leaves and roots, squirrel tails and raccoons, smell of granite stone and just maybe the mingling sweat of old-time quarry workers (have heard there used to be a quarry nearby), and wildflowers and damp mosses, bees' honey, and bristling corn with beets and cabbage from the Greek neighbour's garden just a few doors down through the trees next to Momma's place; and seagull down and owl feathers, pollen, resin, deep brown earth, and smoking tiki lamps, and, now, creeping, just perceptible, the smell of crisp and cooling, forgotten char-black hamburger patties . . .

17.

Of Normal Joes

BLACKY HARBOTTLE POURS cheap whisky into cheap glasses on the coffee table in the house on St. Catherines Street. Jimmy Flood takes a glass, doesn't pass one to Frankie Yin. Frankie Yin sitting on the couch. And reaching forward, takes his own. Frankie Yin of thin, European-cut chintz shirts and hard-creased, high-twist fibre slacks; shiny, gloss leather-look bomber jackets and equally shiny, glossy-look slicked black hair; one Frankie Yin with an eye for the ladies (preferably Caucasian) and a two hundred dollar a day cocaine habit.

"Like I say," says Blacky Harbottle looking at Frankie Yin, "I'm not racist, but I'll tell you, of most Asians I've dealt with, the majority of the criminal types seem to lean toward kidnapping and blackmail an' that sorta shit as opposed to selling dope or simply robbing banks or whatever. Why the fuck is that?"

"Really?" says Jimmy Flood, chancing a wary look at Frankie Yin, Frankie Yin of soft-lidded eyes, round moon face, and hair short-cropped one side and falling long on the other to knife down in a sharp black-sickle curve over one eye. Frankie Yin, leader of the Tai Pai boys, local Asian gang, or, as Frankie Yin will refer to it, the Tai Pai Social League. ("Not a gang," Frankie Yin will say. "It's a club.")

"Really," says Blacky Harbottle to Jimmy Flood continuing his thought. "Kidnapping and extortion, right, Frankie?"

Frankie Yin, puffy rose-coloured lips sipping the whisky.

"Yes, maybe. We could do that. It happens. Good money . . ."

Blacky Harbottle looking at Jimmy Flood.

"Frankie here once kidnapped his girlfriend cuz she wouldn't marry him. Drove all the way to Mani-fucking-toba with a gun to her head and kept her there for two months!"

Jimmy Flood, a mild look of awe on his face and looking again at Frankie Yin.

"She marry you?" says Jimmy Flood.

"No. She doesn't marry. Love is funny," says Frankie Yin.

Jimmy Flood looking unsure, suspecting there may be something here considered ironic, even humorous, but unable to pin it down.

"So, me and Frankie been thinking," says Blacky Harbottle. "Why don't we do something like that? The kidnapping thing."

"You want to kidnap someone?" says Jimmy Flood. "Jesus, Blacky. That's pretty heavy isn't it?"

"Not really, if you think it through," says Blacky Harbottle.

More whisky is poured. A car can be heard outside the window, tires scrunching up the lane.

"Not heavy, no," says Frankie Yin, Frankie Yin of hand-sewn, black leather slip-ons that rise from the floor with his legs and find a place on the coffee table. "Not heavy. Old tradition, part of heritage. My grandfather, father, always kidnapping. Sometimes one, two, three, five different people at once. My uncle get drunk and tell me, drink too much *baijiu* one night and spill the beans on family."

Jimmy Flood not liking this and pouring another drink.

"I don't know . . ."

"It's not so crazy," says Blacky Harbottle. "Of course, you don't pick someone famous or like that. You pick someone simple, a normal joe, someone who won't sort of matter so much."

"Like who?"

"Like who?"

"Yeah, like who?"

"Frankie and me were thinking of Louella, maybe."

"Louella?" says Jimmy Flood, looking wide-eyed now at Frankie Yin, now at Blacky Harbottle, now at the alley-side window that he has so often used as an escape route when the door's come down in the house on St. Catherines Street. "What are you talking about? She hasn't got any money. An' we don't even know where she is anyway."

"Oh," says Blacky Harbottle. "Oh, but we do. And she has."

"We know all this. We do," says Frankie Yin.

"So, we're gonna kidnap, Louella," says Jimmy Flood.

"We're not gonna to hurt her," says Blacky Harbottle. "You remember Little Sue? Sue Rascone? Well, she did a few months with Louella when Louella was in. Word is Louella's mother died, cancer I think. Left Louella a ton of money and a big house in Deep Cove. Five or six cars, too."

"Little Sue's never told the truth about anything in her fucking life," says Jimmy Flood. "Look, you wanna think of something big-money to do, I think I might have got me a helicopter—"

"Spare me the helicopter shit, already," says Blacky Harbottle. "You keep working on that, really. But, in the meantime, let's focus on a deal that's at least tangifuckingble, *capeesh*?"

"She's my ex, you know," says Jimmy Flood.

Blacky Harbottle looks unsettled, stares hard at Jimmy Flood.

"And I think the term 'ex' is the key here, ain't it?" says Blacky. "We'll get the Truman brothers involved. They're in town. They're broke. They have no friends. They have no prospects and they're crazy enough to do it. Besides, Louella ratted me out."

"We were busted in *your* house. Nobody *had* to rat you out," says Jimmy Flood.

"Maybe a point, maybe not," says Blacky Harbottle, slugging a belt of whisky back straight from the bottle. "What the fuck. According to my info, Louella can afford it. What the fuck she gonna do with all her mom's money anyway, besides put it up her nose or in her arm? Not a big deal here, you know. Like I say, we're not gonna hurt anybody. "

"One time I kidnap my sister," says Frankie Yin. "She real pissed off, but when parents pay she gets half. Very happy. Family is funny."

Although somewhat afraid of Frankie Yin (rumours abound on the street about a rather sinister history), Jimmy Flood is beginning to feel a kind of backward admiration. And although the fear is still there, something else is surfacing. Maybe it's the nonchalance that impresses him, the matter-of-fact presentation of facts with an apparent complete lack of emotional involvement. Whatever it is, Jimmy Flood likes it. Jimmy Flood would like to *be* it. Jimmy Flood would like to be like Frankie Yin, Jimmy Flood of a face that could be considered good-looking by some standards if not so gaunt and drug-ravaged, the look some might say of a traumatized forest animal, furtive, on the lookout for predators and with a myriad of premature worry lines that could well tell their own story of displacement from a quite normal middle-class upbringing of minivans and hockey practices, video gaming, and holiday family get-togethers.

And what of the Jimmy Floods of the world, spare, wasting-away men who can't cry deprivation or parental neglect or sexual abuse or anything else as a cause for their present condition, the big mystery remaining, the big question so often asked at family gatherings and social events, "How the hell did so-and-so end up like that?"

This question has been asked many times by Mr. and Mrs. Flood themselves (behind closed doors), with Mr. Flood expressing the old adage that one may as well ask "Why is the sky blue?" and Mrs. Flood pointing out depressingly that one believes that the scientists have at least actually been able to answer that one now. So middle-class Jimmy Flood carries on, undeprived and unabused in childhood, Mr. Flood Senior a successful and hard-working realtor in Kamloops, BC, having provided well for his wife and two children, a boy and a girl. And young Jimmy Flood does not disappoint, not for some time, a good student throughout his early school years and most of high school, out-performing even his high-achieving younger sister. Then just before graduation begins the fall, the gradual but unrelenting slide beginning innocently enough with weekend booze-ups on the banks of the cold and fast-flowing Thompson River, but evolving only too quickly into a full-blown addiction to crack and heroin, the harmless party binges by the river forgotten and displaced by more and more time spent on and in the seedier Kamloopian streets and bars to feed the harsher habit.

And Jimmy Flood is no different than anyone else who "falls," the fall itself being more or less undetectable to the person doing the falling (although there will be more than enough souls along the way shouting warnings), much as a geriatric patient may stumble forward in the hallway of the ward, only to crack one's skull against the unforgiving floor, but feeling all the time that one is still, in fact, standing perfectly straight and quite capable of making it on one's own this short distance to the exit sign up ahead just to have a much-desired smoke outside.

And so it is for Jimmy Flood, having yet another whisky and slouching back on Blacky Harbottle's sofa while beginning to fear less and admire more one Frankie Yin, not as yet aware that there is any real fall taking place, a glitch or two maybe, but all things being relative to one's own experience, life is progressing as usual. And let it be time for his mild somatoform disorder to begin to kick in, as diagnosed and described by the family doctor to his parents when he was thirteen years old, that, when stressed, "distressing physical symptoms are evoked but with a lack of demonstrable findings as a basis for the symptoms." But all that young Jimmy Flood hears at the time is "So, you guys got yourself a nut-job."

The distressing physical symptom that Jimmy Flood most suffers when coming under undue stress is a painful stinging sensation up his right thigh and across his right buttock that can often intensify to a mind-numbing burning of the flesh, or, what feels like a mind-numbing burning of the flesh. There are no medical explanations for the pain, no visible distress of the skin or muscles. For Jimmy Flood, however, the origins of his disorder, he is sure, arise from the experience of watching his younger sister (three years old at the time, Jimmy was eleven) get stung by a jellyfish at a beach in White Rock one summer. She was pulled screaming from the water, angry red welts along her tiny right thigh and buttocks, the welts looking like tentacles themselves, jagged crimson ridges against the pale white skin. But it was the screams, the child-voice screams of sheer fear and agony that affected him most, tingled the very bones not yet fully formed in his adolescent skull. And he experienced the fear, too, the incapacitating fear, the fear that makes you freeze up, want to babble like an idiot, blubber like a baby in your mommy's arms and just keep screaming and screaming until you die.

And ever since this episode, through the years he has felt the heated stinging of those tentacles against his flesh in high stress situations, his right upper thigh and buttock aflame, although there are never any visual signs to suggest any trauma is actually occurring. And as he sits now in the house on St. Catherines Street, mulling over the idea of kidnapping Louella Poule, ex-girlfriend, a meathead proposal at best, it's one's own arse beginning to squirm on Blacky Harbottle's couch, first an itch, then the burn, then the pain. And what would Frankie Yin, his new role model, do about this condition, about any condition? Shrug it off, no doubt, say something like "Pain is funny—" and get on with it. One might take some lessons from this little Asian guy still sipping his whisky, feet stretched out on the coffee table, while one's own thigh and butt catch fire and Frankie Yin suddenly looking over, saying, "What you doing, you? You got to crap? You got to crap, it's okay. Okay to just go. Go crap."

"He's okay," says Blacky Harbottle. "He's got a 'condition' of sorts. Happens when he's stressing."

"A thing," says Frankie Yin. "A crap thing."

"No," says Jimmy Flood. "It's just a nerve thing."

"A nerve thing," says Blacky Harbottle.

"The crap, it's fine?" says Frankie Yin.

"Yes, it's fine," says Blacky Harbottle. "Everything is fine."

"So, it's not a crap thing," says Frankie Yin.

"No, it's not a crap thing," says Jimmy Flood.

"Good it's not a crap thing," says Frankie Yin. "Crap things can be funny."

18.

The Bee Guy

HAVING MET ONE'S NEIGHBOURS to the, say, right of one, even Louella knows that it follows that one may eventually have to meet one's neighbours on the left, they who live in the small rancher-style bungalow half-hidden in the trees bordering dead Momma's backyard.

Louella has heard the man is Greek and lives with his much-younger wife, the wife often seen but seldom known to talk, save the odd "hello" in polite reply to a greeting. The rumour is she's a mail-order bride from the Philippines. The Greek is fairly mysterious, dark skinned and dour; keeps bees and a huge vegetable garden that the young wife can often be seen tending, doing the drudge work. No one's sure of the Greek's name, but most agree it's Something-*apopolos.* No one knows the woman's name. She is not seen alone when off the property, Something-*apopolos* accompanies her every-where in public. She works the garden, helps tend the bees.

The Greek on the other hand, well, no one really knows exactly what he does. Drives a battered, old yellow pickup truck, the rear box crammed with an assortment of tools and what appears to some to be landscaping equipment. One thing is clear to most, at least to the women of the complex Louella has learned, and that is that his young wife seems to do most of the work around the house and in the garden.

Louella had nodded a greeting to her through the lattice-topped fence one afternoon, and the woman had nodded back, Louella glimpsing a pretty brown face smiling from under a wide-brimmed straw hat, a pretty brown face of tropical breezes, thatched bamboo huts on stilts above tidal flats and sloping white beaches, just a hint of typhoon rainstorms in the round, dark eyes peering out from below thick, jet-black hair cut low across the brow.

On the day she finally meets the Greek, Louella stands in her dead Momma's backyard, having just muscled two large cedar planters off the lawn and onto the small patio. Two yellowed circles of flattened dead grass remain perfectly etched where the cedar planters stood, the ground there writhing with a mass of startled wood bugs. She is made aware of the sound, the source undisclosed at first, a buzzing, a frenetic buzz-saw effect, but not piercing, more subdued, Louella looking around the yard, her gaze zeroing in on an area of the fence shadowed beneath the sweeping bough of a large pine growing the other side. And what appears to be a large brown sack hanging from the fence, about two feet across and four feet long. Louella steps closer.

The sack appears to be moving, like there's something trapped inside.

"The queen bee she get out," a voice says. "I come get."

Louella startled, sees the two deep-set eyes of the Greek guy staring at her through the lattice along the fence, then notices that the sack is not a sack at all but what appears to be thousands of bees all grouped together and hanging off one another en masse. A *beard*, a voice in her mind recalls obscurely, *a fucking beard of fucking bees.*

Louella then instinctively backing onto the patio away from the threat, right arm outstretched behind her, feeling for the French doors. The Greek guy appears from the narrow walkway on the side of the townhouse carrying a large cardboard box. Louella sees he's wearing coveralls and a plaid shirt but no gloves and not even one of those funny little hats with the netting to protect the face.

"Not worry," he says and walks straight to the buzzing mass of bees on the fence, drops the box at his feet, and begins scooping bees bare-handed into the cardboard box. They come off in great clumps, like writhing, buzzing cotton candy. The box fills and except for a few errant bees buzzing around his head, they all appear to be in there.

"Not worry," he says again, and with what Louella suspects may have been a smile, he disappears up the walkway along the side of the townhouse the way he'd come.

"Jesus-fucking-Christ," Louella is obliged to say out loud, any predisposition to a somewhat prejudicial outlook pertaining to the suspected dullness and ennui associated with the "normal life" in suburban middle-class neighbourhoods quickly eroding. For that was something to see, by god, and she has already witnessed plenty in the small community nestled under the imposing grandeur of west coast conifers that suggests a certain level of persistent unrest tending to lead to anything but tedium. For instance, she has learned that the Manfreds, Neil and Roxanne, separate almost on a weekly basis (the verbal hostilities invariably occur during the evening hours after social functions or outside in their carport, so all in the vicinity are privy to the drama), and then the breakup is inevitably followed by reconciliation a few days later when the two come together again, as the surrounding neighbours and tall pines await patiently the next eruption of their undying dislike for one another. And even Mona next door with husband Herd and son Shamus also seems to have no end to excitement, the shouting often heard easily enough through the walls, where it's Mona doing most of the shouting and a lot of it seems to address husband Herd's failings as both a husband and a man.

"There is never a dull moment," says Louella to Alcina over the phone.

"Use it, honey. It's a learning ground," says Alcina.

"A learning ground for what, may I ask?" says Louella.

"For what not to do or say in the capacity of normal and/or acceptable behaviour, I'd figure," says Alcina.

"And what about the other side of it?" says Louella. "Like, things *to* do and say . . ."

"Oh, that," says Alcina. "You'll need some kind of self-help book for that stuff, I'd think."

19.

Of Journals and Kitchen Catchers

THE DAYS THEY come and go, and with that coming and going comes yet a new hurdle that tends to accompany any "road to betterment," and that is, what does one do to fill the hours of the day that one used to spend on finding ways to slowly kill one's self? And having forsaken the path of self-destruction, does not one Louella Debra Poule herself fall prey to this very predicament? Gone are the daily activities that one's previous lifestyle demanded, the all-consuming chase to score money to score drugs, the running one's self into the ground stealing, conning, pawning, turning tricks, boosting, and scurrying from drug house to drug house, bar to bar, alleyway to alleyway through rain and hail and dark night violence. It was, at least, a busy life.

And sitting now in dead Momma's kitchen at the circular white table, *The Complete Home Gardener* open in front of her, Louella reads:

Section VII—Compost Heaps: Among the best-known organic fertilizers are dried blood, hoof and horn, bone meal, and fish meal . . .

The mention of fish meal conjures an image, then a smell. The smell can be tracked down to the cupboard under the kitchen sink, Louella Poule leaning down to the cupboard under the semi-pastoral climes amidst the tall trees of Deep Cove, the morning-lit sky outside a fitting backdrop to a display of circling seabirds. And reaching under the sink to pull forth a week or so's accumulated garbage overflowing a glossy white Kitchen Catcher (twist-ties provided) that lines the pale mauve plastic garbage pail sitting there, and a sad irony that running the streets for years trying to kill one's self has all come down to this, carrying the garbage down the hallway and outside to dead Momma's carport, where a bigger, sturdier garbage pail, this one an industrial charcoal grey colour, stands against the far wall. And where one lets fall a week's accumulation of rotting garbage, a resounding *clunk* as it hits the bottom, and a conversation recalled with prison counsellor Jane.

"Well, for that matter, Louella, what is important then? Is it important to wash your clothes? Take out the garbage? Are these things 'important'?" says prison counsellor Jane.

"Um . . ." says Louella.

"Well?" says prison counsellor Jane.

"Yes, I guess—"

"Ask yourself—what would happen or not happen if you didn't take out the garbage? Wash your clothes? Vacuum the floor? Would you die? Would the world suffer? It's unlikely, I think you'll agree, but are these things still important?"

And Louella can remember feeling frustrated, counsellor Jane talking to her like she was a two-year-old, and maybe she is, standing now in dead Momma's carport replacing the charcoal grey lid on dead Momma's garbage container. What *would* happen? Well, the garbage would pile up obviously, invite the spread (maybe) of disease, vermin, mould, slime, and crap in general. And even an idiot can conclude that this would not be a good thing, and one can remember living with Jimmy Flood in a skid row rooming house where the garbage did accumulate and pile up unabated against the far wall next the radiator. The two of them never seemed to bathe either, who could be bothered? In and out of the room only to score and back to the room to shoot up, maybe wolf down a jumbo bag of potato chips or whatever when you got the chance because some part of you says eating is something you have to do, not to stay alive but to be able to score again and get high. And the day-to-day pile-up of garbage could be considered a boon to some living things at least, the cockroaches, mice, spiders, and ants pilfering through the growing pile of garbage against the far wall. The stink you got used to, everything was awful anyway. But one has to admit, for one's self anyway, there was always a distant voice from somewhere suggesting that, regardless of one's own indifference to squalor, wherever there's shit of any kind piling up, someone will eventually have to clean it up.

So it's at this particular innocuous moment standing in dead Momma's carport and pondering the significance, if any, of doing the mundane, that, apart from taking out the garbage on a more regular basis, Louella decides to initiate another small change. At first suggested by prison counsellor Jane and ignored, it has again been suggested by Meagre Deerstone, and that is to just maybe, might, possibly keep a journal.

"I don't see the point," says Louella at first, "writing down your personal shit."

"That's what it's for," says Meagre Deerstone. "Writing down your personal shit. Gets it out of your head. Nobody has to see it, sort of like keeping an eye on yourself."

"You keep one?" says Louella.

"Yes, I do."

"Can I see it?"

"No, you can't."

And so takes place a half-hearted stab at it, a trip down to the Cove and the purchase of a pocketbook-sized, slightly pliable, coil-bound notebook with lined paper and bound in a faux red leather cover; on the inside flap a thin plastic sleeve that holds a small, brightly coloured pen, the whole ensemble (thinks Louella) specifically designed to appear cute and non-threatening in the likelihood of encouraging the release of one's personal and shame-ridden thoughts.

After a week the journal looks like this:

Day 1: ~~Feeling~~
Day 2: ~~Feeling okay~~
Day 3: Feeling O SHIT this is ridiculous /////
Day 4: Feeling //// lonely. There I did it.
Day 5: Feeling lonely I guess. Let's see just write anything

about what you're thinking or feeling or doing Meagre says. Fuck this is hard. Haven't had any cravings. Been going to meetings. Honesty /// fuck nobody's going to see this. Just write crap. So what. Try writing to Matilda Goomba who knows all your bullshit!

Day 6:   DEAR MATILDA GOOMBA: thought all day about going over town to score. Talked to Meagre & got a call from Alcina. Felt better. Took out garbage and it might have even felt GOOD! Fuck. Meagre suggested outpatient counselling. Don't know about that. Sometimes the night is the best time /// feel safe /// the world's asleep. Sometimes the night's the worst time /// maybe want to go running up the walls screaming, but I don't know what at.

Day 7:   DEAR MATILDA GOOMBA: read somewhere that sometimes it's a good idea to write to people you can't talk to. //////// Dear Mom: thought I would write you a small note. Seems kind of dumb you being dead but anyway I'm sorry. For all kinds of things I really fucked up. There's////~~DAMN DAMN DAMN~~

"I've started a journal," says Louella.

"That's great," says Meagre Deerstone. "How's it going?"

"How the fuck should I know?" says Louella Poule.

A Later Page From the LDP Journal

ME///A SHORT SYNOPSIS //////

Well, you got your average girl growing up, a relatively normal family, one parent an alcoholic (the dad), the other (I've since learned) codependent (the mom). Typical teenage years, normal rebellion, parents separate sometime along the way. Kid stays with mother, mother stays with kid. Father comes & goes, appears & disappears but keeps in touch mostly via telephone shouting matches with mother. Father loves kid. Mother loves kid. Kid loves mother & father. Kid/teenager starts using drugs, just starts using them, no deep psychological mystery. Gets hooked, & merrily, merrily, life is but a dream. Kid gets older but not smarter, becomes addict living on the streets. Some ecstasy but more misery, lots of close calls, disasters /// loses a few friends along the way, 3 ladies, Janie, Brook & Laurie, turning tricks off Vancouver's east side, 2 of them found strangled, one stabbed to death. & comes the day, after all that's happened & some things that haven't, the doors come in for the umpteenth time but this time it's different, charges are laid & stick & the kid come young woman does eighteen months, gets clean in the joint & wants to stay that way. She thinks. Anyway her mother dies &, oh, yeah, a whole load of regrets & shitty feelings & she moves into her dead Momma's townhouse on the streets of Straightsville, & what better time & place to try & turn things around, salvage a star before it falls, a heart before it pumps nothing but air from that dark cavity some call the soul ////

—this note is only for me LDP

Oddly Enjoyable Ventures

SO, HOW IT WORKS: A few weeks become four, four becomes more, and more become more yet, Louella beginning to fill some of her time with reading, once a favourite pastime but for a long while set aside like everything else and now slowly the pleasure being reclaimed. And just going for drives in dead Momma's powder-blue Toyota is an oddly enjoyable venture, rediscovering old childhood haunts or driving out on unknown roads to discover new ones. And caring for dead Momma's plants and buying new ones, one's interest in flora and fauna growing in part from reading excerpts over early morning coffee from *The Complete Home Gardener* that remains forever open on dead Momma's circular white kitchen table. One is strangely reluctant to move it, let alone close it, it remains where it is, like a holy book left open on a dais in some small country chapel, and that book, too, left where it is replete with its own locally accepted aura of mystery, power even, *The Complete Home Gardener* holding possibly some folk story of Momma that can reveal tidbits of some of her passions, her reverence and study of the great wide world of non-speaking living and growing things, the great wide world of cultures, human and otherwise, not her own.

And there are the visits from Mona Rose, Aunt Inga, and Meagre Deerstone that provide entertainment and fellowship, not to mention updates on the hidden lives of Cove residents. And taking walks down to the Cove to just sit a while, look around, do nothing in particular. Ask nothing in particular. And it's on one of these walks that she finds herself sitting on a bench down in the local waterfront park watching the sailboats bobbing at the dock, flags flapping from their rigging in a stiff onshore breeze, tarps snapping and whipping in the wind, trees high on the adjacent bluffs shaking their manes and a Park Board garbage can, unchained, bouncing across the walkway, up the slope behind her a group of mountain bikers dismantling their bikes in the parking lot, then the sound of a child's voice. Crying "help" from over her right shoulder and there, up a tree and unable to get down, a little girl. Louella then crawling on all fours through a clump of thick bramble bushes at the foot of the tree to reach her; the little girl is not easily consoled, holding Louella tight as she's lifted down and still whimpering as Louella gently nudges her ahead in a crouch back through the brambles. There is no parent in sight, and Louella walks the little girl by the hand over to the village street where the mother suddenly appears, bewildered, coming out of a shop.

"My god," says the mother. "I didn't even know she was gone."

Louella smiles, shrugs, the little girl burying her face against her mother's leg. The mother then attempting to get the little girl to say thank you, but the little girl will not turn around.

"It's okay," says Louella, and the mother looks embarrassed, held rooted to the spot by the little girl clinging to her leg. And Louella suddenly feels strangely embarrassed, too. For the mother? For herself? Does the mother feel more than just embarrassed, maybe ashamed? A bad mother? And Louella, startled by the awareness that she herself is feeling unworthy, unworthy to even *help* a child, help out a mother, let alone be one, and taking a quick exit back into the park muddling over thoughts of mothers and daughters, mothers helping daughters, mothers losing daughters and mothers finding daughters again. Stands down close to the water where a few stiff gusts off the water can buffet her face, give her a talking to.

But things in general aren't bad—strange maybe, a bit foreign— but not bad. And cravings for drugs, such as they are, come and go, too, but nothing too drastic, too intense, which surprises Louella. One had thought the process of keeping clean once out of jail would be a strenuous, all-consuming exercise in willpower and nail-biting and wall-climbing. But instead, the easy, non-committal flow of daily life, for the moment, seems to be keeping the junkyard dogs of anxiety and angst somewhere at bay. In fact, it seems like forever since she's had to call on the stabilizing powers of Matilda G.

"You're still in shock, my dear," says Aunt Inga. "Dealing with your mother's personal papers and all that stuff can wait. Don't pack her clothes if you're not ready yet. Take your time. I'm handling the financial organization, so that's not a worry. Try to relax. Think of what you may want to do. With your life, I mean. But no real hurry."

"Shock?" says Louella. "Still? My life?"

"See what I mean." says Aunt Inga.

BUT LIFE UNDER the tall trees midst the lush green of Vancouver's North Shore, far from the streets and alleyways of downtown Vancouver itself, well, Louella Poule knows, it ain't gonna be *that* easy. And one is more than aware of the simple, time-honoured dictum handed down through the generations from the annals of drug addict folklore the world over that, while the existing horribleness intrinsic to a drug addict's life is easily maintainable in that horribleness, it is also infinite in scope, and, as a result, the horribleness can forever be added to, and it usually is.

One element, or elements, that can help add credence to this dictum (Louella now learns) is and are "modes of transportation": cabs, buses, and maybe even the bloody astral plane as some may believe; any device that can transport people from one place to another, *any* people, making it more than possible for almost anyone to get to Deep Cove with a minimum of pain and effort if they really want to, for how else to account for the sudden influx of unsolicited visitors to one's fucking doorstep? And the influx begins with Ginger Baumgartner, out of the blue, seen through the peephole of dead Momma's front door and asking, please, just for a place to clean up for a while. And what can one do, anyway? Did not the wacko Ginger Baumgartner front one free dope when one was broke on the street and junk-sick? And give one's own ass a place to crash numerous times when things had become impossible, when bits of Vancouver's back-alley skies had begun to fall on one's own unprotected and drugged-up head?

Then, two days later, the influx continuing with the arrival of Marco Da Silva, bent right out of shape and heard scratching, not pounding, at dead Momma's townhouse door so as not to attract undue attention, and let in reluctantly as one is informed that there is a need to lie low—"A fucking warrant out on me and all that! "—and then one is firing back the question, "What the fuck are you thinking coming here with the police after ya, ya dumb fucker?" And letting the sorry-ass Marco Da Silva, fugitive, letting him know that in this case, and this case only, he can stay two days and two days only, *then has to get the fuck out of here . . .*

And Ginger Baumgartner lives on in the spare room, drug-sick and vomiting, moaning for sugar drinks and more cigarettes while she tries to kick her habit, Marco Da Silva haunting dead Momma's living room with lights off and curtains drawn—"Okay, okay, just drink the water I gave you, damn it, Ginger, and puke in the bowl I put there, please. Hey, two fucking days are up, Marco. Get the fuck out of here and don't come back unless you're clean and not wanted by the fucking cops!"

Marco Da Silva does leave as demanded, a surprise in itself, although he does take the time to voice keen resentment at her selfishness.

"Like, it's not like you earned all this . . ." says Marco De Silva.

"No, you're right," says Louella. "My mom had to die so I could get it."

"What I mean is—" says Marco De Silva.

"What you mean is why can't you have some," says Louella.

"Well, I just—" says Marco De Silva.

"Go, Marco. Get the fuck out!"

"I—"

Slam.

Ginger Baumgartner hits the road three days later, her time up, too, leaving Louella surprised if not rather impressed to see a new name added to the list in dead Momma's kitchen in Ginger's handwriting:

Molly Kool–1939; 1ˢᵗ registered female sea captain in North America.

And how the fuck would Ginger Baumgartner know that? But, if wonders indeed never seem to cease, having certain blasts-from-the-past around is still not good stuff to be happening for someone trying to turn the corner, turn things around, turn over a new leaf. No matter how guilty or responsible one may feel.

"No, it isn't," says Meagre Deerstone. "You got to learn to say no, maybe."

The next day.

"*No fucking way, you fucker!*" says Louella into the phone.

"That's better," says Meagre Deerstone.

"Sorry. Some asshole I used to know. How'd *he* get my number? How'd any of them get the number? And the address."

"Your friend who visited?"

"Alcina? No way. She wouldn't tell anyone."

"The internet?"

"These dinkshits can use the internet?"

"Only takes one . . ."

"But why, though?"

Meagre Deerstone stands at the front door ready to leave.

"Maybe they just love you. Why you think? Got to go. Know anyone with a pink Cadillac? The driver's door looks interesting."

And Louella Debra Poule left crouching in the shadows of the doorway of dead Momma's townhouse as Meagre Deerstone leaves. And peering out. And great leaping shit-sticks, Butch Truman seen climbing over the driver's door of a pink Cadillac convertible, the driver's door secured in place to the car body by what appear to be many lashings of thick yellow nylon cord. (She will later learn that the door was removed by a passing refrigerator truck while the Caddy was parked with the driver's door left open on the shoulder of Highway 1 in Burnaby, Butch himself lucky enough to be searching the trunk at the time for an Abba CD that Baby had insisted on listening to and so was not standing by the door at the time.) From the passenger side emerges a small woman tugging at a thicket of windblown peroxide blond hair. And it's still not too late to shut dead Momma's door. The last time Louella'd seen the Truman brothers was two years ago when cruising the east side in Sandy Shirl's mother's borrowed 2001 Chevrolet Ventura. And Patty Ramm was there, and Ginger Baumgartner, and they all got jammed up in the intersection of Main and First Avenue, a screech of braking tires beside them and Gordy Truman was suddenly at the driver's side door of the Ventura, a size thirteen hiking boot coming right through the driver's window into Sandy Shirl's face as she floors the Ventura, saying, *"Fucking Jesus shit but I'm sorry girls but I ripped the fucking Truman brothers off for a score last night an' I'm not crying but my eyes are fucking watering cuz there's glass and shit everywhere and those Truman brothers are fucking crazy and I'm sorry I got you all into this bullshit an' they're gonna fucking kill us all . . ."*

And still in the shadows of dead Momma's townhouse doorway, Louella Debra Poule sliding open the front-hall mirrored closet doors, a hand reaching for the taped handle of the Petersville Slugger.

22.

The Necessary and the Not Necessary

AS DISCONCERTING AS total darkness can be, as well as being bounced along in the trunk of a car, any real sensations of fear for Louella do not enter into it, at least, not in this circumstance. For one thing, one knows one's kidnappers, the Truman brothers. For another, one cannot feel truly threatened; the whole scenario is just too absurd. The Truman brothers may be many things, but they're not killers, although Gordy Truman especially is no stranger to violent acts in the past (he *is* six foot three and weighs about 230 pounds). Butch Truman, on the other hand, well, no one really knows what he's capable of, but the ambiguity of his criminal potential lends one's self to believe that he is, if nothing else, just a screw-up, but no heavy. So one tends to dwell on other details of the last half-hour's events. Like, why are one's hands tied? Is it necessary? And the blindfold? And the trunk that one is being bounced around in is definitely not the pink Caddy's, too small. So what's that about? And where is one going?

It can be assumed that one's headed west out of the Cove as that's the only direction one can take to get out of the Cove, and the movement of the car dictates that the road one is following is winding, so it's likely to be the lower road along the inlet. Then follows the sensation of a long upward curve and the tires making a different sound, the car now climbing a gradual slope, likely the incline of the Ironworkers Bridge where one is then bounced high to smack the lid of the trunk as the car heads down the other side having just crossed over the crest of the bridge. From this point, one is heading either into the city (west) or beyond (east), up valley somewhere. But now a long stretch (goes on and on) with no slackening of speed, no stoplights, and this supports the notion that the car has remained on the highway heading east and is indeed seeking a destination somewhere up valley. So, with all this figured out, there is nothing more to do than wait, wait and see what exactly the Truman brothers have in mind. Again, it's somewhat surprising to Louella that fear has not entered into it; that one is more just pissed off than anything.

SO, HOW IT WORKS: The bouncing and general weirdness continue, for how far exactly, one can't tell. The drive, at one point almost comical, becomes tedious. One's body becomes cramped, poked and prodded by unknown car trunk parts. Discomfort takes over, becomes the main focus of one's attention. Finally, a couple of harder bumps and the car slows, turns sharply and just as abruptly comes to a stop. The motor cuts, doors open. Another car, maybe the Cadillac, heard pulling up beside and cutting its engine. More doors opening, closing. The trunk latch heard releasing. Then cool night air felt on one's face, hands felt gripping one's arms and yanking one out to stand on solid ground. A knee banged on the rim of the trunk, one's left foot asleep, needling pins and needles. And hands guiding one up a small step, one sensing a narrow opening, a doorway? A few more steps forward and the hands turning one around, pushing down roughly, causing one's butt to sit. The surface under one's butt hard with an equally hard back attached, and in the ensuing rather quiet moment one can take the opportunity to decide just how one will wish to remember this adventure for future times.

Let's see . . . Butch Truman pulls up at the townhouse in a pink Cadillac with a peroxide blond wimpet by his side. Louella can be easily seen in the doorway saying goodbye to Meagre Deerstone, so it's too late to lock the place down and hide one's self away. A pleasant-enough greeting as they come in. Butch and (as she's introduced) Baby, the ensuing conversation is stilted at best, well, stupid really; one should have trusted one's instincts, Louella ditching the baseball bat, she and Baby seated at the circular white kitchen table while Butch makes a pass through the living room. Butch pausing at the French doors out to the patio, mutters something about "Just driving around . . . in town for a couple of days . . . taking a break." And a break from what, thinks Louella as the doorbell sounds, and Louella is on her feet eager to answer the call, hoping it's Meagre Deerstone returning or an impromptu visit from Mona Rose. And in her haste forgetting to check the peephole behind the tiny iron grate, the greatest fucking invention in the world. The front door then pushed inward from outside sending Louella back-pedalling a few steps while at the same time attempting a blind grab into dead Momma's mirrored-door closet for the Petersville Slugger, but Gordy Truman is too fast, too big. And then Butch joining the act, and together the brothers subduing the intended victim, Louella finding her hands bound behind her back with a lady's headscarf and a dark cloth band slipped over her eyes.

"Are you crazy?" she will remember saying.

"You got a bag, a purse or anything?" says Gordy Truman.

"What for?"

"I think I got it!" says Butch.

"Bring it," says Gordy. "And shut the fuck up, Louella."

"Yeah, shut the fucking *right* the fuck up, Louella!" says Butch, sounding excited now.

"Daddy?" says Baby.

And then one is led out of dead Momma's townhouse and thrown blind into the trunk of a car and ending up here, somewhere, sitting in a chair with hands bound and a cloth band covering one's eyes.

The cloth band is suddenly removed, Butch and the blond chick called Baby seen sitting side by side on the bed in what's obviously some motel room, Gordy Truman at the window peering out through a slit in the curtain. And stretched out on top of the bed with an arm covering her eyes, a second woman, brunette, baggy sweater, tight jeans, and bargain-rate sneakers; looks drug-sick. This one must be Gordy's girlfriend and for lack of a better idea or more information, one will call her Bimbo.

"Okay," says Gordy turning from the window and looking at Louella. "As you may have figured, you are now officially kid-fucking-napped. Don't talk, don't say shit. Where's the plastic? Bank, credit card, anything. All that's in that purse of yours is a cellphone, a bottled water and fucking candy wrappers. What the fuck's going on, Louella? We want your bank PIN, cash, whatever you got. An' we know you *got*. Your mother left you a ton. We don't want all of it, but you can part with some. And we're not fucking around."

"Can I talk now?" says Louella.

"Sure, you can talk now," says Gordy Truman.

"Well, first off, this is the stupidest fucking thing you dipshits have ever—"

She feels a sharp blow to the side of her head.

"I told you we're not fucking around, Louella," says Gordy Truman. He's moved close, stands over her with his hand ready to strike again, and one can see the look in those eyes. This is that other look, the look when Gordy Truman is whacked, out of dope and sick and desperate all rolled into one. This is the look Gordy Truman has when he adds to his rep on the street by becoming unhinged and engaging in truly violent and over-the-top acts with no concern whatsoever as to the consequences. This is the look that put him in the Kingston Pen. This is the look of the truly dangerous Gordy Truman.

"Okay, okay," says Louella. "But you know I know that we're only somewhere up the valley somewhere, some sleazeball motel in Abbotsford, maybe."

"Yeah, but *which* motel?" says Butch.

"Shut up, Butch . . ." says Gordy.

"Daaaddy . . ." says Baby.

"Ohh, fuuuuck . . ." says sick Bimbo from the bed.

23.

Crime in Progress

IT'S A FACT KNOWN BY MANY, and no less by the disappointed and more than dispirited parents of the Truman brothers along with others of the Truman family, that the two brothers have never been, nor likely ever will be, troubled by contemplations on theories or actualities of existence, such as one inescapable peculiarity of life that begins even before birth, and that is that anyone who has lived for no more than fifteen minutes on the planet will have been subject to the universal commonality of the phenomenon known simply as "the chain of events." No action in the history of the world, or the universe for that matter, is immune from this circumstance. A night of hot sex, spermatozoa swimming upstream, reaching the egg, fertilization, growth, birth, fifteen minutes of life in the world, and one may be wont to say (if one could actually speak when only fifteen minutes old), "What the hell just happened?" And the answer would be, of course, "Well, this happened, then this happened, and then as a result, this happened, etc. ...." And it's the same for everybody, forever and always irrespective of their station in life, no one is immune. One thing happens, then another, and so on . . .

Chain Link #1: Gordy Truman checks Louella's frequently called numbers on her cellphone, asks her for a family member's number.

"It's my mother's cellphone," says Louella, too late aware of the irrelevance of this information as Gordy Truman makes to crack her skull for a second time.

"But the first number listed is my aunt's," says Louella quickly, thereby thwarting a second blow.

And Gordy Truman speed-dialing the selected number, handing

the phone to Butch. Butch Truman waiting, one ring, two rings. Butch speaks into the phone.

"Listen. We got your niece and want money. Will be in touch with the details. It's no big deal, so don't phone the cops. She'll be okay."

Butch ends the call, looks at Gordy.

Gordy looks at Butch.

"What the fuck was that?" says Gordy.

"The ransom call," says Butch. "Can't stay on the line too long. Gotta keep the calls short so they can't trace us."

"And who would be tracing it, idiot..." moans Bimbo from the bed.

"Hear that," says Gordy. "Who'd be tracing anything, jerk-off? No one even knows she's gone yet. And what was that hokey crap, 'It's no big deal'?"

"Buuutch?" says Baby. "I got to go to the bathroom."

Gordy grabbing the phone, hitting speed-dial again for the same number but gets a busy signal.

Link #2: The reason Gordy Truman gets a busy signal is because Aunt Inga (who answered the phone when Butch Truman called) is on the phone to the North Vancouver RCMP to report a kidnapping. She gives Louella's townhouse address and responds angrily when the evening duty officer suggests that it may have just been a crank call.

"Listen, young man," says Aunt Inga. "My niece knows certain people from her past who are more than capable of this kind of activity, so it would be wise to take this call seriously. I will meet the investigative officers at my niece's address to help in any way I can while they look for evidence or whatever it is they do in a case like this, and I will take your name and badge number to ensure your prompt and correct action in this matter!"

"Um, certainly, ma'am," says the evening duty officer.

Link #3: At the North Vancouver RCMP station, the evening duty officer, after getting off the phone, sits back, closes his eyes, and mutters, "Dingbat bitch," to no one in particular.

And decides not to take the call seriously.

A moment later (something nagging at him, something in the unpleasant tone of that woman caller), he then decides it might be more prudent to take the previous call seriously after all, just to cover his own ass.

Link #4: Moments later, rookie Constable Dusty Yorke while out on patrol gets a call from dispatch. The situation is referred to as an "R1-50 something or something" at 124 Maitland Road in Deep Cove. Rookie Constable Dusty Yorke is only momentarily in the dark about the actual situation that the call from dispatch pertains to; the code means nothing to her. But always prepared and aware that one can't commit to memory every little thing, Dusty Yorke easily refers to her tiny notebook of codes that she always carries with her for just such a contingency. She finds the code, already expecting no more than some sorry-ass misdemeanor call, a domestic disturbance, maybe, or some garbage being dumped illegally somewhere. But spirits rise, literally fly high, upon finding that the code means a possible abduction/kidnapping. A real crime in progress, some true action. And a chance to use the siren.

So with one's jaw set and eyes bright, it's also a chance to pull a four-wheel, rubber-burning U-turn drift in the middle of the road and floor it all the way out to the Cove.

Link #5: Some moments before Dusty Yorke pulls her rubber-burning U-turn and floors it all the way out to the Cove, Gordy Truman has succeeded in getting Louella's Aunt Inga on the phone.

"We have your niece and want—"

Gordy Truman is unable to even begin listing his demands as Aunt Inga takes over—

"I've notified the police," says Aunt Inga. "And you'll get not one red cent from me or the family. If all that my niece has told me is true about you people, and that is that you're no more than cowardly, drugged-up dirtbags, her words not mine, then I will not be a party to it in anyway. Now, I would suggest you let my niece go, in good health, and put an end to this nonsense while you still can."

"Now, wait a fucking min—" says Gordy Truman.

"That's all, I, or anyone else in the family, has to say," says Aunt Inga.

"Look, you fucking—" says Gordy Truman.

"Just how much were you thinking of asking, by the way?" says Aunt Inga.

"Fifty thou—*a hundred thousand dollars, you fucking shithead*! An' we're still asking!"

"Out of the question."

The line goes dead and Gordy Truman goes, well, nuts.

Link #6: Louella Debra Poule gets to watch Gordy Truman go nuts in the sleazy motel room somewhere up the Fraser Valley, probably in Abbotsford. The cheap lamp on the bedside table is the first item to go, smashed against the wall. Then the only other chair in the room is upturned, Butch avoiding injury by leaping onto the bed beside Bimbo. Bimbo bounces a bit as Butch joins her but otherwise remains motionless, still stretched out along the bed with one arm across her face. Gordy puts a fist through the wall, then a boot follows as Baby cries out something from the bathroom. Then Louella thinks she hears the Irish lilt—

> *I kiss the dear fingers so toil-worn for me*
> *Oh, God bless you and keep you, Mother Machree . . .*

And then that familiar sound of wood splintering—doorstop, door jamb, door casings flying—hinges, deadbolt, and strike plate airborne—and timber screeching its last breath as the door to the room comes down and in and enter *Link #7* and *#8,* Gordy Truman doing a leap to safety to sprawl on the carpet beside Louella's feet.

24.

Of Slime-Soaked Alleyways

POLICE CONSTABLE DUSTY YORKE stands at dead Momma's circular white kitchen table, glances down at *The Complete Home Gardener* open there.

She reads:
Diseases—If any plants appear sickly, take them away from their healthy neighbours, for trouble can quickly spread.

"Ain't that the truth," she thinks to herself.

She glances up at the hanging array of plants adorning the kitchen, Aunt Inga watching her a moment. Aunt Inga turns, fidgeting, wanders into the living room, Dusty Yorke following quickly to take charge by the swivel reclining chair.

"You notice anything strange, Mrs. Boehler?" says Dusty Yorke.

"Strange?" says Aunt Inga.

"Well," says Constable Dusty Yorke, her eyes travelling the sectional sofa, the low dark-wood coffee table, and the beechwood combination wall unit. "There doesn't appear to be any signs of a struggle, no signs of anything out of the ordinary."

"No, there appears not," says Aunt Inga. "Should there be?"

"Yes, well, you know we don't usually investigate missing persons until the subject is missing for twenty-four hours. Except in the case of children," says Dusty Yorke.

"Yes, I'm aware of that," says Aunt Inga. "But in this case there has been a phone call saying my niece has been abducted. I feel that immediate action is necessary in a case like this, don't you? Will there be other officers coming?"

"Just me for now," says Dusty Yorke, "until it's a positive for an actual abduction. Did you tell the dispatcher that you know the people who are supposed to have taken your niece?"

"I didn't say that," says Aunt Inga. "I said I know the *type* of people who are supposed to have taken my niece."

Constable Dusty Yorke leaves the room, mounts the narrow stairs to the upstairs.

"Better have a look. Your niece do drugs, anything like that, Mrs. Boehler?"

Aunt Inga following.

"Is that important?"

Dusty Yorke standing at the top of the stairs, looking down.

"It could be," says Constable Dusty Yorke.

"Well, if you must know. Yes, my niece has had a drug problem, but she's cleaned herself up and is doing just fine now."

"I see," says Constable Dusty Yorke, her excitement rising. This could be the real deal if the abductee is a drug user. A possible drug deal gone bad, a rip-off of some kind. A junkie in too deep.

The door to the smaller room at the top of the stairs stands open, a view of an unmade bed, clothes strewn across the floor. The door to the room opposite closed, Constable Dusty Yorke standing close, sniffing.

"This the master bedroom?" she says.

"Yes," says Aunt Inga standing halfway up the stairs, her head eye-level with Dusty Yorke's shoes.

"Better stay back a minute," says Constable Dusty Yorke, nose against the door, seeking a scent—cannabis, methyl alcohol, or turps—anything chemical. "You never know..." she says half to herself as she tries the door, opening a pinch and peering through the crack, imagined booby traps or blinding fluorescent lighting hung precariously overhead and a room crammed with marijuana plants, or better still, the acrid odour of chemicals bubbling over in rusty kitchen pots on poorly wired hot plates. "*Just a'cookin' up de ol' crystal meth.*"

"You never know what?" says Aunt Inga from behind, head craning for a better view.

"Just what you may find..." mutters Constable Dusty Yorke, entering the master bedroom and biting her lip to keep from voicing her disappointment. A neatly kept bedroom, hardwood queen-sized platform bed and armoire, chest of drawers with brushed nickel handles, cubbie storage bench, and a native dream catcher with eagle feathers above the bed. Aunt Inga gaining the bedroom doorway, standing beside Constable Dusty Yorke on the native print decorator rug and looking down at the RCMP issue firearm now clutched in Dusty Yorke's hand.

"My god," says Aunt Inga. "What were you expecting, constable?"

And Constable Dusty Yorke (often inclined to the dramatic) would love to say—*"Every godawful, filthy corrupt thing you could imagine, sweetheart, the things that can kill yourself and your children, kill your dreams like maybe a drug-crazed homicidal maniac or just the skeletal, rat-gnawed bones of a drug- and alcohol-overdosed once-human being jumbled on the floor, the stuff of ugly real life like the blank stare of the homeless, or the tears running down the face of a prostitute at the end of the line sprawled on her bottom in some slime-soaked alleyway, skirt hiked to her waist to reveal the track marks up her thighs, and all this with many thanks to the sideshow we call politics that seems to favour the rights of criminals over the rights of the common blinkin' citizen—"*

But Dusty Yorke doesn't say that, doesn't say any of it. Instead, Dusty Yorke says: "Like I told you, Mrs. Boehler, you never know..."

And leaving Mrs. Boehler (Aunt Inga) to say, "Um, no, you never do, I guess..."

SO, AS CONSTABLE DUSTY YORKE and Mrs. Aunt Inga Boehler explore the ambiguous world of that which one will never know, the Truman brothers experience the harsher but much more vivid world of the clear and concise in a motel room somewhere up valley, and this in the form of a thorough and unprovoked beating at the hands and boots of the Cuban and the Mick (*Links #7* and *#8*), the two plainclothes cops careful to rain blows only on torsos and not the heads of the brothers so as to limit any incriminating signs of an assault, Butch Truman ending up sandwiched between the motel bed and the far wall, expelling breaths while older brother Gordy makes an involuntary circuit of the room and lands once more at the feet of Louella, arms crossed over his sides attempting to protect a freshly cracked rib. The motel room then tossed by the Cuban and the Mick, mattress flipped, drawers from the natty motel desk flung afar, and the entire bed upended as the Truman brothers' women seek shelter in the bathroom, Baby whimpering and repeating her man's name and one Sherry Kinsella dazed and drug-sick, muttering unanswered queries about just what is going on.

At last the Cuban stands over Gordy Truman, shaking the stuffing of a pillow down around him, Louella still sitting in the chair, hands bound, and the blindfold now slipped loosely below her chin. A small man noticed standing in the motel room doorway, sixty watts' worth of yellow light from the ceiling bulb straining to reflect off his face, a face reflecting back the rubescence of long, sordid nights in his chosen vocation, night manager of a rat's-nest motel, the tired, pale flesh projecting in turn the long guest lists of undesirables, of hookers, pimps, thieves, and murderers on the run, and forlorn salesmen on forlorn stopovers, drug addicts, alkies and the mentally ill, and unfaithful husbands shacking up for one-night stands with office secretaries, and the emotionally scarred and physically battered, and it all projecting up at the Mick who stands balancing on top of the toppled door and looking down.

"I brought you the pass-key," says the man.

"Kind of late for that, me father," says the Mick. "But, thanks."

"Who's gonna pay..." says the man.

"Oh, oh, oh," says the Mick. "Hold it right there, buddy. This is a drug bust. Cleaning up the streets so guys like you can sleep safer at night, and you want to put a price on that? I don't think so, my friend. Be grateful these guys didn't have a chance to slit your throat for the few measly bucks you got in that cash box out there."

"Well, I..." says the man.

"And just what the fuck we have here?" says the Cuban, noticing

Louella Debra Poole, bound and partially gagged for the first time. "What the fuck you people got going here, anyway?"

Looks are exchanged between Butch and Gordy, between Louella and Butch, between Gordy and Louella. The silence is uncomfortable to all but the two narcs, Louella tempted to just rat the Truman brothers out.

Butch is the first to speak, drawing from yet another dream he's had since adolescence that goes along with the dream of driving to the West Coast in a pink Cadillac with a blond by his side.

"We're making a movie," says Butch, sweat shining along his nose. "A documentary . . . sort of . . ."

Another silence, but this time it's of the stunned variety. The Mick stoops, leaning over to the space between the upturned bed and the wall, and smacking Butch Truman across the head, disseminating for the moment any and all dreams.

"Yeah? And you're the fucking director, I suppose. Where's your fucking cameras?" he says.

"We don't need the gear yet, we're just doin' rehearsals . . ." says Butch lamely.

"And it takes place in a shit motel room?" says the Mick.

"Some of it . . ." says Butch.

"And what's the name of this movie you're all so intent on makin'?" says the Mick.

"Ah . . . *Daddy and Ba*—" says Butch.

"How 'bout just callin' it *One Great Big Pile of Fucking Bullshit*, like it fucking is!" says the Mick.

Gordy Truman drops his head, yet another dream of Butch Truman surfacing. The Cuban stands in front of Louella.

"We do know you—Rubella, or something—busted you and your buddies and that goofball Jimmy Flood, wasn't it? And now you're hanging with the Tru*dick* brothers? Why can't all you fuckers get a life? Jesus."

"Looks like we might have the Trudicks on abduction charges, eh, Mr. Rourke?" says the Mick.

"I haven't been abducted," says Louella.

"Sure, sweetheart," says the Cuban, "you're rehearsing for a movie. And it's gonna be one fine fucking masterpiece, an' Mr. McFadden, cuff the Trudicks, cuz we're taking them in because we knew when we saw that freaking Cadillac that we'd score something with you fucking bozos if we just followed it."

"Hey," says Butch Truman, still lying between the upturned bed and the far wall. "You guys aren't even in your jurisdiction! Gordy! These guys are out of their jurisdiction! They can't arrest us can they?"

"Shut up, Butch . . ." says Gordy Truman.

"Jureez-fucking-diction," says the Mick. "What exactly is that, anyway, *jureezdiction*? Is that, like, something we need to be *in* to arrest you dipshits? Like a pair of pants? We gotta be in a pair of pants to arrest you guys?"

The Cuban has moved to the doorway of the bathroom.

"You girls, outta there. I gotta take a dump."

Baby and the Bimbo coming out of the bathroom, taking a seat on the carpet beside Gordy at the feet of the Mick. Baby's crying now, loud sobs, two rough smudges of black eyeliner under her eyes. The Mick hollering to the Cuban, "Hey, can you take a dump somewhere if it's not in your jurisdiction?" and a hearty guffaw had by the two plainclothes narcs, the Mick wiggling his fingers down at Bimbo and Baby.

"ID, ladies. We already know who your boyfriends are."

Bimbo and Baby rummaging through handbags on the floor, Louella sitting quiet. The Cuban and the Mick were crazier than the Truman brothers and could do a hell of a lot more damage if riled up.

"You, too, dearie," says the Mick.

"Can someone undo my hands?" says Louella.

"Oh, yeah, the movie," says the Mick. "Hey, blondie. Untie the leading lady."

And Baby crawling over to the chair, undoing the scarf from Louella's wrists and using it to blow her nose.

"Ah, that's nice, girlie," says the Mick. "Honk it up, love."

Louella stands pulling cash, a bank card, credit card, and a driver's licence out of her right-front jeans pocket, thereby demonstrating to an angry Butch Truman an age-old rule of the street that only the idiot broads carry money in their jackets or handbags, Butch eyeing the cash and plastic in Louella's hand and Gordy giving him an evil look. The toilet heard flushing, the Cuban back in the room and the Mick handing ID back to Baby and Bimbo. Then wiggling fingers at Louella, Louella handing over cards and cash. The Mick looking things over, handing back her driver's licence and cards, then counting a total of six twenties in cash, pocketing four, and returning two to Louella. Louella says nothing, pockets her two remaining twenties and sits down. Not because it's the right thing to do, but because it's the smart thing to do. Then the Cuban standing tall in the middle of the room, scuff-toed Daytons, blue jeans, hunter's vest, and lumberjack shirt, setting forth their immediate itinerary.

"Okay, this is what's gonna happen. We're taking the Trudicks downtown and towing that pink pile of shit parked out there, and since it don't seem that Rubella here or whatever her name is gonna press any charges, it won't be a problem for us to come up with something. And since we haven't found any dope, it rips my heart out that we can't arrest all of you, so you ladies can go, and not to be too disappointed, we'll get you for sure next time. Any questions, whining or talk about 'rights,' and it'll be considered resisting fucking arrest."

The Mick guffaws again, the two narcs trundling Butch and Gordy, wrists cuffed, out the door and into the parking lot, the night manager still in the doorway catching the dull glow of light off his head and stepping aside as the two plainclothes narcs and their charges stomp by. Back in the room, Louella sits back down on the chair, the only stick of furniture left standing. And removes the blindfold that has slipped down under her chin. Baby and Bimbo are still seated at her feet on this worn cigarette-scarred carpet, Baby wide-eyed and teary staring after the vanishing backside of Butch, Bimbo bleary-eyed and spent, not watching the exodus of the

Truman brothers but instead staring up at Louella as if awaiting direction, a word as to what comes next. Louella, on the other hand, is experiencing an unexpected evocation of childhood, kindergarten to be exact, as she sits on the chintzy motel room chair with Baby and Bimbo seated obediently at her feet. One feels just like Mrs. Orlander, one's old kindergarten teacher, who used to sit on a time-worn, old oak chair in Reading Circle and read stories to the class, who sat obediently on the floor at her feet in the same way, the carpet of one's kindergarten class a lot cleaner and exhibiting a more cheerful rainbow design back then, but all the kids, just like Baby and Bimbo, staring up expectantly, maybe a little confused and, yes, even a little frightened, a vague fear and intuition of the lady in the chair's undisputed authority that can show itself at any given moment when a simple classroom rule is broken.

And so it feels now to Louella Poule, *Miss* Louella Poule. The tables have turned, hers is the upper hand now, the voice of authority. And gazing a moment at the cheap print that until a few minutes ago was hanging over the motel room bed before the Cuban and the Mick tossed everything, it now lies on the far side of the room angled against the wall, one corner of the frame stabbed into a pillow. A standard pastoral scene it appears, of crudely brushed purple mountains, vague shadowings of green and brown tumbling across the foreground suggesting forest, grey slashes and circles depicting boulders and stones on a rising cliffside, two small and very stiff-looking renditions of what one assumes are mountain goats staring out from a rock ledge over the canyon at the observer.

She's spacing out, Louella looking back down at her wards, Baby and Bimbo. This is the slow class and the pupils have been very bad, very bad indeed, Louella remembering Mrs. Orlander's upright position on the chair, the authoritative no-nonsense tone of address.

"Okay, ladies," says Louella. "I'm not calling you Baby and Bimbo, so what the fuck are your real names?"

"Tina," says Baby.

"Sherry," says Bimbo.

"Okay, Sherry and Tina. I've got forty bucks cash left here, and it's yours after you give me a ride back to town. You can buy dope with it or whatever you want, I don't really care because I feel sorry for both of you dickheads getting mixed up with the Truman brothers, who are complete assholes and I know none of this shit was your idea."

And to the night manager still hovering in the doorway: "You, I'll give my phone number. Take it or leave it, I'm past caring what anyone does. I just want to go home, and you can call me with the cost of repairs and I'll cover it compliments of my dead mother's estate and in honour of her memory. Understand?"

The night manager nodding, "It'll have to do, I guess—"

"*That* is so fucking right, mister-sir," says Louella smacking her hands. "At last someone who has a handle on the way things are gonna work around here. *It will have to do.* Everything will *have to do.* Now, I'm going to make a call to let people know that I'm okay and to expect me back soon. Then you two ladies are going to drive me at least to the fucking bridge where I'll probably just call a cab because I really just want to get the fuck away from here and away from you two fuck-ups, too."

Tina "Baby" Blout rising to her feet, looking hurt and willing to cry some more. Sherry "Bimbo" Kinsella rises, too, shouldering her purse, marching forth across the wobbly fallen door out into the parking lot, face sullen, expressionless, just another tired, junk-sick soul impervious to ridicule or insult.

"Sorry about your mother . . ." says the night manager as Louella motors by him, but the words are heard only by maybe the night gods of sleazy motels and the night manager himself, Louella now deaf to all conversation, questions, complaints, woes, travails, problems, doubts, fears, or any damn thing anyone has to say for the rest of the night. But one may in fact thank the night gods of sleazy motels or any others that Meagre Deerstone will a short time later not also be deaf to all conversation, questions, complaints, woes, travails, problems, doubts, fears, etc. for the rest of the night, as two-and-a-half hours later Louella is on the phone to tell her that she's screwed up and scored some dope with Baby and the Bimbo and took out more cash on her bank card and scored more dope and now she's totally wrecked and high and lost and her whole life is once again going down the shitter and she wishes her mother were here and what the fuck's the use of anything anyway?

"Get a cab," says Meagre Deerstone. "Come to my place, not yours."

"*It's too fucking late,*" Louella wailing, slurring, babbling woes. "*Goo, goo, blah, blah . . . O' sweet Matilda Goomba . . .*"

"A cab, Louella."

"Okay. Coming . . ."

And Louella in the back seat of a cab racing across the bridge over the narrows, nose pressed and running snot against the window, the cab cresting the span and rolling onward down the other side, headed for home—well, almost—a few doors down, anyway, and one glimpsing tall trees racing by all-black against a distant city glow left behind over the black water as the cab heads deeper into the shadow of the mountains, somewhere up the creek, up the inlet to granite bluffs and high creaking pines, dark ferns, and tethered moss, moon-glow on white fungi clenching red bark, and one's eyes streaming, eyes streaming tears down one's cheeks, down onto one's chin and neck and collar, and down across one's favourite jeans and shoes and onto the floor of the cab where the back seat begins to fill with the salty water and the tears won't ever turn off, the Cove around the next tree-lined bend and one weeps on into the still morning and along the dark ribbon of road, weeps for all the bad things, the terrible things, the sorry things, and weeps for all the lost things, the hidden things, the forgotten and missed things, and weeps on for all the dead-and-gone things, too . . .

25

Of Rummaging
Underground Rodents

IT'S FOUR THIRTY in the morning when Meagre Deerstone greets Louella at her door after the cab drops her off. It's thought prudent that Louella stay at Meagre's for a few days following her relapse and not return to dead Momma's townhouse. Louella is grateful for the suggestion, finding it necessary to admit (yet again) that, yes, she may need a helping hand from time to time.

"You can stay in my spare room," says Meagre. "You'll get through this."

Louella stands in Meagre's living room and sobs uncontrollably.

"Sorry, I let you down," sobs Louella.

"Don't be an idiot," says Meagre. "Let's get you to bed."

Louella following upstairs, lying down on the spare bed. Meagre turning on the bedside lamp. Louella rising from the bed, stands in Meagre Deerstone's spare room. And sobs uncontrollably.

"You probably won't want anything to eat yet, but try to drink lots of water," says Meagre. "And lie the heck down."

Louella lies down, sits up, and lies back down again.

And sobs uncontrollably.

LOUELLA ALONE, LYING ATOP the spare bed in Meagre Deerstone's spare room. She leaves the light on; darkness would be unbearable. Some native prints on the walls, one that looks like a bird, a raven or an eagle. Another larger one on the opposite wall, a killer whale maybe, black and red. On the bedside table, a smudge pot. And thank god, or Matilda Goomba, a small TV positioned at the foot of the bed that she turns on without the sound. Doesn't matter what's on, just a need for meaningless images for the eyes to focus on and allow the time to pass. She's talking out loud to herself but can't recall a moment later what she's said. But that doesn't matter either, really. As long as whatever happens in the next while is completely devoid of any meaning, please. Meaning at this time would be too much to handle and would be wasted. Wasted on the wasted. Time to advocate meaninglessness for a while and just exist. Be sick. Be awful. You deserve it.

LOUELLA SLEEPING THAT first day and the following night away, left alone to stay in bed watching the muted TV. Meagre Deerstone does look in occasionally, once in the morning and once in the evening.

"Checking for breathing only," she says from the doorway.

Louella smiles a thanks but can't summon the energy or enthusiasm for conversation.

On the second morning, she awakes before dawn. The birds have started outside, but there is as yet, thankfully, no sounds of human life—vehicles, voices—just a few birds and the pleasant airborne scent of spruce and pine, cedar and coast forest. Of dark, wet earth.

Funny how the early morning chirping of birds, the sound of the world waking up, was not that long ago a sound so feared and unwanted, a sound that heralded nothing but the coming horrors of a new drug-seeking day when all one wanted was to stay hidden and anonymous under a reassuring camouflage of night, wishing for night to be forever, where all the sordid details of one's existence can creep around in shadow, hiding the mottled puffiness of one's skin, the dark rings around the eyes, the sniffling nose and chewed fingernails, or the fresh green-purple bruises along the jawline, and one's hair pasted damp and oily across one's forehead. The beginnings of days for a long time meant nothing more than more grunge, jangled dope-sick nerves, and the daily awakening of the fear that followed you around like an acetylene-torch sky that would hang over you the entire day, trying to burn a hole in your brain, causing you to wear sunglasses even indoors or adopt an angry squint like some rummaging underground rodent that's anything but cute and cuddly, tiny teeth bared as it pokes its head up out of the trash pile, while all the time keeping a watch for the talons or claws of bigger, meaner predators that can swoop down out of nowhere at any time and take its head off in a New York minute.

But lately, for the most part, there seems a noticeable difference in mornings, those beginnings of days. Not so much a nightmare, and one now lies safe under the covers in Meagre's spare room. Pitcher of water beside the bed, compliments of Nurse Deerstone. Sure, there's guilt. Shame and angst. One knows one has screwed up; it's the price to pay. But at least now terrible events seem to have a perceivable beginning and, more importantly, a perceivable end.

"And you seemed such a bright, happy child growing up," Aunt Inga has said, not coming forth with the obvious questions, the questions she really wants to ask. The hows and the whys. The questions everybody wants to ask when confronted with any sense or form of disaster. And they're the same questions she herself has felt compelled to ask many times about others over the years. She remembers the surprise—no, the shock—when she had realized that the junkies and crooks and general castoffs she'd ended up with had all, at one time, been *kids.* Had been *raised*, had *lives.* And beyond that even, had become, at some time, *adults.* They had all had parents and childhoods, and it seems nobody is just born a degenerate. They all came from homes of some kind, went to school, had birthday parties, and swam in lakes and swimming pools from sun-up to sundown on summer vacations.

There was Jeanne White, last seen leaning up against a wall downtown waiting to score, she who had run a successful boutique in Toronto until losing it all to a crack habit. And Old Stu, now in his late fifties and had done ten years' hard time for manslaughter or something, a trained architect, for god's sake. And Bobby Southern, last seen stretched out on the sidewalk at Main and Pender babbling incoherently while jonesing on crystal meth and who once sold high-end real estate in Saskatoon and owned two houses to boot. The list goes on and on, the commonality of an actual normal life that existed before everything went south on the back of poor decisions and just plain shit-luck. And on that list, Louella knows, sits the name Louella Debra Poule, no better, no worse than all the others, walking the drug-botched stumble through the side streets and alleyways needing a fix, looking like death itself and who once carpooled daily out to the University of British Columbia, freshly showered in crisp, clean jeans and snowy white halter tops in pursuit of an Arts diploma in psychology . . .

Whoa—Jesus—

Louella Debra Poule lies on top of the covers of Meagre Deerstone's spare bed in Meagre Deerstone's spare room as the world awakens to another day. But, really, that's all it is, just the start of another day. Not a unique occurrence by any means; just something that happens, well, every day to everyone, the killer whale on the far wall arching its back in a hard, graceful stylized curve, its brow and back inky black and smooth, a harsh white orb implanted on the side of its head, assured, frank, and accommodating one blazing red eyeball.

WHILE THUS ABSORBED in such revelations pertaining to the collective parallels in everyone-in-the-world's lives, Louella would be surprised to know she is not alone (for she is still self-centred enough and believing in her own uniqueness enough to not believe that anyone else can really think or feel the way she does), and she would be even more surprised and disbelieving to know that the person who is at the same time undergoing a similar episode of jumbled thought and memory is none other than Blacky Harbottle himself, this similar episode of jumbled thought and memory sparked, perhaps, by the crass inherent loneliness cherished and nurtured by all lost and drug-ravaged souls. He lies at this same moment on this same morning full length along his sofa in a semi-conscious drug stupor of his own, while his mind, unrestricted by any controls, tells him not that everyone was at one time a child, but that he, himself, was at one time a child! His life actually began (like any other) with a childhood!

He groans here, and it's not obvious if it's from physical discomfort or the immensity of the realization.

There's this boy, see ("Must be me," his semi-conscious mind says), spending summers playing baseball on the local park diamond in the village of St. Gabriel-de-Valcartier, north of Quebec City. And there's swimming in the brisk, icy currents of the Jacques Cartier River. And taking rafting trips and paddling trips with the family, English father and French mother, younger brother and older sister, and everyone screaming in fear and excitement while being bounced down the rapids. And fishing for pale blue river trout and sea-green lake pike off sandbars or from a canoe while drifting downriver under spreading, sun-dappled overhangs of birch and maple. And playing leapfrog and tag among the marble and granite headstones of St. Gabriel Church, a small army of kids with Blacky among them, and then suddenly as if by some mutual consensus everyone tiring of the game and vaulting the antiquated low stone wall of the graveyard to roll en masse down the grassy slope that bolsters the tiny hilltop churchyard. And at the bottom, dumped helter-skelter at the side of the road, the mishmash of bicycles waiting, deposited there earlier by the same mob and now sorted out by small dirty and scabby hands, disentangled and jerked upright, bantam-sized legs thrown over seats and dusty running shoes jammed onto pedals and legs pumping, bike wheels rattling over the gravel of the back roads that twisted their ways through those rural Quebec woodlands, everyone racing to get ahead, to be the one in front on the mad pedal home so as not to be caught in the dust cloud . . .

He jerks awake.

Paws the air.

Mutters something unintelligible and dozes off again, dreams of his mother and large bowls steaming, large bowls of poutine.

IN KEEPING SOMEWHAT with the same theme, that of drug-induced stupors, there is yet another who is at the exact same time immersed in his own stupor in an apartment on Vancouver's south side, although Jimmy Flood is not so assaulted with disturbing thoughts of childhood and general reminiscences. But it remains that if he were so plagued by this mode of thinking, it would be quickly apparent that to the best of his knowledge, he, too, has had a childhood along the way and is still at least loved by his mother and father, although not particularly liked. As far as his sister's affections go, he would (if he were thinking about it) have to assume that here, too, he is somewhat loved, but, again, definitely not liked either. And, if given the ability or desire to build from here, he might attempt to differentiate between the two. As it is, he can only perceive a general disapproval of his behaviour and lifestyle (or lack thereof) as being a general disapproval of his very self.

There are memories of a happier time; a childhood lurks in the fog with birthdays and schoolyard games and Saturday afternoons at the movies. But these images are for the most part very fleeting, like shy birds shaking the branches of a tree, shadows momentarily visible and then gone again, the branches left trembling with naught but an inference that something was ever there at all, and leaving no real impression of what exactly it was. And so might be encapsulated Jimmy Flood's very life up until now: things that are there momentarily, then just as quickly gone. Of course, Jimmy Flood, throat constricting for a moment while lying semi-conscious and sprawled on the living room floor of the apartment on Vancouver's south side, is not ready to "build from here" in any way, shape, or form. Instead, he coughs, gurgles, jerks both legs upward and outward, joints stiff and forming a V of limbs in mid-air, and then allowing them to fall again. These twitches, spasms, gurglings, and accompanying moans and groans will go on for several hours, the brain misfiring for the most part but occasionally getting back online long enough to proffer the one coherent thought that is at present the most important if one is to make one's life in any way better, and that thought is: "One must find, *and retain,* the phone number of that pilot guy, goddamnit!"

26.

Of Destinies and
Heavenly Attire

IN SPITE OF Constable Dusty Yorke's more than apparent limita-
tion of life experience and, well, just plain maturity, let it not be
said that Constable Dusty Yorke does not take her job and its duties
seriously. On the contrary, under a thin veneer of what may at times
appear to be just frivolous feminine wiles (at least to some of her
male colleagues), there lies a heartfelt and sincere concern for the
welfare of others, most specifically for the safety and protection of
the old and infirm, the very young, or anyone who displays a state
of helplessness in the face of adversity. Dusty Yorke, to her credit,
does in her world aspire to be no more than a champion of the mis-
treated, seeking justice while remaining devoid of cynicism and
prejudice. (These two elements will, of course, manifest promi-
nently only later on in her career.) So, it's not too surprising that
she does, in fact, pursue the alleged abduction case of this Louella
Debra Poule woman with a fair amount of zeal.

After speaking with the girl's aunt, she inspects the backyard for
any signs of intruders or anything else suspicious. She comes up
with nothing and in turn inspects the carport. Again nothing. Not
deterred, she questions the neighbours, gathering what information
she can, which is not much. A few people report seeing a pink
Cadillac, older model, parked a short while out front. But it was
dark and no one got a look at the actual occupants. And, no, there
were no sounds of any altercation between their neighbour Louella
Poule and any supposed assailants.

Officer Marv Klep is to ask the next day, "Any viable leads on
this supposed abduction thing?"

"Not really," says Dusty Yorke. "A pink older-model Cadillac convertible was seen parked at the scene sometime last night . . ."

"Sounds like a lead to me," says Officer Klep.

"What I said," says Dusty Yorke.

"Um, you did?" says Officer Klep.

"Yes, I did," says Dusty Yorke.

The conversation is interrupted by a call for Dusty Yorke from the aunt of the alleged abductee stating that her niece had just called and she's okay and there's just been a misunderstanding and it's a long story. Dusty Yorke masks her disappointment; it could have been a good case, but she handles it well, confident that all is not yet done with the goings-on at the townhouse complex in the Cove. This confidence derives from a firm if somewhat naive belief in the idea and subsequent power of destiny. A not widely known side of Constable Dusty Yorke is that, while not in the least spiritual, she is decidedly religious. This apparent contradiction, in reality common enough among many of the planet's population, led to a short, never-to-be-repeated argument with Marv Klep one day when Dusty insisted that she was, in fact, spiritual as well as deeply religious.

"Religion is a 'thing,'" Marv Klep had said. "Spirituality is a 'state.'"

Dusty Yorke had not replied, instead offering a silent apology for Marv's ignorance to the god of her choice. Hers is a strictly optical relationship with the divine, seeing all aspects of religion in pictures, usually cliché renditions. The Maker is seen with long, white hair and flowing beard, and is often sprawled somewhat majestically across fluffy, white clouds while casting a critical gaze downward upon the Earth and deciding, perhaps, what events to set in motion next. She harbours pictures of angels, too, these clothed in various standards of heavenly attire, always incorporating a quantity of whirling sheer white linens while transparent wings unfold and reflect the brilliant rays of the Sun. Any biblical human character is, in turn, reproduced in the mind's eye, appearing very much as depicted in brightly illustrated children's books relating stories of the Bible. These images are more than enough to provide the imaginer with any necessary sense of faith or belief in the "good," but with none of the perplexing and annoying mystique that often accompanies "that which is unexplainable." In times of stress or undue anxiety (and these times do come often enough for Constable Dusty Yorke, considering her line of work), a visual image in one's mind of, say, the Virgin Mary standing with hands clasped beneath her chin in prayer, head slightly bowed; this image will be enough to instill a feeling of calm coupled with a sense of obedience that will more often than not dispel any nagging feelings of doubt and uncertainty.

And so it is when Dusty Yorke takes Aunt Inga's call, she is able to say, "Well, that's good news then," and mean it and not mean it. "I'll need a full report from you and your niece," she continues, "about what exactly the circumstances were in this incident."

"Of course," says Aunt Inga.

"And if your niece will want to press charges against anyone . . ."

"Absolutely, I understand," says Aunt Inga.

"Please have her contact me as soon as possible so we can clear everything up," says Dusty Yorke.

"I will," says Aunt Inga. "And, thank you very much, constable."

"You're welcome," says Dusty Yorke, in reality no longer really talking to Aunt Inga but instead to the long, white hair and flowing beard of the Maker somewhere above as he looks down upon all, watching and directing events—*creating* events—pointing her (and all others, too, of course) to her (and their) destinies. And this time, there is just a barely discernible nod of the white-maned head as if in consensus that all is, indeed, not finished at a specific townhouse complex in the Cove.

27.

Cry-Baby Stuff

LOUELLA READS:
Lime-Haters—Many of the gift plants simply survive for
varying periods before dying and being thrown away.

SHE HAS RETURNED to dead Momma's townhouse after her much-
needed respite at Meagre Deerstone's and, although still a little
unsettled, is trying to move on from her slip those few days ago and
the insane debacle with the Truman brothers. She has her
suspicions about who set the whole ridiculous thing up, but Meagre
has suggested that it's irrelevant unless Louella has plans to exact
revenge of some kind, which Louella admits she doesn't. No,
Louella faces a more frightening dilemma than simple kidnapping.
She is attempting to strengthen her resolve, first by a lot of self-talk
along the lines of gaining the proper perspective on the matter,
using phrases like "It's no big deal" and "People do it all the time,"
but this doesn't help much to lessen her anxiety, and, yes . . . her
blatant fear.

One initiates a pathetic attempt to manifest images of a fierce and
reckless individual (namely one's self), like that guy she watched
on TV who tried to break the speed record for catapulting down a
fifty-degree slope of solid ice on a bicycle just to be the fastest person
to ever catapult down a fifty-degree slope of solid ice on a bicycle.
The bike disintegrated at the finish line, sending the guy to the
hospital with multiple injuries, but in its own way and at this
particular moment of crisis in one's life, the act seems to Louella to
make as much sense as doing anything else in life. And, *Oh, sweet
Matilda Goomba, why was one born such a coward?*

No answer is forthcoming to this question, but Louella knows that a so-called crisis like this one she's contemplating, debating, turning left and right and trying to hide from, would be met with raised eyebrows and a look of amused pity if not downright laughter by any normal person. When the subject was first broached by Meagre Deerstone, first lightly and then more strenuously the other afternoon while Louella was still recovering at Meagre's place, one's mind had flailed madly for some kind of excuse, some valid written-in-stone reason for one to be excused from partaking in the suggestion, but all ensuing excuses sounded lame, cry-baby stuff, until she thought she'd hit on the obvious one that could not be denied.

"I can't go on a trip with you to Mexico or anywhere else," says Louella. "I've got a criminal record."

"This is true," says Meagre Deerstone, appearing unperturbed.

It's an ugly afternoon with a heavy rain beating down and a mean north wind coming hard off the mountains. There's a long silence, and one has learned that silence to a First Nations person is a lot different than silence to a white person. To a white person, it's uncomfortable, often plain unbearable, and the white person in question will be obliged to ease his or her white discomfort by yapping away to fill the void, saying anything to maintain some kind of resonance, most of what is said being completely mundane and trivial to the point of the illusory. She knows at the point of this particular silence that it's probable she has lost any argument there may be to sway things to her side, but she must wait to learn how. In fact, since hanging around with Meagre and experiencing these emphatic silences, one has only become more aware of how much talking people do, non-stop yaking reinforced with the increased use of cellphones, which makes it possible for one to remain in a blissful state of non-stop chatter, even when physically alone on a deserted country road. One has always been somewhat fond of solitude, not to the extreme of wishing to live in a hermitage or spend life alone on a desert island, but god love a duck, some fucking silence, please. And even as a little girl, Louella would think adults seemed to go on forever when together, talking about everything in the world it seemed, but at the same time young Louella would think, pulling her dolly's hair back with a plastic comb and fixing it in place with swatches of Scotch tape, she'd think: "But, what does all the talking do, Mommy? What does it *do*?"

And sitting there that rainy afternoon in Meagre Deerstone's living room, waiting for Meagre to speak, to do something, Louella feels herself getting restless, becoming more and more *white*. Can't give Meagre the satisfaction of giving in to one's genetic deficiencies, a sudden image of heavily bearded English crewmen peering over the sea-worn bulwarks of a sailing ship in the year whatever and about to meet the Coast Salish tribes for the first time, their white man genes getting ready, gearing up, to talk the Indians' fucking ears off.

Instead, one had sat quietly on one's hands on Meagre's living-room couch and focused one's attention on the large black-and-white framed poster on the wall above Meagre Deerstone's non-speaking head, the quality of the photo on the poster looking circa turn of the century or around there, and a man, a native man in his fifties or sixties, stands on the edge of a small creek against a backdrop of tall trees, knee-length buckskin jacket, large fur cap, and one hand hanging straight at his side, the other with a thumb hooked into a wide beaded belt.

"That your grandfather?" says Louella, the silence broken by the white person as no doubt any folk of the First Nations could have predicted.

Meagre laughing.

"No," says Meagre. "It's a picture of Chief Joe Capilano, although my grandfather did know him."

"Guess by his name he was from around here, eh?" says Louella.

Meagre Deerstone placing her coffee cup on the side table.

"Yes, he was 'from around here.' Took a delegation of our people to Ottawa in 1903 to meet with the prime minister. They were grieving land claims, native rights, stuff like that. It wasn't appreciated, and when he returned to Vancouver he was thrown in jail."

"Oh," says Louella.

It's her turn to be silent, sit quietly and look at the framed eight-by-ten photograph of a young native boy, Meagre Deerstone's son, who died very young of something, and Meagre doesn't talk about him and no one who knows of it feels invited to ask.

"A direct flight," says Meagre suddenly.

"Huh?"

"A direct flight, from here to there. No stopover in the States. Just need your ID for that. No passport."

"What if they run a check?" says Louella.

"A check on what?" says Meagre.

And silence again, Meagre Deerstone content sipping her coffee, Louella Poule not so much. A knot growing in her stomach as she sits back against the couch, looking at the poster of the chief, a mountain of obstacles forming in her mind—flight bookings—hotel reservations—how to pack a suitcase properly. And feeling that one is a little, helpless kid again sitting on a big person's couch where one's feet shouldn't yet be able to touch the floor. But then again, Meagre will surely know how to do all that stuff, Meagre Deerstone will know how to pack a suitcase.

And that had been that, Louella now turning slowly in dead Momma's blue leather swivel chair. One's going then, one guesses, to Mexico. Meagre Deerstone will tell her when exactly. And how. One will simply have to wait, follow directions as they come, interspersed with long silences. And one can do that, why not? Get psyched. Don't call it a trip. Call it an adventure. A *growth experience* sounds even better. And what's the worst that can happen? Turned back at the airport? No big deal. Would be a bummer for Meagre, but one could make a deal that if it happened, Meagre would continue on by herself. At least her trip wouldn't be ruined. And one can take some heart from that Chief Capilano's story. Look what happened when he took a trip. A guy who probably didn't even have a criminal record to begin with and was only trying to do some good. Anything can happen to anybody for any reason, so it follows (reasons Louella) that it's stupid to worry about it. Leave it in the hands of fate or whatever. And stop being such a chickenshit.

Louella into dead Momma's kitchen, setting on a pot of coffee and attempting an unwavering, determined stare out the window at the far tops of trees. One is able to admit to one's self that it's not really the legal bullshit that one's scared of. It's not customs or airports or even flying (although she hasn't been on a plane since she was seven years old). No, one admits quietly to the far treetops, it's an illogical (or is it logical?) fear of the unknown, fear of the unknown *she*, really, and who that *she* will be in a foreign place without drugs, without the familiar.

28.

Codes of Conduct

FRANKIE YIN BEGAN putting the squeeze on other kids while still "fresh off the boat," so to speak, entering grade seven as a new Canadian in an ESL program at Champlain Heights Elementary School in southeast Vancouver. It begins as a two-man operation, the squeeze game, young Frankie and best friend Pauly Chin shaking down the younger grade five and six kids for lunch money, portable electronic equipment, and occasional articles of footwear or clothing if the item was cool enough and the right fit.

During the whole of these early years (and throughout his criminal career for that matter), Frankie Yin has never thought of himself as a bad person or, back then, as a particularly bad student, explaining to his less bright cohort Pauly Chin that the school's actual official Code of Conduct lauded the qualities of Respect, Empathy, Achievement, and Cooperation, all four of which young Frankie Yin was easily able to transpose in a positive light onto the intimidation and fleecing of the younger students.

The respect aspect he saw as something he himself and Pauly Chin gained from the frightened students upon their being relieved of their worldly goods. Empathy was there, too, illustrated by the fact that he did feel "a little bad" for those kids smaller and younger than himself whom he terrorized, many of them bursting into tears when giving up whatever precious commodity was asked for, young Frankie often inclined to give a couple of sympathetic pats on a trembling shoulder and reassuring them, not unkindly, that he'd kill them if they told the teachers or their parents. The achievement part he felt was self-evident, with Frankie Yin and Pauly Chin achieving not only notoriety, but also monetary and material status. And cooperation, to young Frankie Yin at least, appeared rife in the schoolyard community. How could it not be with only a tiny percentage of students attempting to be uncooperative when asked to cough up the goods?

This ability of Frankie Yin to transpose almost any axiom of moral or ethical behaviour into a form to suit his own agenda, right or wrong and at any given instance, would serve him well into his adulthood. As it eventually comes to pass, however, the good school-day times do come to an end when some of the braver kids discover their own axiom of "strength in numbers," banding together and ratting both him and Pauly Chin out to the school principal, who in turn talks to Frankie's parents. The Yins take it personally, mortified by the loss of face for the family and, to ratify this new and unwanted social stigma, endeavour then to enrol young Frankie in a Montessori alternative program, where if they had read more carefully the program's description of its actual aim, they would have read the part that said: "and to impart a learning experience that promotes the development of intellectually reflective individuals who are caring and ethical members of the community."

It's easy enough for Frankie himself, if not for his parents, to see that this program will never work for him in a million years, and he promptly skips school altogether, and town, for three years. It will always remain vague and subject only to speculation where exactly young Frankie Yin goes during this time and what exactly he does. Clear explanations are never forthcoming. The best anyone gets from Frankie Yin are statements such as "I went up north..." "Some cousins I visit, the Interior..." "Can't remember..." "Memory is funny..."

But one thing is clear when Frankie Yin returns to Vancouver. School was out, the Tai Pai boys are in. *"Ah! It's not a gang, it's a club we make."*

One minor glitch to returning to Vancouver is he's forced to move back in with his parents for a time, but this doesn't cause Frankie Yin too much concern as his father, Mr. Yin, had been a bit of a gangster himself, partaking in his fair share of criminal activities when living in the Chinese province of Zhejiang before immigrating to Canada. Although Mr. Yin has never disclosed this information about himself directly to young Frankie. Frankie knows all about his father's secret history from his uncle (Mr. Yin's brother), who boasts an ardent fondness for a good belt of *baijiu* or unlimited bottles of Canadian beer at any given time, a practice that makes him more than a bit talkative, and it is he who most suspect Frankie Yin stayed with during his three-year absence. The only reply to all Frankie Yin's direct inquiries to his father as to his father's actual vocation in Canada were the words: "Businessman, Frankie. I am a businessman."

Frankie Yin is now sitting in Blacky Harbottle's living room listening to Jimmy Flood's account of the Truman brothers' kidnapping debacle. Jimmy Flood had received the details via a short conversation with Butch and Gordy's girlfriends the day before, after a chance meeting downtown where he ran into the two of them wandering the streets in search of a score.

"These Trumans," says Frankie Yin, "fuck-ups, eh? I could have taken three, maybe four people by the time they take to mess up taking one. You make the big mistake with those guys, Harbottle."

"Tell me something I don't fucking know, Yin," says Blacky Harbottle. "But just remember it was your dipshit idea."

Jimmy Flood watches Frankie Yin for a reaction. There appears to be none. How cool is that? Another positive impression for Jimmy Flood to emulate, now vowing silently there and then not to react to anything ever again. Frankie Yin remains reclined on the sofa, legs stretched out stiffly with feet resting on the coffee table, wearing what look like actual suit pants and a pale pink cotton dress shirt, a thick gold chain dangling from his left wrist and aviator sunglasses tinted orange across his nose. Jimmy Flood slouches back in his chair, stretches his legs out stiffly, and rests his feet on the coffee table.

Blacky Harbottle lights a cigar, doesn't offer one to anybody.

"I give you good idea, you fuck it up," Frankie Yin says simply.

Now Jimmy Flood watches for Blacky's reaction and here, too, there appears to be none.

"They should have made *her* make the first call," says Frankie Yin. "Make it more family. The family pay, not take chances. Maybe wheel and deal a bit but come to an agreement. Everybody happy."

"Word is Butch and Gordy are leaving town, anyway," says Jimmy Flood.

"Word is? What word?" says Blacky Harbottle.

"Well, you know," says Jimmy Flood. "The word . . ."

"The fucking *word*?" says Blacky Harbottle.

"Well, yeah. The word is they somehow got that stupid Cadillac fixed and they're okay to leave town," says Jimmy Flood.

"We maybe put the word out on these Trumans," says Frankie Yin.

"Again with the fucking *word*!" says Blacky Harbottle. "I don't give two shits about the Truman brothers. I just want to know what that dipshit Gordy's done with the rental car I signed off on for him!"

"Guess how many shits I give about the Trumans," says Frankie Yin.

Blacky Harbottle walks into the kitchen. Frankie Yin looks at Jimmy Flood.

"Go on, guess."

Jimmy Flood looks back at Frankie Yin. A sound of glasses tinkling comes from the kitchen.

"Um . . . none?" says Jimmy Flood.

"Five hundred," says Frankie Yin. "I give five hundred shits about the Truman brothers. Cuz I give them five hundred up front for the kidnap deal."

"Oh," says Jimmy Flood, and, although somewhat fearful of Frankie Yin, the wheels begin to turn. Blacky returns to the living room with three glasses of whisky. Jimmy Flood downs his in one gulp, an attempt to summon courage, call up some recklessness. It might be now or never.

"I got a plan for something," says Jimmy Flood. "But it's not kidnapping."

"Yeah?" says Frankie Yin.

"But it will need maybe quite a few more, um, shits up front."

"Quite a few more shits up front it needs," says Frankie Yin. His bracelet makes a jingle as he raises his glass to his lips.

"What the fuck you guys talking about?" says Blacky Harbottle.

29.

Kidding and Not Kidding

THE TRUMAN BROTHERS are not new to the city of Vancouver and its environs by any means, having made the trek out from Alberta on numerous occasions over the years. And although the specific details of each visit may vary, the basic pattern prevails, that basic pattern being: things go bad in Alberta, one thinks things can only be better in Vancouver, one takes off for Vancouver until things go bad in Vancouver, then one goes back to Alberta.

And this visit has been no different.

Unable to cite the Truman brothers on any viable drug charges, having (surprisingly) found none on their persons or in their vehicles, and having forgotten to secrete a drug stash on themselves that they could plant, the Cuban and the Mick are left with only traffic violations, charging Butch Truman with driving an unsafe and defective vehicle, namely the pink Cadillac that still has the driver's side door lashed to the body with yellow nylon cord. The charges are a disappointment to the Cuban and the Mick, and to a certain extent the rest of the Vancouver Police Force who are also familiar with the infamous Truman brothers.

"Not to worry, Mr. McFadden," says the Cuban to the Mick. "Assholes like these only be destined to deliver unto themselves a twenty-year sentence in the not too distant future . . ."

"Ah yes, Mr. Rourke," says the Mick to the Cuban. "'Tis naught but ordained,' as me dear Catholic mother would say."

He sings: *Just before the Battle, Mother,*
              I'm thinking most of you,
              While up on the field we're watching
              With the enemy in view . . .

ON BEING INFORMED in the holding cell that his car would be impounded pending payment of legal citations and a commitment to undertake the necessary repairs to the car to make it roadworthy, it's Butch Truman's turn, not Gordy's, to go crazy. This is only ample reward for the Cuban and the Mick, who stand grinning from the doorway into the holding cell, Butch's obvious distress bringing if not actual tears, then a slight glistening to the eyes of the two plainclothes narcs that imports no little contentment and almost (for them) no small amount of actual joy.

"*You gotta be fuckin' kidding!*" says Butch Truman, forgetting who he's talking to.

"Not kidding, dipshit," says the Cuban. "And you might think of you an' yer brother there as lucky, an' you might also think that when you get out of here, you keep on going, maybe."

"But the Caddy—" says Butch Truman.

"Butch," says Gordy Truman, "leave it be. Let's just concentrate on getting the fuck out of here."

"Smart man," says the Mick.

"But my guitar!" says Butch Truman. "*Can I at least have my guitar out of it?*"

Butch's guitar, that part of yet another dream of Butch Truman. Butch Truman did dream of driving to the West Coast in a classic pink Cadillac with a blond by his side and that had happened. And Butch Truman did dream of making a movie as he alluded to back in the motel room when busted by the Cuban and the Mick. (It was to be a high-production visual account of the fulfillment of the first dream, that of driving to the West Coast in a classic pink Cadillac with a blond by his side.) But yet another dream of Butch Truman was to be a singer and songwriter, having learned the rudiment fingering for the three basic guitar chords in the key of C from an older fellow inmate while serving time in detention in Alberta for possession of stolen property a few years ago.

"With these three chords, sonny boy," the older fellow inmate made the mistake of saying, "you can play any fucking song in the world!"

Butch Truman is hooked. Being devoid of any sense of rhythm, rhyme, reason, or lyrical and singing sense is not a problem. Butch Truman dreams. And writes songs, many, many songs. Pretty well all have titles like "I Love Baby, It's True," "Baby Loves Daddy, Doesn't Everybody Know," and Baby & Daddy this and Baby & Daddy that. "Baby & Daddy Will Forever Together Stay" he's particularly proud of, being obliged to comment on the title whenever playing it: "See how I fucked up the order of the last three words there?"

Gordy Truman, who indeed had been feeling lucky as the Cuban had said, especially upon hearing of the impounding of the heat-score Cadillac, at the mention of the guitar no longer feels all that lucky.

"Guitar?" says the Cuban. "You got a gig or somethin', music man?"

"They can't confiscate your guitar," says Gordy. "They can't confiscate any of our stuff from the car."

"Sad but true, there, Mr. Truman," says the Mick. "Or is it? Would take a fuck of a search through your guys' shit to find anything worth taking anyway, I'd figure."

"Ha, ha, ha," says the Cuban.

So in keeping with the patterns and traditions of trips to the West Coast for Butch and Gordy Truman, things are no longer good in Vancouver and its environs, so things will be better back in Alberta. The word on the street is that Frankie Yin is not happy about being out five hundred smacks and nothing to show for it. And word is that Blacky Harbottle is not happy either because Gordy Truman reneged on their deal for the rented car and stopped making payments to the rental company. As a result of this, Blacky Harbottle is on the receiving end of threatening phone calls from the car rental company to either pay up or, at best, "Just return the fucking car, sir," the exact words of the rental company's account manager at the conclusion of the last heated phone call. All of this in itself is not good for the brothers, but added to the mix is the general resentment and dislike from the entire Vancouver and environs police forces, fuelled energetically by the free-speaking mouths of plainclothes officers Ruben McFadden and Peter Rourke.

The result of all the unpleasantness is Butch is forced to call Mrs. Truman back home in Edmonton to please wire money so he and her other son, Gordy, can get the Cadillac out of hock and back on the street so they can come home. Mrs. Truman does wire money behind Mr. Truman's back as she has many times before, Mr. Truman having long ago thrown in the towel on his two sons and being dead set against offering them any aid to help get them out of "shit-bombs" they've gotten themselves into. In his words, the two boys "would've robbed their mother's womb if there was any cash in it." In Mrs. Truman's words, however, they are, and forever will be, "still my boys."

To the Truman brothers, the parental setup is half good and half bad, the latter being, of course, the father part. The mother part (as is not uncommon between mothers and sons) remains the good part, being susceptible to entreaties, promises, desperate apologies, and imaginative renderings of events in one's sorry sons' lives as not being their fault. Butch Truman is even inspired to write a song about the family dynamics (one of the early ones before the coming of Baby), perhaps in some attempt to put voice to that which is unsettling but that one is not confident enough to hash over in any form of a "family meeting." In truth, Gordy Truman doesn't think this one song by brother Butch is half bad and has been known to sing it to himself on the odd occasion.

He can sometimes be heard singing: *"Pappa don't like us, don't want us around . . ."*

30.

The Pelican Lines

LOUELLA REREADS THE SECTION ON DISEASES.
. . . if any plants appear sickly, take them away from their neighbours, for trouble can quickly spread.

THREE WEEKS AFTER the kidnapping ordeal, Louella Debra Poule, free and clean of drugs, once more finds herself in a cab racing along the dark ribbon of road aside the inlet, this time heading the other direction, bound for the Vancouver airport in the still-dark of early morning with Meagre Deerstone seated beside her sipping coffee from a stainless steel travel mug.

"No more questions," says Meagre Deerstone. "My grandfather okayed the whole thing weeks ago. We're on our way."

"And your grandfather?" says Louella.

"Will meet us there," says Meagre Deerstone.

At the airport, Louella follows Meagre's lead, checking her bag when directed, ordering coffee at a coffee bar and two jelly doughnuts and a Frisbee-sized chocolate chip cookie. And the sheer size of the place, the chaos of movement, and one realizes that one has never really "taken a trip"; one has only gone on drug- and liquor-fuelled road trips to parts unknown just outside of Vancouver, Louella mentally and physically clinging to Meagre Deerstone, the fucking stoic native, one feels like a frightened little girl, a little girl who's afraid something will go wrong, something will mess the whole thing up. And sitting in the waiting area on the grey plastic seats ill-designed to fit any human body, watching the people go by, some in a panic-confused rush, others looking bored with their luggage trailing on tiny wheels behind them.

Finally, it's time to board, and walking the long tunnel onto the plane, carry-on bag stowed in the space above the seat, the plane shuddering as the engines power up and then the plane moving out on the runway, whistling down the tarmac, and one is pushed back in one's seat as the plane points its nose skyward, a feeling of lightness, floating, one's own anxiety seems to have disappeared, while for other of the passengers, it appears to have heightened. A feeling of calm, no, relief. Like everything's out of one's hands and at last in the hands of someone or something else, a feeling of leaving, leaving things behind that already seem a distant memory; dead Momma's townhouse; the Cove; the tall trees and the idiot Truman brothers; the shadows of one's past and a still-empty aquarium in the living room.

Meagre gives Louella the window seat, Louella looking down on the city below growing smaller, details obscuring and becoming just patterns, then lines and colour, wisps of cloud drifting by and on the flight goes, Louella glued to the window while other passengers read, sleep, stretch in the aisle. Louella's eyes following mountain ranges, rivers, deep valleys, and green and yellow mosaics of farmland, thin winding ribbons of grey that must be roads, and tiny dots visible now and again that must be vehicles or roadside buildings, and a sudden amazement at the sweeping size of the land, the sweeping size of the very globe, the curve of which one can see against the far horizon and consequently (some hours later) a sneaking sensation forming of the relatively insignificant size and importance of the individual in all this, a portent that as the individual shrinks, it stands to reason that the individual's problems and shortcomings shrink, too, and a sense of things falling away like siding off the wall of a house in a gentle, non-lethal hurricane, if there is such a thing, and outside the cabin window, wisps of cloud tumble over the wings.

She sleeps.

And awakened by a nudge from Meagre, a high metal tray standing in the aisle and a coffee with a ham sandwich set on the plastic fold-down table built into the back of the seat ahead. The view outside the window has changed, no longer a mosaic of greens and yellows and browns but stretching out below one flat plane of blue-grey.

"Where are we?"

"Somewhere over the water," says Meagre, the airplane trembling slightly, rising, then falling, banking to the left, and Louella's view through the window angled sharply toward the ground for a moment. A sense of going down, losing altitude, the white froth becoming discernible on the tops of waves below, a large ocean bay and white block clusters of buildings hugging the shoreline, and roads becoming visible, spiked swaths of palm trees and the amoeba-shaped green of a golf course emerging, blue blobs of swimming pools from the hotels and resorts, white oblong smatterings of small boats on the water of the bay as the ground rises up.

THE AIRPORT, PUERTA VALLARTA, small in comparison to its Vancouver counterpart, no profusion of glass and steel but more like a downsized functional facility crowded with unhurried tourists and nationals, already a slower pace evident to Louella while lugging her suitcase out through the main doors to the drop-off zone.

The air outside blows hot, whipping dust into one's eyes, con-stricting the nasal passages, Louella following Meagre following a Mexican guy in a crisp, white short-sleeved shirt to a tiny yellow taxi with a battered roof rack strapped at an odd angle across its roof. Louella handing over her suitcase, then crammed beside Mea-gre in the sweltering back seat as the taxi bounces over the curb onto the road, the languid pace of the airport terminal now succeeded by a more frantic pace, the driver leaning forward over the wheel as the taxi accelerates, the driver and the cab driven by a mutual sense of reward: the more fares in a day, the higher the day's pay. And for a mute Louella, a visual onslaught of fresh images flying by the open window offset by the noticeable difference in the general upkeep of roads and sidewalks, a mild bout of culture shock making her feel even more displaced than she has already been feeling back in dead

Momma's townhouse. But thoughts of anything "back there" have for the most part been successfully ousted, toppled, dispersed by distance travelled and the passing display of all this new stuff: low, square block houses on dirt lots; shops with open fronts displaying various hodge-podges of bright clothing, clay pots, leather belts, exaggerated sombreros, and shiny, highly decorative porcelain lizards and exotic birds. And two- and three-storey emporiums with huge signs in Spanish hung from banners a mile long—*Botas! Cuero! Chaquetas!*—giant plastic palm trees vaulting from buckling terracotta rooftops.

Louella's eyes taking it all in, a humming in her ears, heat blowing in through the open cab window, whipping her hair until it hurts, and sunlight suddenly blasting off the surface waters of the bay and reflecting painfully off the white hulls and silver rigging of moored yachts of a marina. The taxi slowing, the road has turned to red brick, or stones, or something, with wide, humped speed bumps painted bright black-and-red stripes. A more upscale neighbourhood, maybe, no dirt lots anymore. No open-front shops but instead lush green jungle plants and tall palms lining the road obscuring more modern and newer buildings. And white sidewalks with no cracks or chips, crisp blood-red curbs lining them, and the cab climbing suddenly a ridiculously steep black driveway and around a slow, easy curve to the left.

The cab pulling to a stop, broad awning of green and orange canvas stretched overhead, the driver in white short-sleeved shirt out his door and opening the rear doors. All manners, he places the suitcases at their feet.

"For *las senoritas*—"

Then a quick directive in Spanish to the young hotel staff who have approached at a trot, they, too, in crisp, white short-sleeved shirts, and from the cab driver as he drives away a wide white smile that to a jet-lagged and displaced Louella appears completely unpretentious and genuine. And now up the hotel steps under the broad front awning, a vast lobby the size of at least three gymnasiums, open-aired at both ends. The flip-flap, flip-flap of thongs and sandals smacking across a highly burnished floor of large, dark blue ceramic tiles, Louella stepping cautiously at first, the polished floor appearing slick and dangerous. But then confidence returning as one discovers the traction is actually quite good and making one's way past shoulder-high, big-bellied clay planters embellished with Mexican motifs and playing host to mini-jungles of thick draping plants, loud screeches emanating from wide-leafed trees housed in a colossal bamboo cage that reaches to a skylight in the ceiling, a dozen or more parrots of bright reds and blues and yellows visible high in the branches, and on one a solitary long-beaked toucan. And on past the wicker and leather ensembles of easy chairs, sofas, and dark wood coffee tables, trying not to look like an awed and stupefied tourist, Louella making her way to the long front desk on the heels of Meagre, a nagging, whimpering voice from somewhere back of her brain accompanying her, nagging her, saying: "This isn't you, you've no right to be here . . ."

But, nagging, whimpering voices or not, slowly, ever so slowly, observe Louella Debra Poule becoming a tourist, giving in to the rhythm of another place, another culture, another manner of inhabiting the Earth. And slowing down enough to initiate a drop in heart rate and blood pressure, a slowing of the mind (or is it a "taking control" of the mind?), and walking with Meagre Deerstone instead of trailing timidly behind. And sleeping in until whenever, then the two of them sipping coffee on their balcony that affords a not-unpleasant view over the tops of palm trees of the city in the distance gleaming white from the base of the hills across the curve of the bay. And watching the brown pelicans in their daily flight, this daily ritual that becomes one's own, the pelicans flying north every morning in a long line single-file following the shoreline and returning every evening coming back south over the bay, always flying in a line, never a V. And the two of them sitting out on the balcony in the evenings, too, watching as the sun goes down as below one's feet propped on the balcony rail, the hotel pool lights and courtyard lamps come on to illuminate the easy flow of guests wandering the walkways.

"I notice a lot of Mexican families are staying here," Louella is to comment.

"That's why I like this place," says Meagre. "It's affordable for their vacations, too. Who wants to come to a different country and spend the whole time with other tourists?"

"Good point. Your grandfather teach you that?"

"Yes, as a matter of fact. He has also suggested we rent a car and see a bit of the *real* Mexico."

"And?"

"I talked to the very sweet tour guide girl to see if she could recommend a car rental place."

"And?"

"She told me it was a bad idea. It was not safe for two lady tourists to go exploring on their own off the beaten track."

"Maybe it isn't."

"So, where in the world would be safe, you figure?" says Meagre.

"Well, is she going to help us or not?" says Louella.

"She wasn't happy to at first," says Meagre. "But then I told her I was Coast Salish Indian and was protected by Tsonokwa, the Wild Woman of the Woods . . ."

"And this, Sonok-whatever. She does what?" says Louella.

"She can revive the dead and make the ugly beautiful," says Meagre.

"That sounds good," says Louella.

"Yes, it is good," says Meagre. "I think I scared the tour girl a bit, but she'll help us out. As far as I'm concerned, she might as well have said it may not be safe to walk under the trees tomorrow cuz a coconut might fall and bust your head."

"You think a coconut could kill you?"

"The *Palo del muerto* will kill you," says Meagre. "Tree of the Dead. If you drink the water near it, you go crazy and die."

"And you know this how?"

"It's inside beside my bed. A visitor's guide to local plants and wildlife I picked up for you. You seem to have taken an interest in plants back home."

"Does it have the names of things in it?" says Louella.

"Of course."

"Because I need the names of things," says Louella.

TWO DAYS LATER a car rented (blessed by Meagre in Tsonokwa's name for the reassurance of the tour guide girl), and an overnight road trip to the south undertaken, defying all well-intentioned warnings from the good folk working in the tour guide offices, at some point along the way Meagre veering inland from the main highway and navigating dirt roads that twist and weave their way into thorn forests. Acacia trees and mimosas identified by Louella from her book; the strangler fig (*matapalo*) and the cardinal sage flower; the spider lily; the *mala raton*. And she is also able to spy and identify some rust-coloured spider monkeys, parrots, macaws, tricoloured herons, and squirrel cuckoos. That night a stop in a small village, no other tourists but a small hotel of sorts; close, muggy air with the sounds of the jungle around them, authentic Mexican dishes (contents unknown, it would be impolite to ask) set before them at a table outside on the rustic veranda and grateful for the crate of bottled water stashed in the car to quell the spicy fire in the mouth, sweat pouring forth down one's temples, from under one's eyes.

"This is great," hacks Louella.

"We may die or we might not, but we gotta eat it all," says Meagre. "The owner and his family are watching, and I don't think it's cool or polite to waste food out here."

And taking a roundabout way back the next day along narrow, claustrophobic dirt roads closed in on either side by thick jungle, a glimpse occasionally of a hut or clay building through the dense trees, smoke rising from a small fire, scruffy Indian children running over packed ground around the yard toward the dirt track to get a look at the car and standing at the edge of the road, offering handfuls of fruit, handmade trinkets, large-eyed and wide-mouthed carvings. Then that evening once more back at their hotel, the perfect, ill-advised road trip over, no ugly incidents as advertised, just discovery and a new ambience setting in. Louella more relaxed, more go with the flow, although the nagging, whining voice somewhere in the back of her brain is still present, not as loud but still there. But one keeps up one's end, following Meagre's lead, who appears to relax even more than normal, too, laughing more, and one day renting a panga to take them by water down the coast inaccessible by car and skimming the shoreline to villages with names like Las Animas and Quimixto. Or the itinerary for a day may comprise just a quick taxi ride into town to walk the *Malecon* along the edge of the bay, eating ice cream; or a walk over the *Rio Cuale,* deeper into the old town where Meagre purchases a Mexican sink for her bathroom back home, the inside of the bowl decorated with flowers and animal heads and Louella standing in the shop impressed as Meagre has the shopkeeper pack it up in a cardboard box, asking him to pad it enough to take the punishment of the jaunt back to Vancouver in the baggage compartment of the airplane, the shopkeeper laughing like he doesn't mind a bit and he's done this a thousand times before and Louella taking in the whole episode and wondering, *Why does everyone in this country seem so happy all the time*?

"Maybe they're laughing at *us*," says Meagre.

They've stopped at a street-side fruit drink stand for a break from the heat, Meagre resting her feet on the neatly packed box containing her sink.

"Maybe," smiles Louella. "But even the people in the jungle we saw, they don't seem to have all that much but they seem happy. And I don't think it's phony, just an act for the tourists."

"Happiness is relative," says Meagre, "to your state of mind or spirit. They go with life, not fight it."

"You think that's it?" says Louella.

"I think that's it," says Meagre.

"I think I fight it," says Louella.

"I think we all do," says Meagre.

"You know what I'll miss?" says Louella.

Meagre doesn't answer.

"I'll miss the pelicans," says Louella. "The way they fly all in a line. Up the bay in the mornings, back down in the evenings. I don't know why, but I really like those pelicans. You know, the crows do that in Vancouver. Not in a line, but in the summer thousands of 'em fly down the valley in the mornings and fly back up in the evenings. I used to like to watch them, too. Why is that, you think?"

"Maybe it's just nice to see something that seems to know what it's doing," says Meagre, "for whatever reason."

They sit.

"Are you going to get that watch?" says Meagre.

The Watch, spied in a small shop on their first visit to town and crafted in gold in the form of interlaced reeds that compose the band and a turtle that forms the timepiece, the shell opening to expose the watch face and costing three hundred and fifty dollars, and that Louella has (possibly not aware of it) hummed and hawed over whether to get ever since.

"It's pretty expensive," says Louella (more humming and hawing).

"And you don't deserve it," says Meagre Deerstone.

"Well, I probably don't," says Louella.

Silence.

"What would I need a watch like that for?" says Louella.

"To tell time," says Meagre.

IN THEIR SECOND WEEK another car is rented for a few days to visit nearby beaches; the crisp white sands on the Playa Mismaloya; the stony, more rugged Couchas Chinas; and lastly the lagoons of Boca de Tomatlan. At Boca de Tomatlan, some more rentals, two kayaks, to "scout the lagoonery," says Meagre, and the two of them paddling the network of glassy tributaries bounded on both sides by mangrove rising thick out of the water, Louella able to spot, and name (with the help of the visitor's guidebook to local plants and wildlife), a red crown parakeet, the odd jay and woodpecker, and even a yellow-winged cacique.

"You're getting good with those names," calls Meagre Deerstone, her kayak drifting a little distance behind.

"Damn right," Louella Poule calls back. "Keep your eyes open for a west Mexican chachalaca."

"Does it play Mexican music?" says Meagre Deerstone. "Cuz that's what I'm hearin'."

Louella hears it, too, and around a bend a long, timbered wharf appearing out of nowhere running parallel to the lagoon along the shoreline, the jungle cut back from it and housing a crowded outside bar shaded with blue-and-white striped awning. Beyond the bar, a series of low terraces support a small hacienda-looking hotel and a large, meandering swimming pool and red clay walkways, well-tended gardens, and three or four tennis courts.

"Want a drink?" calls Meagre, aiming for the wharf.

"Where the fuck did this come from?" says Louella.

And moments later the both of them seated on white plastic lawn chairs under the blue-and-white striped awning, sipping virgin pina coladas and watching other kayakers and pleasure boats drifting by on the lagoon.

"Should've stayed here, maybe," says Meagre Deerstone.

"Yeah, it's pretty cool," says Louella. "But a bit claustrophobic, I think. Got a nice view of the mangrove, I guess, and this little stretch of lagoon in front of us."

"Yes, you're right," says Meagre Deerstone. "You'd miss your pelicans and I the open sky of the bay."

A Mexican man suddenly hollering in Spanish from the wharf, another younger man running down. And together the two of them unfolding a rickety wooden stand and placing a circular bull's-eye target on it, facing up to the bar and the hotel, the younger man then running into a tiny shed and coming out with a rifle.

"Everyone!" calls the man on the wharf. "Everyone welcome to hit target. Get free drinks, *muchachos*!"

A crew of tourists gathering on the red clay walkway by the bar where the younger man is now gesturing holding the rifle.

"Hit target! Best shot, free drinks!"

And the rifle handed to those wishing to take part one by one—three shots each—the tourists giving it their best, the man standing on the wharf occasionally waving his arms and shouting "Stop!" as a pleasure boat or some kayakers make their way by on the lagoon, passing behind the target.

"This is one fucking bizarre—" says Meagre Deerstone as someone misses, the pellet or bullet (they're not sure which) can be heard crackling into the mangrove across the water. A kayaker passing idly by, and still in the line of fire, jerks at the sound whizzing overhead and paddles hard out of sight. Pleasure boats full of people putter slowly past, the people waving up at the people at the bar, the people at the bar waving back; some notice the rifle, some not. Then, when they're barely out of the line of fire, the man on the wharf signalling to fire again, the next contestant raising the rifle awkwardly and pulling the trigger, a hooray from the crowd when the pellet (or bullet) makes the smack on the target, a good-natured groan when it misses and crashes into the bush across the water.

Meagre is laughing now, Louella has not closed her mouth since the first shot.

"I don't quite believe this," says Meagre.

"The people on the boats," says Louella. "They gotta be wondering what the fuck."

"Obviously considerations of what is safe or what is a hazard to the public differs from culture to culture," says Meagre Deerstone.

"This is the best fucking country in the world!" says Louella Poule.

THEIR LAST NIGHT they spend sitting on their balcony as they have done most evenings since arriving, watching the sun setting over the water and the pelicans appearing on cue overhead, flying in a line up the bay, and Louella thinking what she always thinks when she sees them—*They don't look like they should even be able to stay up there.*

"Yes, I'll miss them," she says, flicking the turtle shell open and closed on the gold watch on her wrist.

"Me, too," says Meagre.

"Meagre, tell me about your son," says Louella.

And, to Louella's, and her own surprise, Meagre does.

31.

Unknown Detritus

"YOU MIGHT WANT to move your stuff upstairs at some point," Aunt Inga had said. "That's what bedrooms are for, dear."

And so after sixteen weeks in dead Momma's townhouse, Louella Debra Poule dragging her personals up the stairs from the living room. One can concede that it's time to make use of the upper floor, move into the spare room at least, but not dead Momma's, not yet. And turning right at the top of the stairs away from the master bedroom to the spare room at the end of the hallway, a nice queen-sized bed of beech veneer with headboard, a rattan swivel chair near the window. Handwoven cotton rug stretched out along the floor, depicting a tropical motif complete with palm trees, blue sea, and exotic birds. Not so bad, really; it reminds one of Mexico, as do a couple of square coconut palm leaf baskets stuffed with what appears to be clothing. Two large earthenware pots hold dried, ceiling-high, reed-like plants. And in a corner against the wall, Poppa's old wooden desk, the only noticeable vestige of Poppa in Momma's townhouse, except for the photos downstairs. Against the other wall, a low-slung, six-drawer bureau, and this is how the other half lives, one guesses, different rooms slated for different functions. One sleeps in a bedroom, eats in a dining room, entertains in a living room, etc.

Louella dropping her things on the floor; when in doubt stand still a minute. Think things through. And can one really sleep up here, tucked away at the top of the stairs with a whole floor empty below. There suddenly seems to be a surplus of room, so much *space*. One may have to get a companion to fill the void—a cat, maybe—or a dog. A parakeet to better match the decor. And now with all of one's personal belongings safely piled in this one room on the upper floor, can one really make the nightly trek all the way from the downstairs to the upstairs just for the sole purpose of sleeping? It's near-impossible for one person to make full practical use of the premises, isn't it? And what about the terrors, those night terrors that do come off and on. How will they be at the top of the stairs? At least when one is crashed in the living room, one has quick access to the exits. But then again—Louella staring into the spare-room closet stacked with cardboard boxes, each labelled in felt marker in dead Momma's hand—then again, one is not living downtown anymore. One is in dead Momma's townhouse in the Cove midst the tall green forest woods. Midst the downy mosses and well-meaning neighbours, where surely any threats from the street are at a minimum, if even there at all.

But moving upstairs is not what she's really been dreading, not what she's really been avoiding. No, what she's really been dreading and avoiding is the dreaded and necessary foray into the unknown detritus of dead Momma's life, Momma's life without Poppa, Momma's life without Louella.

"You really have to do it, Louella," Aunt Inga had said. "It's respectful of your mom and respectful of yourself in a way. You might learn something, get connected. Reconcile things. Who knows. I can help if you like."

So the two of them are found one evening on the living room floor of dead Momma's townhouse, foraging through the many boxes found in the bedroom closets and the storage space underneath the stairs and all labelled in felt pen by dead Momma's hand. An intimidating accumulation of paper gaga: old greeting cards, postcards, yellowing scraps of electrical bills, phone bills, official looking forms stamped with various letterheads, what appear to be tax documents, bank statements, credit card statements, mortgage registrations or something—Louella can't possibly know. And one can thank god for fearless Aunt Inga, who begins sorting the more mysterious papers into piles while leaving the letters, postcards, photos, and anything that appears personal to Louella, Louella dutifully fingering envelopes, unsure what to look at, what to ignore, a guilty feeling opening Momma's life like this, fearful but curious, tracing the path of someone's life, stumbling the path of one's own.

Miscellaneous Photo #1: Louella, age four or five, riding a bike, a small two-wheeler with the training wheels that day removed, and she wears a smile a mile wide, having mastered the feat of balance, and beams that look of accomplishment at the camera, the bike pink with white wheels and red streamers glittering off the handlebars.

Miscellaneous Photo #2: Louella, T-shirt and shorts, about eleven years old in this one, with a large blond dog licking her face. Toby. And how one did love that dog, died quietly one day while one was at school. And found her lying flat out under the aspen tree in the backyard, and Poppa covered the body with a tarp, and nobody did anything with her for three or four days, and then one day she was gone and marking the spot a silhouette of Toby's body lying there rendered perfectly in the dead yellow grass where her body had lain, like a police chalk outline, and the dead grass image of Toby remained there for months displayed in the backyard where one ceased to play until the silhouette turned green again and finally disappeared.

Miscellaneous Photo #3: Momma in a hospital ward where she worked as a nurse in palliative care and standing beside an old lady in a wheelchair, Momma smiling in her whites and her arm draped over the old lady's shoulder, the old lady not looking at the camera but appearing to be staring at something on the floor.

"Don't go through all those now," says Aunt Inga. "Set them aside for another time. This is hard enough, I imagine."

Louella grateful to be relieved of the task for the moment and setting the photos aside. And flipping instead through some postcards, one from France and another from Spain. More from Mexico, Italy, the Bahamas, South Africa, and New Zealand, dead

Momma's friends travelling the world and keeping in touch, cheerful messages of fun and goodwill, and one is somehow comforted to know dead Momma wasn't really alone. In fact, just the opposite. And here, surprised to find a jumble of technical drawings from Poppa's work, the mysterious alien world of a Mechanical Engineer, and snippets of conversations suddenly rising from one's memory with Poppa describing engines, power trains, kinematic chains, and vibration isolation equipment, a young Louella enthralled with words like *antifriction, drifting, thermal expansion,* and *yield strength,* all of it incomprehensible, but at the same time aware that Poppa seemed the happiest when talking about this stuff, and it was better than hearing him argue with Momma, or knowing he was sitting alone in his workroom at the bottom of the basement stairs in the old house and not talking or arguing with anybody, instead just sitting in a basement silence, the furnace rumbling just outside the doorway of the workroom, and Poppa drinking whisky while staring ahead at some blueprint or other impenetrable technical rendering tacked to the wall.

And so continues this evening, a shuffling and gentle spilling of cards and photographs, letters, memorabilia, and keepsakes—a child's drawing of various seed plants and scrawled under each hand-coloured rendition the name of the country the plant comes from—a lined primary school exercise book from grade three, one believes, a notation "Good work, Louella" inscribed in the teacher's handwriting in the upper left-hand corner—and why would Momma keep that? And child's handmade cards and notes celebrating birthdays, Mother's Day, Christmas . . .

She stops.

One is unprepared for the amount one is obliged to absorb in one sitting; one is already experiencing a tightening in the chest and throat, a dissociation between one's present setting and the cascade of memories from the past—images—smells—sounds—one's mind trying to hang onto the actuality of the present, that one is doing no more than sitting in dead Momma's townhouse and sorting through things, getting things in order, but it's hard to stay rooted. An impulse to just pack everything back up and convey to the nearest dumpster. It may just be too much, the hodge-podge of someone's existence in the world (especially your mother's), and none of it making any sense (then again, one suspects it makes *some* sense). And beneath it all, a non-distinct rumbling, not one's stomach (ate a bunch earlier) but a distant roaring like of water, a tsunami-style wave or flood rushing head-on toward, around, and through you. And it's the weight; it's the weight that defines its purpose, not the possibility of drowning, the lack of air, water in the lungs. It's the crush of it all, the slow, relentless pressing down, slow and measured, flattening one into an amoeba-like form beneath it, one becoming fluid in mind and body, a part of the water surge, becoming the water surge, and one is swept away by a power greater, rolling on and away, one small dipshit individual unable to fight the flow of others' lives and the story they make of it without you. And throw in abandonments along the way; there is someone or something responsible, isn't there? Old school friends, parents, completely indifferent strangers that carom off the boarded-up brickwork of one's life, as one caroms off theirs, and there's no point looking off in the distance to the past or the future—nope—the thing or the someone is near, always near, *sweet Matilda,* this stuff, there's all this fucking *stuff* . . .

"Aunt Inga . . ."

Louella clasping a bundle of pale blue airmail envelopes postmarked England, finger flicking the thick brown elastic band holding them together.

"These are—"

"From your father," says Aunt Inga. "He did write your mom often enough. Mostly to ask about you."

"I guess Mom did mention they kept in touch."

"Oh, they did," says Aunt Inga. "You were not that approachable on the subject, however."

The water surge, a slow, relentless pressing down.

"You can read them or not, of course," says Aunt Inga. "But I wouldn't recommend putting them in the garbage pile just yet."

Louella Debra Poule holding the bundle of letters, loosely, almost timidly like holding a pale blue bird that one does not wish to harm, or, in this case, perhaps fearful of having harm inflicted back.

"I don't think Mom would want me to read them," says Louella.

"Oh, I doubt that, Louella," says Aunt Inga. "I doubt that very much."

Louella setting the bundle aside, finding two more like it at the bottom of the box. And wondering how many more evenings like this there may be (for how would anyone know?), and is the whole world perhaps doing the same thing tonight, searching the past, taking stock of losses as Louella Debra Poule is doing now, as unbeknownst to Louella, "three peaks down" Meagre Deerstone *is* doing the same thing, thumbing a photo album of her own with pictures of her little boy who died in a house fire at age five while Meagre was out somewhere blind drunk...and as Officer Marv Klep is doing, sitting at home and twiddling with his wedding ring and thinking of Mrs. Klep and their last days together before the separation...and as an old Taiwanese man is doing, sitting alone in the all-night Denny's on Hastings near Boundary, stirring his coffee, watching the white swirls of cream blend in his cup and reminding him of the coffee-coloured amusement ride in his homeland where children and grandchildren played on a grassy knoll...and as Melody Tenbrink is doing, sobbing hard tears in a rundown dive off Powell Street in downtown Vancouver after shooting up some bad dope and thinking back to a happier time when her family loved her (they don't now, of course, how could they?) and how she's messed things up so bad and it's so scary to live and so scary to die...and as a young couple of newlyweds originally from the Maritimes are doing in their one-bedroom condo off Main and Broadway, holding each other tight and weeping soft tears (unlike Melody Tenbrink's) over news of the passing of a favourite uncle on the husband's side...and as far up as on Vancouver's east side, for even Jimmy Flood is not immune to the inexorable burden of loss as he searches through the garbage of his flop, not looking for old photographs (of which he has so few) or old letters from loved ones (of which he has none whatsoever), but searching instead for that which dreams are made of, his chance for the big time, the big score, a chance to never regret anything ever again, by godawful god, and all he needs is to find that fucking telephone number, that little fucking business card...

32.

On Knowing Death, Somewhat

16) FUN PLANTS FOR CHILDREN—Flycatchers: Insects are attracted to the leaves but fall into the fluid and drown.

ONE DAY, AS a rigorous child of six years four months, she is seen scampering up over a grassy hill from the lake and is gone. Tied to the trunk of a tree with a weathered remnant of old rope at the lake edge, another six-year-old wails, her dilemma the result of some argument and young Lou-Lou's revenge, young Lou-Lou heading back to the cabin with gleeful images of the tide coming in, waters rising about her friend, teaching her a lesson.

The lesson, of course, will be for young Lou-Lou and will concern, among other things, the difference between the behaviours of lakes and seas, lakes being tideless, and an hour later young Lou-Lou sitting on top of the grassy hill under an orange sky at dusk, her mother down the grassy slope with orange on her shoulders and untying knots and wiping away the friend's tears. The two girls, of course, remain friends, these episodes nothing more than the preordained and generally accepted travails of childhood.

On the day of knowing death (such as it was, anyway), she is, for those moments, entirely alone and on her own. Twelve years old and asserting a hungry energy at the world and a member of the school diving team.

Young Louella hates diving. The height, the fall, head down into the arms of fate. She wonders what she's doing there, in the diving club. In later years, one will speculate that it was mandatory, but this is unlikely. The why will always remain a mystery.

On the day, the white, purple-veined feet of Ms. Claire, diving coach, are slapping through the shallow puddles poolside. Voices echo off the walls and vaulted ceiling of the diving pool. The smell of chlorine tickles noses, the water in the pool rippling an unnatural blue. And one by one they ascend the tower.

A body spins, falls, hits the water, diving coach Ms. Claire admonishing, praising, keeping it all moving. Young Louella's toes gripping the rubber footplates on the climb up to the high-diving tower, eyes now coming level with the platform at the top. And seen there for a moment at the end of the platform, her friend from the lakeside, now twelve, too—turning—giggling—and she's gone.

Louella waiting a moment, hears the splash from down below, the voice of Ms. Claire echoing up from beneath the platform, some advice and encouragement. Young Louella advancing along the platform, a mile up if it's a foot. Her feet moving forward, the water below ice blue and kid-hungry.

"Next!" from Ms. Claire.

Young Louella at the end of the platform, taking off, free fall of terror, body turning over, spiralling, maybe twisting, like jumping off the edge of the frigging world, her head down and meeting the water. At the moment of entry, the power fails, the building plunged into near total darkness. Shrieks explode from the other girls, Ms. Claire appealing for calm; all that's visible four red battery-operated EXIT signs shining in the four corners.

UNDER THE WATER her body knifes downward, then checking her descent, arcing, her eyes, shut at the moment of impact, now open. And nothing, just black and unaware the power's gone off.

One is dead is the only conclusion one can draw from the darkness, must have died hitting the water. No white light asking one to come into it. No celestial voices. No nothing.

She sinks, feels the bottom, and, as perhaps only a twelve-year-old is able, is not afraid. This is cool, sort of.

Then through the dark, through the black water around and forever, a memory of another death when nine years old, that of a great-aunt. This aunt was unfamiliar, mysterious, talked about but never visited when alive. And travelling to Prince Edward Island for the funeral, her, Momma, and Poppa, an old farmhouse outside Priest Pond. Mid-January and Poppa taking young Lou-Lou out through the snow to the back shed.

"Come look at this, Lou," he says.

In the shed her great-aunt stiff and cold, standing in a boarded coffin leaning against a stack of old tires.

"One of the things winters on PEI are good for," says Poppa. "She'll keep forever."

YOUNG LOUELLA SITS on the bottom of the diving pool. Dead.

A writhing sensed overhead, her lungs about to burst. And rising instinctively to the surface where one receives a bump on the head, just like when one was alive. An arm hitting something, her friend's voice heard beside her. And scrawny arms thrashing the water, her friend has leapt into the watery blackness for her friend Louella.

Now young Louella gulping air but still blind. Can hear the shrieks of the others, all of life's sounds, smells, feels, tastes, but no sight yet, one and one's friend grabbing black water, black air, and starting to giggle.

"Glub, glub, save us."

A surge of splashes as the lights come back on, the rest of the team responding to one's call. Then nearly drowned in the rescue attempt as the whole team plunges into the water on top of her, young Louella dragged from the water, Ms. Claire still demanding calm, young Louella breathless on her stomach on the cement by the side of the diving pool, arms extended, all one can see white puckered toes around her.

Then Ms. Claire, "Are you all right?"
Louella sitting up, hair matted over her face.
"I thought I'd died."
"I listened," says her friend. "But you didn't come up."
"Holy, Jeez. I'm sorry."
They can't contain themselves.
"It should be so funny," says Ms. Claire.

33.

On the Covert Nature of Miracles

COIFFURE RUINED AND broken damn stiletto heels, one feels no better than some East End skank, Alcina Omojolade Ajunwa navigating the ten or so metres out of the alley onto Broughton Street, just a night spent in the West End club scene with the beautiful people (those motherfuckers), making it out to Robson Street where the Saturday-night crowd buzzes in and out of the nightlife venues and for the most part gives her a wide berth—who wouldn't?—this tall black woman with the maniacal gaze and long, crazy legs, the ravaged coiffure and broken damn stiletto heels.

Her knuckles are scraped and bleeding, having given as good as she got from the three of them, three arsehole honky johns wanting their fun for free and figuring they could get away with it, but the three of them forgetting to consider the man-woman nuance of the situation. And this shit's been happening a lot lately: the bozos want to goof off with the "she" part but fail to understand that the "he" part will come to the rescue (as any gentleman would) if the lady part is disrespected. And Alcina's been clean for close to two months now, which is no small task living as she does, but now the feeling is that maybe one should just say to hell with it all and get loaded, shut down the system that controls any and all sensation—

"Louella? I'm thinking of using. Getting wasted. I've been in a fight and who gives a shit."

"Alcina? Where are you?"

"I want you to sing along—*half past the monkey's dick and a quarter to his balls . . .*"

"Are you loaded?"

"Not yet, love. Just enjoying some West End whimsy along Robson Street."

"Can you get out here? Want me to come get you?"

"A generous offer. A taxi from here to the Cove should only cost a thousand dollars . . ."

"Stay put—"

"Don't bother, dearie, I'll make my way. I don't want you down here."

"You sure?"

"I'm sure. Have you ever noticed how Robson Street actually 'buckles' on a Saturday night under the weight of so many dipshits?"

"Turn off your cellphone, Alcina. And get out here."

"On my way."

It will not for some time become apparent to Louella (a few years of clean time, actually) just how dehumanizing and violent her existence had become running all those years through her addiction, careening from the temporary highs to the interminable lows and back again. Her acquired immunization, not only to any sense of reality, but also to any appreciation of the inherent danger and pain with which she lived, will remain with her a long time and diminish only slowly, receding almost reluctantly like the jagged claws of a glacier across the scarred face of a favourite escarpment. This immunization is no more noticeable than now in her simple acceptance of Alcina's dilemma—there's concern, but no horror. *This is the stuff that happens—all the time.* And so blind and ignorant of this condition will both remain once Alcina arrives by cab in the Cove with the comment: "Obligatory transportation is one of the terrible things, dear Lou," and after paying the exorbitant fare with her face bloodied and her limbs scraped and bruised, it's understandable that neither Alcina Omojolade Ajunwa nor Louella Debra Poule is yet able to stand away from the scene that unfolds and see what is really happening—a small miracle, really—two drug-addicted ladies *without* drugs and doing no more than one comforting the other and sipping herbal tea in a respectable part of town while listening to music and the odd, mad scrapings of small night creatures across the roof as the two of them do no harm to anyone, including themselves.

SOMEWHERE FAR AND AWAY across Burrard Inlet, a notion of miracles can also be said to be at least partly alive, too, in none other than the mangled psyche of Louella's ex-boyfriend Jimmy Flood, but only in the barest form, Jimmy Flood's belief being that miracles consist of just two parts. The first part would be just getting through another day on Earth alive, and the second part, dependent on successful fulfillment of the first part, would be getting through that particular day with a minimum of upset that includes not alienating everyone you've met during that day. This simplistic equation of the miraculous should in no way be viewed as a spiritual measure or true reflection of any parental or other mentoring influences during Jimmy Flood's formative years.

In fact, his parents, Mr. and Mrs. Flood, do in their own individual ways believe strongly enough in the actuality and goodness of miracles, but also hold the opinion that *some* work is involved in attaining them. Mrs. Flood, for example, since her marriage years ago to Mr. Flood, attends a rigid nightly regimen of prayer to a number of benevolent saints and always in the same order.

The nightly litany of invocation begins with a prayer to St. Philomena, patron saint of babies, infants, and youth. Prayer number two goes to St. Monica, patron saint of wives. Prayer number three goes to St. Catherine of Siena, patron saint of fire prevention (Mrs. Flood having a deep-seated childhood fear of death by fire). Prayer number four goes to St. Teresa of Avila, patron saint of headache sufferers (Mrs. Flood suffers migraines). Prayer number five goes to St. Anne, patron saint of Canada. *("What, you kids too good to pray for the country you live in, my god?")* Prayer number six goes to St. Claire of Assisi, patron saint of television (yes, it's true) for the daily uplift provided via the miracle of daytime soaps. Then, deemed necessary at a later date when son Jimmy begins getting heavily into drugs, two more are added as a precautionary measure: St. Dominic Savio, patron saint of juvenile delinquents, and St. Leonard of Noblac, patron saint of danger from thieves.

Mr. Flood maintains a simpler and less strenuous regimen of faith in the miraculous, putting forth only occasional invocations to St. Matthew, patron saint of bankers (*"Please protect one's savings and conservative investments, however humble..."*), and St. Augustine of Hippo, patron saint of brewers, and without whose help, Mr. Flood believes, when things get unbearably awful, one would be unable to cope. (Mr. Flood will on occasion forgo the saints and any prayer altogether and just speak directly to God himself, this act revealing an inherent belief under the surface in the *possibility* of miracles at least, these moments taking place usually just after a home visit from son Jimmy and upon finding money or items of value missing. In fact, to further assert a deep if not fully acknowledged belief in the possibilities of miracles, Mr. Flood has often been heard to say in a loud voice and with face raised to the sparkles glittering from the plaster of the ceiling, "Dear god-in-fucking-heaven but if that kid *doesn't* kill himself one day it will be a bloody miracle!")

Son Jimmy, on the other hand, evokes help (or salvation) when needed from an obscure representation of celestial power sketched and fuelled by his own addiction, a mishmash of clouds broiling high in the heavens that are rent with flashes, not lightning really, but more like bolts from a comet entering the Earth's atmosphere and a vague image (much like Dusty Yorke's) of a half-naked gentleman sporting a heavy white beard and head brimming with piled metres of impenetrable white hair and looking sternly but benevolently down from above.

And so now, while Louella Debra Poule and Alcina Omojolade Ajunwa take part in one small quiet miracle with no incantations, so does Jimmy Flood call on his celestial benefactor with an incantation that is not the usual *"Please, God. Please, God. Please, God,"* but instead is the more positive and less desperate *"Thank you, God. Thank you, God. Thank you, fucking God!"* for he holds in his hand no less than a miracle found wrapped in a stinking bundle of dirty clothing, a miracle no more than three-and-a-half inches wide by two-and-a-half inches high, a business card promoting heli-skiing at a mountain resort area up the coast, three-and-a-half inches by two-and-a-half inches with a name and a phone number.

34.

Night Skies

JIMMY FLOOD, OF all people, has certainly never been spared the ramifications of the core perplexity that comes with simply existing, that core perplexity being the essential unpredictability of life's events. Nor is he now so spared while entertaining a certain anxiety over his present predicament, even though most would be inclined to say that everything at last seems to be working out for Jimmy Flood and that Jimmy Flood, in fact, could appear to some to be quite the agent of prediction, for he has at last, finally, "got himself a helicopter."

A Bell 206B-3 Jet Ranger to be exact, from High West Heli-Skiing Enterprises that services the ski resorts of Whistler and Blackcomb in the mountains north of Vancouver. On the surface it could be asked why, when things are apparently working out, would anyone be filled with fear and anxiety? In Jimmy Flood's case, although it's true that he does at last have the use of a helicopter, it also follows that he also has to have the use of a helicopter pilot, and though the machine itself may be checked and approved for reliability, the pilot may not be. The pilot at this moment at the controls comes in the person of one forty-seven-year-old Arnold Archie Bridger, a self-confessed cokehead and "impresario of opportunity" (his own words), who has claimed in a verbal resumé of his abilities to having flown thousands of hours all over the vast wilderness reaches of British Columbia in the most *"fucking bullshit conditions any asshole's ever seen!"*

Credentials of any kind, on the other hand, have meant little to Jimmy Flood in recruiting the use of a helicopter and a pilot. Beggars can't be choosers, and there's not really a big market of helicopter pilots who want to risk flying illegal contraband.

"I've flown the timbers, the glaciers—all the fucking fishing lakes and rivers!" Arnold Bridger is saying above the roar of the rotors as he sucks hard on a reefer the size of a cigar. Although equipped with headphones to cue in to any radio in-calls that may be out there, Arnold Archie Bridger seems incapable of speaking in anything less than a shout, a nerve-rattling element that only adds to the whole nerve-rattling experience for Jimmy Flood, who sits in the seat next to him, the air in the chopper cabin blue with smoke. Jimmy Flood takes a toke himself, exhales, and snorts a line of cocaine off a small mirror that he then holds in front of Arnold's nose. Arnold snorts a line in turn and draws back on the reefer again while managing the controls, the chopper bumping and grinding its way through a rain-swept night sky.

They'd made the pickup in a farmer's field up the Fraser Valley just east of Abbotsford, seventy-five kilos of plastic-wrapped bundles of homegrown BC marijuana, now stacked in the space behind the front seats. They're flying back down the valley en route to a drop-off point just over the US border in the farmlands of Washington State. They have attempted a route that runs west more or less parallel to, and thirty or so kilometres north of, the border. The reason they're not flying directly south to the drop-off point just over the US border is because Arnold Archie Bridger has just intercepted a garbled radio message from Central Aviation Control at the Vancouver Airport that an RCMP helicopter is in the air with a directive to investigate a possible unidentified aircraft flying somewhere in the skies over the Greater Vancouver Lower Mainland that appears not to have registered a flight plan.

"That's got to be us!" says Arnold Archie maintaining a course due west and making for the open and deep waters of Georgia Strait. *"We gotta dump this shit!"*

Jimmy Flood almost reaches for the controls, an instinctive reaction when one's deal of a lifetime, one's dream of a successful stab at something, appears about to be dumped out onto the foam-tossed waves of the open sea.

"We can dump it somewhere safe!" he shouts as the sympathetic or emergency branch of his brain kicks in, and his forebrain, that part of the brain whose job is planning and problem-solving, and although rarely used in Jimmy Flood's case, does at the same moment also kick in.

"Somewhere I can get it back later!"

"Chopper lights!" says Arnold Bridger, peering over his left shoulder through the window into the rain-streaked night. *"It's gotta be police. They're onto us!"*

The Bell 206B-3 banks hard to the right, and Jimmy Flood for a moment finds himself looking straight down from above on the lights of Vancouver, able also to make out the sweeping black mass that would be the University Endowment Lands to the west and the lighted skeletal frame of the Lions Gate Bridge that spans the harbour mouth to the east. The Jet Ranger levels out as Arnold Bridger takes another long drag on the reefer.

"Head up fucking there!" points Jimmy Flood at a dark void ahead running between the lights of Vancouver on the one side and the lights of the North Shore on the other, the unlit void marking Burrard Inlet which leads to Deep Cove.

"Where's that you talkin'?" says Arnold Bridger, hunched forward now with eyes straining into the night ahead, a High West Heli-Skiing Enterprises baseball cap pulled tight across his brow and his paunch lifting against a T-shirt with the slogan *You Can Kick My Wife & Kids But Don't Kick My Dog.*

"Deep Cove!" says Jimmy Flood. "I know a place in Deep Cove!"

And Jimmy Flood does know a place in Deep Cove, that place being, of course, Louella Debra Poule's dead mother's townhouse, where he'd shown up one drug-shuddering night a month or so ago after getting the address from a babbling, drug-sick Ginger Baumgartner. He'd only wanted to talk, perhaps renew the old flame, and ask for money. And met at the front door by a baseball bat–wielding Louella Poule and some Indian chick, who had appeared calm but potentially menacing. One has a general sense of the actual location of the place from the ground, and now, thanks to the ingestion of cocaine and the copious amounts of pot inhaled in the cabin of the chopper, the synapses in Jimmy Flood's brain lie packed with enough dopamine to render a feeling of confidence (however false) and almost euphoria that could make anyone certain he or she could easily locate a specific location from the air and in the middle of the night. He does know that the townhouse complex in question sits adjacent a large sports field and Louella's is the townhouse on the end closest the field.

The Bell 206B-3 dips violently, banking steeply to the right again and Jimmy Flood can see the lights of the North Shore skimming by directly beneath them now, the lights of downtown Vancouver across the harbour bouncing along the corner of his field of vision over his other shoulder.

"We gotta dump it somewhere!" says Arnold Archie. *"We sure ain't gonna land an' unload, fucknuts!"*

"I know! I know!" says Jimmy Flood, thinking he may have seen a faint flashing light moving through the night sky at the same altitude coming toward them from over the city core. "We gotta get lower so I can see!"

Arnold Archie Bridger, divorced from his wife and estranged from his children, and not yet able to construe any good reasons why, not even withstanding the sentiments relayed by the slogan on his T-shirt, leans over to look out Jimmy Flood's window.

"Those are signal lights there—anti-collision fucking strobes— another chopper!"

The Jet Ranger bucks, falls steeply, and then levels out again but maintains a rocking movement from side to side as Arnold Bridger attempts to keep an eye on the unidentified signal lights.

"This fucking thing flying okay?" shouts Jimmy Flood, his hacked voice full of apprehension, his potential windfall so close yet so far. And Arnold Archie Bridger taking one last deep drag on the reefer, popping the roach in his mouth and gulping it down.

"Flying okay?" says Arnold Archie. *"High inertia rotor! Rupture resistant fuel tanks! Attenuating skid gear! It fucking flies itself most of the time an's safer than your fucking mother's arms!"*

And Jimmy Flood does feel a dim reassurance, not at the

reference to the safety of his mother's arms, but at the sound of these technical terms, a suggestion that the Bell 206B-3 Jet Ranger is crafted by higher minds that are way beyond the two of theirs, and the Bell 206B-3 Jet Ranger is, therefore, probably quite reliable.

Jimmy Flood now peering below into the nighttime landscape and attempting to discern geographical clues of their position from light patterns of streets and buildings. Can see the outline of the Ironworkers Memorial Bridge approaching ahead, which means they're at least heading the right way.

"Keep going straight!" says Jimmy Flood.

"*Flew a chopper for the BC Forest Service fighting forest fires out of Terrace, too!*" babbles Arnold teasing the controls. "*Honking great flames a mile fucking high! Up drafts and down fucking drafts! And smoke—you wanna talk smoke? Can ya see that other chopper?*"

Jimmy Flood can't see the other chopper or much else, but he does think he recognizes a brightly lit intersection below.

"We're close! Look for a big blacked-out area—should be a playing field! Gotta go lower!"

"*We gotta watch the power lines!*" says Arnold Bridger, the sweat on his face reflecting the colours off the instrument panel lights.

"Where?" says Jimmy Flood.

"*Now that's the fucking question, isn't it, numbnuts?*" says Arnold Bridger lifting the tiny mirror to his nose.

Jimmy Flood doesn't answer, sees a large dark area below, no lights, and at the far end and half-hidden by what he guesses are trees, that which can only be Louella's townhouse complex, what *has* to be Louella's townhouse complex. And directing Arnold Archie to get the chopper in a hover above the townhouse at the near end of the complex, Arnold Archie nudging the controls, the Bell 206B-3 slowing, beginning to hover, then making a wobbly, cautious descent. Jimmy Flood already unbuckling his seat belt and leaping into the back of the cabin, flinging open his side door. A sudden rush of noise and air, rotors whining and rain slicing through the opening. He's immediately soaked and can see the wind-buffeted tops of trees thrashing back and forth below in the strobe from the chopper, hellishly close, and a flash of time for one to wonder: *"Where the fuck* are *the power lines?"*

Then tossing out plastic-wrapped bundles of perfectly good homegrown British Columbia bud into the yard barely visible through the chaos below, Jimmy Flood is surrounded, *engulfed* in a frantic broil of sound and movement, all of it unpleasant, and the tossing of plastic-wrapped bundles and the tossing of the Jet Ranger, one's body staggering, straining, huffing and puffing, eyes blinking away this curtain of falling water fanned into a particular meanness by the rotors, Jimmy Flood's mind and body awash with more than sufficient stress hormones of adrenalin and cortisol to awaken in his brain his until-now sleeping hippocampus (that part of the brain responsible for memory), and with its awakening, he is forced to recall who staked him to this venture and that Frankie Yin had ended up coughing up a lot more than a few hundred "shits" to finance this deal and expected a large return on his investment.

The last plastic-wrapped bundle disappears into the night, Jimmy Flood sure he could see an imprint of Frankie Yin's face on the last bundle staring up at him as it falls and through the sound of wind and rain and rotors Frankie Yin's voice saying, "Not paying back is *not* funny."

With the contraband load dumped, one would think that one could almost relax now, but then suddenly aware of jellyfish-like stings crawling painfully up one's right thigh and spreading across the right buttock, the good ol' somatoform disorder coming to the fore in full force fuelled by the ongoing stress of the situation, Jimmy Flood pulling fast the chopper door and falling painfully into his seat.

"Shitfuckingcrapcrapcrap!" he says.

"Jesus! You fucking okay?" says Arnold Archie, giving power at the controls *("Throttle on collective and a Rolls Royce 250-C20J engine!")* and the Jet Ranger rises straight up and away, climbing high into the night and only arresting its ascent when eye level with the tops of the near mountains, their peaks now silhouetted in a

faint early dawn. The chopper hovers there a moment, rotating an unsteady circle, much like one of those dorky juggling acts where a guy spins dinner plates on the top of a number of long bamboo poles, thinks Jimmy Flood appropriately, the whole night venture having taken on a somewhat vaudevillian air.

Then the nose of the Jet Ranger pointing north, Arnold Archie Bridger demanding maximum performance from the Rolls Royce 250-C20J as he guns it full throttle to make as hasty a return to base as possible and seeming to exhale only once during the entire twenty-three-minute flight home to utter the words: *"Well, don't just sit there rubbin' yer ass, Flood, boy! Roll another doobie, asshole, an' don't piss yerself on the seats!"*

35.

A Terrible Thing

RIDING THE RAILS of a cellblock dream where all the female inmates are wearing pretty little-girl party dresses and eating ice cream (although the guards have strictly forbidden birthday parties), and she sits apart against the gaily decorated cinder-block wall, waiting nervously for a visit from her mother, yes, she's coming to visit, and a stifling heat (it seems) and a dull roar, *whump* and *whump* repeated faintly then getting louder, and it's hot as hell at this jailhouse birthday party and they've turned the ceiling fans on, the ceiling fans are on an'—what the fuck—did they even have ceiling fans in jail?

Louella waking suddenly, her bare feet touching the carpet before her eyes are open. And trying to identify the noise, *whump*, *whump*, it's coming from above, that's for sure. And through the spare-room window that looks out over the backyard bright lights seen flooding the area for a moment, and then gone, and then the *whump*, *whump* sound receding and then it, too, completely gone, leaving only the sound of rain pelting the roof and hissing down through the branches of the trees. Louella over to the window, face against the glass and seeing through the trees backing her lattice-topped backyard fence, the motion-sensor floodlight come on from the Greek's front porch in the lot next door. Her view partially obscured, but she is able to catch a glimpse of the Greek in boxer shorts running off the porch toward the hives that blaze bright white in the floodlight glare. Some are toppled; some appear smashed. Light reflects off what appear to be duct-taped Cellophane bundles that lie scattered over the area like poorly placed garden masonry. The Greek is yelling, grabbing at the disassembled hives, his young wife with him now, her thin nightgown drenched and clinging to her body, her long hair wetted down along her back, and she's screaming too, pulling at the Greek's waistband trying to get him away from there.

Phone Conversation #1

"You heard me," says Alcina.

"I *think* I heard you," says Louella.

"You heard me," says Alcina.

"This guy wants to marry you," says Louella.

"Lock, lanky stock, and barrel, baby," says Alcina.

"Is he—does he know about you?" says Louella.

"Everything," says Alcina.

"Is he a very strange and very lonely man as well as being short?" says Louella.

"Yes, to all three, you clever girl," says Alcina. "How did you know?"

"Well, who else would be—um—so inclined, dear heart?" says Louella.

"You mean, so desperate?" says Alcina.

"I don't mean that," says Louella.

"Well, who indeed," says Alcina.

"And," says Louella, "what have you said?"

"Oh, I have said things like 'My, isn't life unpredictable' and 'How much money you got?'"

"No shit."

"No shit. We have a very open relationship. We come right to the point."

"And this guy's okay with that?"

"He says he has money and plenty of it."

"And what's this guy do?" says Louella.

"You mean besides frequenting escort services?" says Alcina.

"Yeah, besides that," says Louella.

"He buys and sells things," says Alcina.

"Things."

"Yes. Things."

"Okay. What sort of things?" says Louella.

"Well, money-making things, apparently," says Alcina.

"Quit farting around."

"I don't know the true nature of the *things*," says Alcina. "Enough to know they're lucrative things."

"Is this guy a gangster? A business man? What?"

"He's a man who wants to marry me, unfinished transformation and all. He says he'll pay for the rest of what I need done. He's nice, has money, and this old cranky bitch could do a lot worse, sweetheart."

"You haven't answered my question, cranky bitch."

"You're right, I haven't. And when I have an answer I'll let you know."

"You do that."

"I will."

"Better."

"Will."

"Right."

"Ta."

"I'll believe it when I see it," says Louella.

"Oh, I don't know about that," says Alcina.

Phone Conversation #2

"Something happened last night, Aunt Inga," says Louella.

"Are you all right?" says Aunt Inga.

"I'm fine," says Louella. "You know the weird Greek guy next door?"

"Yes," says Aunt Inga. "That is, I know who you mean."

"Well. He's dead," says Louella.

"Dead?" says Aunt Inga.

"Bees got him," says Louella.

"What a terrible thing," says Aunt Inga.

"A helicopter came over, middle of the night," says Louella.

"A helicopter?" says Aunt Inga.

"Dropped a ton of shrink-wrapped marijuana bundles the size of suitcases into the Greek guy's yard."

"What on earth for, I wonder," says Aunt Inga.

"They crushed the beehives. I noticed in the morning a few of the bundles had landed in Momma's backyard, too," says Louella.

"What a bizarre thing to happen," says Aunt Inga.

"The Greek guy tried to get his bees. Saw him out there in his boxer shorts trying to find the queen, I guess," says Louella.

"Yes," says Aunt Inga. "They need the queen to attract the others."

"I guess the bees freaked. Swarmed him and stung him into a coma," says Louella. "His wife, the little Filipino woman, she kept hollering at him, 'The queen, she in your pants!' 'The queen, she in your pants!' He died at the hospital."

"My god," says Aunt Inga.

"Thing is, Aunt Inga," says Louella. "I saw the wife out there with him trying to save the bees, and she was pulling on his shorts and I thought she was trying to just get him away, but now I'm not so sure."

"What are you talking about?" says Aunt Inga.

"Well, maybe she dropped the queen—"

"You're not serious," says Aunt Inga.

"Well, she had hold of his boxers. Plenty of time to—"

"You saw it?" says Aunt Inga.

"Well, no," says Louella.

"You think she did that?" says Aunt Inga.

"What do you think, Aunt Inga?" says Louella.

"Well, *I* don't know!" says Aunt Inga.

"Well, I think I do," says Louella.

Phone Conversation #3

"Okay, listen good, Jimmy," says Louella. "Don't call me anymore."

"But what about the weed I dropped there?" says Jimmy Flood. "I need it back!"

"I *thought* it might be you," says Louella.

"I got to get it back, Louella," says Jimmy Flood. "The backer's gonna kill me!"

"Not my problem," says Louella.

"*Please, Louella*," says Jimmy Flood.

"Can't help you. The cops got it. Most of it landed in the yard next door," says Louella.

"Oh, fuck, *nooo* . . ." says Jimmy Flood.

"Oh, fuck, *yeees*," says Louella. "Where'd you ever get a helicopter?"

"*Shitshitshitshitshit!*" says Jimmy Flood.

"I'm changing this number," says Louella.

Phone Conversation #4

"I've changed my number," says Louella, "that's why I'm phoning."

"Thank you, love. How's things?" says Alcina.

"Jimmy somehow got hold of a helicopter," says Louella. "And the Greek guy next door got stung to death by his bees after I'm pretty sure the wife put the queen down his pants. And I've got sixty-odd kilos of weed buried in the backyard."

"Let me call you back, Louella," says Alcina, "when I have something anywhere near as interesting to say."

"Okay. Ciao, lady," says Louella.

"Ciao, baby," says Alcina.

Phone Conversation #5

"Okay. I'm going to marry 'Very Strange and Very Lonely and Very Short,'" says Alcina.

"No effing way," says Louella.

"His name's Richard," says Alcina.

"That's nice," says Louella. "You can call him *Ricky*."

"Of course," says Alcina. "What's new with you?"

"Not as much as that," says Louella.

"Ha! I knew I'd win," says Alcina.

36.

Dead Momma

SHE IS BORN Shirley Anne Wilcox in September 1957 and dies of pancreatic cancer in April 2009. Remembered by those who knew her growing up as a boisterous, exuberant child who swings fearlessly from the orchard trees in the backyard, removes the learner wheels herself from her bicycle at the age of four, and roller skates rough and tumble down the gravel-strewn sidewalks of a suburb of Edmonton at the age of five. Although city raised, her face is a face of Alberta wheat fields, cattle ranches, and straight, horizon-seeking prairie highways, the cliché of "farmer's daughter" who has sun and wind in her blood, the light blue of the prairie sky running willowy veins under the skin. And retains throughout her life a recondite connection with nature and all things distinct and diversified.

At the age of fourteen, she sees her first dead body, an old woman slumped at a bus stop outside the Hudson's Bay department store. Her friends cringe; Shirley Anne approaches and pokes gently at a still shoulder, says, "She's dead," without horror, and waits until help comes to remove the body. Later she takes nurse's training, psychology studies, mental health training. And marries David Alan Poule.

They have one child, a girl, and sometime later move to Vancouver, British Columbia, on the coast. At that time, jobs are easy to come by: a position as a mental health nurse in Ward 7 at Lions Gate Hospital on the North Shore. Later, after the separation and divorce, purchases a townhouse and begins work at a palliative care facility, where is awakened a cryptic understanding and empathy for the dying, as well as an up-until-now suspected but undeclared kinship with the realms of the spiritual.

Loses her child to drugs, her husband to alcohol, her self to her patients and their families.

Discovers through a neighbour the fundamental benevolence of other cultures, an attribute that appears lacking in her own, and begins to devour books on the First Nations peoples, the Inuit, Australian Aborigines, the Huichol Indians of Mexico, and the Yanomami tribes of Brazil, and the list goes on and on and grows and grows, until, of course, April 2009.

Finds solace and satisfaction in cultivating plants and flowers, something she never seemed to have an interest in or have the time to take an interest in when living with her daughter and husband, David Alan Poule. And lives a beautiful life (for she knows, by the time her end comes, just what a beautiful life is), though she has also come to know through her work with the dying that very few people ever believe that about their own life when their time comes, and it's this, this denial of regard and delight, this air of futility and failure and wishing it had all been more, that most disturbs her about her work.

No, Shirley Anne Wilcox lives a beautiful life, imperfect and replete with joys and sorrows, victories and defeats, pains and raptures. This she believes as she lies dying (although she tells no one because who would believe her, how could they?). And she says a prayer for her daughter, having never used her illness as a weapon against her, loves her still above all, and wonders what will become of her girl once she's out of jail and out there on the streets and finds herself wishing—it is somewhat funny— wishing for her daughter's sake, it had all been a bit more.

37

The Legend of Louella Debra Poule

Legend: A marvelous story handed down from
earlier times; a non-historical narrative.
Legendary: Fabulous; traditional; mythical.

—*Webster's*

FOLLOWING THE DISASTROUS helicopter drug-deal attempt,
Jimmy Flood flees the immediate Vancouver area as anyone would,
hiding out at a nondescript motel far out in the valley fearing reprisal
from none other than his backer (and, ironically, his hero), Frankie
Yin. True, Frankie Yin is not happy with what went down; he'd put
up a large sum of front money to finance the scheme. But, as Jimmy
Flood will learn later and to his eventual relief, Frankie Yin had not
confided in the rest of the Tai Pai boys about the deal, running it solo
under the table thereby planning to reap the profits for himself only.
This will work out well for Jimmy Flood, for Frankie Yin is dead no
less than a week after the screwed-up helicopter drop, shot dead
while eating zong zi dumplings and mu shu pork in a downtown
Chinatown restaurant (although a gangster and a thug, Frankie Yin
always maintained a keen respect for the Eight Great Traditions of
Chinese cuisine). In a twist of fate it's learned that the shots were
actually meant for a rival gangster, Charlie Woo, at the next table,
who escaped with minor injuries, these being slight scaldings on his
hands from splashed sizzling rice soup. Frankie Yin's second-in-
command, Bobby Phat, takes over as head of the Tai Pai Social Club,
a move that is agreed to by the remaining Tai Pai boys in keeping
with a nebulous tie to Chinese dynastic traditions handed down

through the centuries. "We [the Chinese] invented the clock, gun-powder, and fucking video games!" proclaims Bobby Phat at his inaugural piss-up, receiving resounding applause from the rest of the gang, all imbued with a confidence that this kind of affirmative think-ing can do nothing but good for the Tai Pai gang whether based on a biased interpretation of history or not.

So, Frankie Yin is mourned by some and missed (it's supposed) by a few, and Jimmy Flood is free to come out of hiding and attempt to take credit for what is, or was, his crack at the big time, and at the same time, although not altogether consciously, initiating The Legend of Louella Debra Poule. In another small ironic twist, Jimmy Flood himself will be one of the few who will truly miss Frankie Yin, even though Frankie had made it clear that he would want his money back or blood, Jimmy Flood feeling that Frankie Yin would undoubtedly have said about his own flukey demise, "Gangland shootings are funny."

THE LEGEND OF Louella Debra Poule can be said to qualify as an actual legend if one takes into consideration that it is "a story handed down from earlier times" (although the time frame of the "earlier times" is, in fact, only a few days or weeks), and it does have its fair share of the marvellous and the mythical. The storyteller can be none other than Jimmy Flood himself, of course, having been at the centre of the storm that sowed the seeds of events. Jimmy having lost his shipment of prime British Columbia bud, and the fact that Frankie Yin is no longer a threat, it's too much to expect that he will keep his mouth shut, for the story does hit the BC media and even gets a spot on the CBC national news, and Jimmy Flood is witness to the awe and respect registered by those on the street for the pluck and audacity displayed by whoever it was who tried to pull off this caper, even though the outcome, after only a cursory investigation by the authorities, suggests that it was a thoroughly botched job at best. But a man did die in the fiasco, however indirectly, bestowing upon the whole event even more notoriety.

Jimmy Flood does blab about his part in it; the fact that it was his idea and he was *there*. How many people actually believed him couldn't be known, but many had to admit that Jimmy Flood's apparent knowledge of details did vouchsafe a certain credence to his claim. Notwithstanding his attempt to reap some of the fame, if having at the same time to accept the complete loss of any monetary gain from the whole fiasco, Jimmy Flood does let it be known as a solid God-is-my-witness truth that Louella Debra Poule is the one who actually ended up with the cache of prime British Columbia bud as it was her dead Momma's townhouse where he and his cohort dropped the load when being chased through the night skies by the police. It is also of no big surprise that the actual amount of marijuana involved grows with each telling.

"The police only recovered *some* from the neighbour's yard," Jimmy Flood is to say. "Most of it landed in Louella's yard and where's all that dope, eh? A hundred—no—two hundred—no—more like three hundred kilos! And where's *that* dope, you think?"

Response to the growing Legend on the street is quick, a nerve is touched, that nerve of possibility, the proverbial big score, the fact that someone has a lot of something they shouldn't have by law, so it's not really a crime to steal it back.

Adding to the growing lore around Louella Debra Poule, now exposed as a bona fide drug dealer of no small consequence, is the widely shared information concerning her recent inheritance from her mother, who, in the rumour-fuelled scheme of things, turns out to have been a prominent drug dealer herself who left a fortune of drug money to her dopehead daughter. The Cuban and the Mick hear all about it during relentless shakedowns of the drug community, although they find it hard to believe that that lowly scumbag Jimmy Flood could have had anything to do with such a nervy operation. Still (and although they don't necessarily realize it about themselves), they are also evolved products of the street and answer to the same warped instincts and misplaced priorities as any crackhead they habitually shake down and figure at best that maybe a simple, illegal late-night home raid on the Deep Cove townhouse might be the way to go.

Blacky Harbottle, on the other hand, still miffed by the kidnapping fiasco with the Truman brothers but feeling it to his advantage to maintain ties with the Tai Pai boys, believes that simplicity could carry the day for him, too. He attends Frankie Yin's small memorial service to more or less mime allegiance to Frankie Yin's successor, Bobby Phat, at the same time proposing to the new head of the Tai Pai boys a possibly lucrative straightforward home invasion on the townhouse in Deep Cove, citing that "Frankie would have wanted it this way" and hinting that the "kidnappee" in the ransom job, namely Louella Poule, sort of owed it to Frankie.

This act could also be regarded as a meaningful tribute to Frankie Yin's memory, to which Bobby Phat solemnly agrees, dabbing an eye with a hanky, which leaves Blacky Harbottle wondering if it's a wiping away of actual tears or just some ratty city dust flung on the breeze.

Marco Da Silva is also one of those seduced by the power of The Legend, but, to his credit perhaps, opts for a less criminal approach to maybe attaining some undeserved riches, and that would be to make his way back out to Louella's and just ask, beg, or plead for a modest handout based on their past friendship, or, if not actual friendship, their mutual reliance on drugs and the dirty, lowdown things they used to do together to attain them.

Ginger Baumgartner, for her part, hears about it all and believes in The Legend wholeheartedly, contemplating wheedling for a position as Louella's roommate, with a hope that after a short time and faithful companionship she would be asked to become a partner in the drug ring or even second-in-command, eventually ripping Louella off (no hard feelings—just business) and become her own boss.

Melody Tenbrink, lacking at best imagination but not to be left out, has no plan as such, plotting a course much simpler than any others that consists of somehow just getting to Louella's front door, "And, well, seeing what gives." Jimmy Flood, having convinced himself that the whole Legend is not a legend at all, but true, just wants his dope back.

38

Loose Screws

BUT NOT EVERYONE CAN BE caught up in the buzz generated by
the growing Legend of Louella Debra Poule being propagated on the
streets of Vancouver, Constable Dusty Yorke being one of them for
simple geographical reasons. If ignorant of the growing Legend, she
remains no less suspicious of this Louella Poule, but also, somewhat
surprisingly, has managed to keep both RCMP-issue police shoes
firmly on the ground in spite of recent events. She is called out on
the cold, blustery night when a Deep Cove resident meets with
tragedy while trying ostensibly to save his bees after some hives are
smashed following a bizarre incident involving a large shipment of
marijuana dropped from a helicopter, Constable Yorke arriving
eagerly on the scene and it does not escape her that the scene they've
been called to is right next door to the townhouse where a month
earlier she had been involved in the alleged abduction of the
occupant that turned out not to be an abduction, apparently, or so
maintained the alleged "abductee." The ambulance is already on
site when she arrives on the call, the medics attending to the male
resident of the house who lies prone on the wet grass with shirt off
as they apply CPR. The wife stands over them, arms clasped tightly
across her chest, her dark hair matted down over her face. Someone
had thought to drape a rain slicker over her shoulders.

Constable Yorke peruses the yard as forensic cameras flash,
Constable Yorke treading carefully between the scattered plastic-
wrapped bundles. She makes her way through some trees to the
lattice-topped fence that backs the familiar townhouse. The beam of
her flashlight darts around the backyard of the townhouse but reveals
nothing out of the ordinary. Then shining the beam directly on the
sliding French doors of the small patio, the same doors suddenly

slide open, Louella Poule standing in the opening wrapped in a robe and shielding her eyes.

"It's me again," says Dusty Yorke. "Constable Yorke, RCMP. Louella isn't it? Did you see any of what happened?"

"No, I didn't," says Louella. "I think it was a helicopter, though."

"I'll have to talk to you later," says Dusty Yorke.

"Sure," says Louella.

Dusty Yorke returns to the crime scene through the trees. Marv Klep is there talking to another officer. The ambulance has left.

"What do we know?" says Dusty Yorke.

"The guy's been taken to emergency," says Marv Klep. "Doesn't look good. Bee stings."

"Bee stings?" says Dusty Yorke.

"Yup," says Marv Klep. "Looks like the poor guy got stung by the whole kit an' kaboodle."

"Jeepers. And the bud?" says Dusty Yorke.

"That's a bit of a mystery," says Marv Klep, hunching his shoulders in the downpour and casting a glance around the yard at the plastic-wrapped bundles. "It appears to be a drop of some kind, but in the middle of a stormy night in a densely populated area? Somebody's got a screw loose."

Dusty Yorke shields her eyes, looking upward into the night.

"How'd they miss the power lines, you think?"

"Like I said," says Marv Klep, "a screw loose."

Regardless of all the unanswered questions, Constable Dusty Yorke cannot help but feel a rush of excitement. It would appear, on the surface anyway, that here was one of the drug deals she'd been speculating about. A big drug drop in the middle of the night in a supposedly innocent residential neighbourhood, something obviously goes wrong, and the intended drug-dealer recipient has an accident and is sent to hospital. She silently hopes that an officer accompanied the patient and has the wherewithal to cuff the perp's sorry ass to the bed.

"You might like to go to the hospital," says Marv Klep. "Talk to the wife, she went in the ambulance. Better a woman do it, I think."

"I'm on it."

"Make sure you take it easy. She seemed pretty shook up."

"Like I said," says Dusty Yorke.

"You—?" says Marv Klep.

But Dusty Yorke is gone.

"Oh, to be that young again," thinks Marv Klep, "and sure as the stink of cowshit about everything."

AT THE HOSPITAL Dusty Yorke finds the wife being comforted by a nurse in a waiting area off the emergency ward. Her husband has just been pronounced dead, and Dusty Yorke can't help noticing the faint yellowish-blue marks of bruising below the wife's left eye and along her forearms. The wife is quiet, no tears. But Dusty Yorke is at least savvy enough to know that people respond to shock and grief in different ways and to her credit acts accordingly. The wife doesn't purport to know what exactly happened. There was a helicopter, it was dropping something, her husband ran out to tend to his hives, some of which were damaged. It all happened so fast. And, no, her husband never used drugs.

Upon further investigation in the next few days, there will be no real evidence uncovered that would support the theory that the whole incident was anything more than a colossal screw-up by criminal parties unknown.

"I still think that Poule lady in the next-door townhouse has something to do with it," Dusty Yorke will say.

"And why is that?" Marv Klep will say.

"Because she's been a drug user herself," Dusty Yorke will say. "And that whole abduction thing was suspicious, too."

"Well, if that's what you think, better get some evidence then," Marv Klep will say.

"I just might," Dusty Yorke will say.

"Well, good," Marv Klep will say.

"And the neighbour who died. His wife. Didn't seem all that upset."

"And this means . . ." Marv Klep will say.

"It means that maybe the two women were in on it together . . ."

Marv Klep will then say nothing more, deeming it better to afford instead what he hopes will come across as a sympathetic expression that will convey at least the possibility that Constable Yorke could be right, although one doesn't believe it in a million years, and at the same time one will stifle an impulse to expound openly and at length on the inherent dangers of coupling uncomplicated, regulated police work with complicated, unregulated imagination.

"You think I could be right, don't you?" Dusty Yorke will then say. "I can see it on your face," leaving Marv Klep thinking about his face and how the hell, considering the present circumstances, a message anywhere close to that could have possibly got on it.

39.

Marie Jereni Philena Papadopoulos

MONA ROSE SITS at dead Momma's kitchen table, turning slowly the pages of *The Complete Home Gardener*. She's brought over some homemade Nanaimo bars and a sizable chunk of coffee cake, all heaped together on a large porcelain platter-tray, its petal-curved lip ringed with brightly painted dancing bluebells and colourful renderings of ducks of varied species. Louella absently gazes at a brown-and-white striped one with a wide yellow beak and a bright green head.

"You reading this, Louella?" says Mona Rose.

"Mom's book? Yeah, sort of," answers Louella.

A not-unpleasant smell of burning scrap timber drifts on the air from somewhere outside. The sound of a chainsaw can be heard someplace distant, muted, then braying high as the user revs it. Some crows put up a fuss from the backyard.

"We ought to pay our respects," says Mona. "The neighbourly thing to do."

"I don't even know her, really," says Louella.

"Who the heck does?" says Mona. "Now's our chance."

THE FIRST THING Marie Jereni Philena Papadopoulos does after her husband, Leonidas (Leon) Papadopoulos, dies from multiple bee stings is to cut down the dead raccoon her husband had hung from a branch of the cherry tree as a deterrent to other raccoons. She will leave the aluminum flange on the trunks of the cherry, apple, and pear trees to prevent the raccoons from climbing and possibly destroying the trees in the process, but come ripening time, she will systematically climb each tree and shake down a generous amount of fruit, making it easily accessible for any and all foragers on the ground. The second thing she does after her husband, Leonidas (Leon) Papadopoulos, dies from multiple bee stings is to call her two Filipino friends Marifel and Perlita living in Vancouver to inform them of the *natay* or death. The two friends come immediately out to the Cove to assist their friend Marie Jereni in any way they can, be it simply to comfort or, more importantly, to ensure that all burial rites are undertaken correctly. The main concern of the three women is the potential for haunting from Leon Papadopoulos's *kararua* or other evil *anitos*. The fact that Leon Papadopoulos was a brutal and abusive man lends credence to their concerns that his kararua would love to hang around and cause more trouble for Marie Jereni.

"We must say the novena," says Marifel. "Then we must move the bed. We can't take chances with anitos."

The three women deliver the appropriate prayers, then drag Marie and Leon Papadopoulos's king-sized bed out into the yard. Perlita soaks it with sugar wine that she has brought for just this purpose. Marie scatters rice grains about the bed and Marifel burns some straw.

"I can't remember all that we are supposed to do," says Perlita.

"Neither do I," says Marifel. "But I remember when my uncle died, there were lots of prayers. And the 'bed thing' to prevent my uncle haunting it. You got to leave it outside for nine days. And everyone played cards—*pipito*—all night long to stay awake and keep vigil, and you're not allowed to sweep the house either for nine days."

"No housework and playing cards all night for nine days?" says Marie Jereni. "I can do that!"

The three women laugh, throw more rice around, sprinkle more sugar wine. That night they make *kare-kare* and *pochero*. Then some *bagoong* and plain rice. Marie throws the broom out the door and Marifel puts the vacuum cleaner out on the back porch. They drink gin *pomelo*, ginger tea, and *pandan* iced tea with lemon grass.

They hear the raccoons come after sundown rattling the garbage cans. They throw remnants of the *kare-kare*, oxtail cooked in peanut sauce, out onto the lawn near the cherry tree. They watch the raccoons waddle out of the darkness into the light cast from the porch.

"You want some *pochero,* night bandits?" says Perlita, throwing beef and banana onto the grass.

"Come tomorrow and every day if you like for *agahan* and *merienda*," calls Marifel.

The raccoons hesitate, sitting up on their haunches.

Marie Jereni, slightly drunk on gin *pomelo*, spreads her arms.

"I grant you access, my *banditos amigos*," she says and tosses high an entire bowlful of rice. "No more *la tiranía*!"

MONA, MEAGRE, AND LOUELLA walk up the gravel driveway from the roadway. It's surprisingly warm for late fall, a fluke in the weather that releases the sharp, rich smell of damp earth into the air. The three women have never really seen the Greek's house, his driveway, his property. Only glimpses over the lattice-topped fences through the trees.

The driveway curves, obscured by clumps of large spread-leafed ferns and thick, wild shrubbery that borders its edge. The Greek's old pickup parked against a tree trunk around the curve, its truck bed still full of tools and equipment. And on past a shed as the driveway onto the property ends, the yard opening to a larger grassy area where the whiteboard beehives stand along one side, some of them smashed. From the ones still intact, bees circle, buzzing the air. A flat-stone pathway sunk into the ground traversing the vegetable garden, the vegetable garden only ever partially glimpsed, like everything else, over lattice-topped fences through the trees. This time of year the garden is practically bare, of course, but one can see the straight lines of stakes, the neat heaped rows of earth. Farther on and standing in the grass by the flat-stone walkway, a king-sized bed completely made up, quilted bedspread and all, and smelling strongly of wine or spirits and what appears to be rice scattered everywhere, radiating white off the grass. The front porch of the house sits partially obscured by high untamed brambles and blackberry bushes. Then voices heard, women's. And speaking Spanish, maybe. Laughter.

Two low steps lead up onto the porch, three brown-skinned women sitting there, the Greek's young Filipino wife and two others. They stop laughing, the Greek's young wife still smiling as she stands up. A yellow T-shirt with I Like Bananas emblazoned across the chest, blue jeans and white sneakers, no socks, her arm extended toward some weather-worn wicker chairs.

"Hello. I'm Marie Papadopoulos," she says. "Please sit."

Mona moves forward, offers a basket of white flowers.

"I'm Mona," she says. "This is Louella. And Meagre. You probably know we live in the complex next door. We've come to pay our respects to you for the loss of . . . "

"Leonidas?" says Marie Jereni.

"Yes," says Mona Rose. "For the loss of Leonidas."

"NOW, THAT WAS not quite what I expected," Mona is to say later.

"Not at all," says Louella.

"Oh, I don't know," says Meagre.

"She speaks good English," says Mona.

"Yes, she does," says Louella. "And she's quite funny, actually."

"I like her," says Meagre. "And she's handling the loss of 'Leonidas' exceptionally well . . . "

"You noticed that, eh," says Louella.

"And what was with the bed?" says Mona Rose.

"No idea," says Louella.

"It was kind of fun," says Mona. "Was it supposed to be? I mean, she seemed quite happy."

"I think she is," says Louella.

"I liked that meat and banana dish," says Meagre. "Did you know that *Marie* means 'bitter sea,' derived from the French?"

"Um, no. I did not know that," says Louella.

"I didn't know that either," says Mona Rose.

"Well, now you do, don't you," says Meagre Deerstone. "Bitter sea…"

40.

Poppa

DURING THIS TIME there is another who is fitfully unaware of the propagation and growth of The Legend of Louella Debra Poule and that person is Louella Debra Poule herself, although she does have her suspicions that something beyond her is in the making. Her first clue is the arrival of Ginger Baumgartner at the door of dead Momma's townhouse one cold, grey afternoon two weeks after the helicopter fiasco. The smell of winter is in the air and the birds have been making themselves scarce departing for warmer climes. Ginger Baumgartner sits at dead Momma's circular white kitchen table, emanating what feels to Louella is definitely an aura of unconfirmed expectancy. Ginger makes trivial conversation, drinks three cups of coffee, and finally Louella is forced to ask just what it is she wants, Ginger Baumgartner humming, hawing, and interspersing these manifestations with the odd reference to having no place to live, nowhere to go, and does Louella need a reliable roommate or partner to assist her in her, um, business?

"Business? What business?" says Louella.

"You know," says Ginger Baumgartner. "Everyone knows."

"I know I don't know what the hell you're talking about," says Louella. "Look, Ginger, you can't stay here. Sorry, but it's not an option. This is the best I can do."

Louella gives Ginger forty-five dollars and change for the bus. It's not much, but one has to be careful with handouts to one's ex-associates, lest they become regular visitors. It's not that Louella holds no affinity for the girls on the street, quite the opposite. She knows it's the girls who actually run the street, not the men. Most of the guys have girlfriends who turn tricks and are responsible for any income. The guys are supposed to be "protection," but Louella knows that most of them are useless in a crunch and run the other way when there's trouble. The women make the money, score the dope, and keep the whole thing going. And so it is she also helps Melody Tenbrink out a bit, too, when she shows up, sending her on her way with a bit of cash and a polite but firm notification not to make a habit of it. Melody Tenbrink does leave a surprise impression on Louella who notices, after Melody Tenbrink has left, a fresh annotation on the list in dead Momma's kitchen:

1752—Elizabeth Bushell—published first newspaper in Canada.
"Now how the hell would Melody . . ." thinks Louella.

Things do go a bit differently for Marco Da Silva when he once more makes his way to the Cove to scratch at the door in the early morning hours. He doesn't even rate a face-to-face meeting, sent on his way with a strong rebuff delivered through the greatest invention in the world on the bolted door of dead Momma's townhouse. Marco Da Silva does manage to let it slip in an angry, wailing voice that everyone knows she has a ton of money and is *"dealing a ton of dope in there!"*

Louella Poule allows herself a shake of the head, then allows herself to breathe a heartfelt prayer from behind the door—*"C'mon, Matilda, do something. Keep poor dead Momma's house safe from all the fucking dipshits."*

LOUELLA READS:
Pruning: Correct pruning can stimulate a plant to grow in the way you want . . .

Oh, if it were only that simple for people, she thinks, feigning a deeper philosophical interest (if only to herself) in the possible homespun horticultural counsel of *The Complete Home Gardener.* She's stalling, two pale blue bundles of Poppa's letters to Momma brought out and sitting on dead Momma's circular white kitchen table. The most recent one just brought in from the seldom-remembered-to-check communal mailbox out at the curb, a standard airmail envelope postmarked England and still holding the cold air from outside. She sets it aside, reaching for one of the bundles, the snap of the caramel-coloured elastic band holding the bundle together as the band is released and shoots across the room.

And Louella then (and finally) reading her Poppa's collective letters to Momma, all handwritten in Poppa's steady engineer's hand, Louella reading phrases like "Hope things are well with you" and "Haven't had a drink in some time."

And, "Tell Lou I love her."

And what can one make of all this in one's present state of emotional and physical flux, though on the whole, one's feelings and senses are on the heal, one believes, but still subject to the confusion of conflict of opposites, hot and cold, up and down, the so-called normal life of which one still seems to be more fearful than the dark, life-sucking existence of the other? The letters, above all, seem to be congenial, Dad talking to Mom, telling her what and how he's doing. And then in turn asking her how and what she's doing, no hint of the animosity one strung-out daughter has always taken for granted after the separation and divorce; after all, *she* hated Poppa for leaving, so why not suppose Momma did, too. And Momma kept them all, all Poppa's letters. Why? For her? For Louella? And there are enough references in the letters to things Momma had written to substantiate that it was a two-way correspondence, and what's more, the two of them appear to have been, if not friends exactly, definitely *caring*.

A weariness, a sense almost of desperation descending, and a coffee and a cigarette taken out onto the small back patio. Definitely winter in the air, a cold, biting wind. The firs and pines heavy with moisture, the grass thick, fuzzy with frost. And Christmas is being promoted in the stores, looming on the horizon—good god—what is one to do with that? And maybe this low feeling is no more than a natural progression when faced with the change of season, the general hysteria and predictable complications that traditionally accompany the Christmas madness, and these coupled with the fact that one is dealing suddenly with so much that's not exactly the way one has thought it's been for so long. Like, who were Momma and Poppa, anyway? Two people who, it's starting to turn out, didn't hate each other. In fact, they shared something: regardless of their personal problems and differences, they shared something. They shared Louella Debra Poule.

And back in dead Momma's kitchen, the new, unopened letter warm now, room temperature, part of its surroundings. And Louella tearing open the flap, Poppa's handwriting below a letterhead that says *Marisco Tavern—Isle of Lundy*. Poppa's opening line "Dear Lou..."

She reads, able to glean only a broken chain of phrases, the brain feeling pressured to perform but distracted by this wadded ball in the gut.

Talked to Inga... Very sorry about Mom... Difficult to write... Remarried... A younger stepbrother and sister... Angry with me... Don't blame you... I'm sorry... Keeping it short...

But she is able to focus on the last part:

PS: Don't worry about the letterhead. It's not what you might think. Was rock climbing St. James Stone here on the Isle and took a spill off the Devil's Slide. Resting here a few days with friends. Am okay. Haven't had a drink in a long time now. Much love...

And Louella once again hearing the clink and chime of carabiners, bolt hangers, and descending rings being stuffed into a sports bag, Poppa gathering static rope, belay devices, and other paraphernalia to head out the door for another Saturday of rock climbing, and even at a young age, she thought it a somewhat ludicrous passion for a heavy drinker to pursue. But Poppa never got seriously injured, attempting, but not too energetically, to get her interested in the same sport. And the day would end late in the evening, Poppa standing tipsy in the doorway, a dusting of climbing chalk smattering his hands, his La Sportiva climbing shoes laced over his shoulder and his Rock River mountain boots tumbling dried mud on the mat.

Louella glancing down, tears running down her cheeks off her chin, etching the open pages of *The Complete Home Gardener* with darkening circles.

SHE READS:
Indoors, poor ventilation encourages fungus diseases...best to remove dead vegetation.

41

Predatory Natures

THE GUIDING FORCE that is about to fuel yet another of many forays to places and municipalities beyond their jurisdiction is, simply, obsession. And possibly, plain boredom. Neither plainclothes cop Peter Manfred Rourke nor Ruben Gerald McFadden has ever pretended to spend much time on inner deliberation. Or dissecting any suppositions (or even vague ideas) on cause and effect. Or questioning why they, or anyone else for that matter, do the things that they do. Why other people do the things they do—and this diagnosis is freely applied by the two narcs to practically everyone, not just the criminals on the street and fellow officers—why other people do the things they do is because they're "just assholes." But it's also a fact that both plainclothes cops are single, and this condition may only contribute to pre-empt any inclination to explore the intricacies of human emotions and behaviour or manifest any sense of empathy to the masses that experiencing a true relationship with another might instill.

Both do have girlfriends; they are not without need of some personal connection and sense of sanctuary, however artificial. The two women who mean the most to them, though, are their mothers whom they revere in established Irish fashion. But the main, all-pervading reason for either to get up in the morning is, simply, the job. A predatory nature flies the two psyches like a pair of frenzied, tunnel-visioned sparrow hawks. In short, the two narcs hunt.

So it's no big surprise that both succumb to the sudden and vehement condition of that frenzied sparrow-hawk tunnel vision when cruising the downtown streets of Vancouver in the early morning hours, spying one skinny, pale-faced Jimmy Flood passing by in the other direction in a 2004 light green Dodge Neon *and at the wheel, no less,* for it's none other than this skinny, nondescript, strung-out *blighter* who has become their main obsession.

"Where the fuck did that shithead get a car?" says the Mick.

"I have no fucking idea, but what say we follow the prick and find out?" says the Cuban.

And it isn't until they pass the PNE fairgrounds and head north onto the Ironworkers Bridge that Peter Manfred Rourke puts it all together.

"Our little friend is off to visit his ex, methinks," says the Cuban. "The one that's supposed to be dealing heavy and has a ton of money from her mother who died, who was a big dealer herself the word is."

"The broad with the Truman brothers in that motel a while back?" says the Mick.

"One and the friggin' same," says the Cuban. "She lives in the Cove, remember? And we both know this little bastard has been up to something, but I'm fucked if I can really believe the shit on the street 'bout him being in on that North Shore dope-drop fuck-up. Still, you never know with this little prick. Maybe his 'I'm just a dumb junkie' thing is just an act. We've known dumber assholes that have had their thumbs in some pretty big pies."

"Aye, Mr. Rourke, that we have," says the Mick.

"Aye-fucking-aye yerself, Mr. McFadden," says the Cuban. "We're gonna bust this little dickhead's sorry ass, I daresay, brother..."

"It will 'bring out the lilacs on the O'Shea Dale,' Mr. Rourke," says Ruben McFadden.

"Yes, indeedy," says Peter Manfred Rouke. "The O'Shea-fucking-Dale..."

VINCENT JULIO PREVOST is on his cellphone, but then again, Angela Romano (who takes phone orders at Abruzzi Pizza situated just a little above Deep Cove along Mount Seymour Parkway in the Parkgate neighbourhood) knows Vincent Julio Prevost is always on his cellphone. But he's reliable, delivers the orders efficiently, and seldom complains. Vincent Prevost finishes his call, diverts to the washroom to no doubt comb his hair, and returns to the front counter.

"Whatcha got?" says Vincent Julio Prevost.

"These four," says Angela Romano and slides the four steaming pizza boxes into the heat-retaining delivery case. Vincent Julio Prevost grabs the case and heads for the door.

Angela Romano watches him through the window, Vincent Prevost placing the case in the Suzuki hatchback outside, the words *Abruzzi Pizza—One of a Kind* emblazoned in flame-coloured letters along its side. She watches Vincent Prevost drive off as the phone at the counter rings and Angela Romano takes another order, large steel oven doors behind her banging shut as her father tosses discs of spongy dough in the air and the smell of flour, sliced meats, and tomato sauce permeates the heated air.

Vincent Julio Prevost will make a number of stops, only four of which will be deliveries of the pizza variety. The others will be of a private nature but will not interfere with his job responsibilities. The last actual pizza delivery is for the Cove, a #6 large, double cheese, pepperoni, Italian sausage, mushrooms, olives, and extra banana peppers. The customer's a regular and always tips well.

THE CUBAN AND THE MICK crest the span of the Ironworkers Bridge, bidding farewell to the grain elevators rising up from the south shore of the inlet and bidding hello to the dry docks and moored houseboats that bob the shoreline on the other side of the bridge. The light green Dodge Neon ahead takes the Deep Cove exit and the Mick's stomach rumbles.

"Hungry..." says the Mick.

"Fucker's taking the Cove exit," says the Cuban. "Told ya."

"I'm fucking starving," says the Mick.

"Relax, Mr. McFadden," says the Cuban. "We will soon dine on heart-o'-junkie..."

"And after that, I could go for an extra hot an' spicy shrink-yer-dick pizza, methinks," says the Mick.

"A shrink-yer-dicker it'll be, Mr. McFadden," says the Cuban.

42.

Of Crack Cocaine, Normal Cocaine, and Rotgut Whisky

A FORM OF HUNGER is also afflicting Jimmy Flood, too, at the wheel of the light green Neon, but not a hunger in the biological sense. It's more a hunger for a lucky break, a good hand, some freaking good karma as his stomach is beyond rumbling and is choosing instead to boil noiselessly with a concoction of fear, anger, and panicked anticipation of possibilities, real or unreal, it doesn't really matter which, possibilities of what could conceivably arise of finally seeing some return on his big score, his big scheme that for all intents and purposes appears at this point to have failed completely. But one thing is sure, and that is that Louella Debra Poule is not about to get away with the big rip-off, living the high-and-mighty life in the fancy-ass Cove in her fancy-ass townhouse off the spoils of his, Jimmy Flood's, master plan.

And such are the thoughts of Jimmy Flood, firm believer in The Legend of Louella Debra Poule as he speeds through the night and crests the Ironworkers Bridge at the wheel of the Dodge Neon, the car borrowed from that useless slimeball Rudy Decker, who, after being promised a generous cut of the proceeds once Jimmy Flood regains possession of his now-legendary shipment of BC bud, handed over the keys to his precious green Neon and wished Jimmy luck. And indeed, an overblown sense of being lucky has deeply suffused the unsteady psyche of Jimmy Flood in recent weeks, beginning with the demise of Frankie Yin, his chief creditor, and Arnold Bridger's constant references to their extraordinary luck that night at evading all power lines during the helicopter-drop debacle. (This particular feat was also played up in the media, only adding to a growing sense of impunity—*O, luck be a lady tonight.*)

He has no real plan at the moment, just a circulatory system swimming with crack cocaine, normal cocaine, and rotgut whisky he'd downed with Rudy Decker while talking him into lending him his car. His somatoform disorder is in high gear, too, with his right thigh and buttocks taking the brunt of it, burning with the imagined welts of a hundred jellyfish. And now he sees the tips of the rusty green monoliths of the old CPR retractable bridge passing by in the moonlight on his right and beyond them just up the inlet the ghostly white mists rising from the small refinery lit up on the south shore below the university.

Taking the Deep Cove exit at the north end of the bridge, he follows the lower road along the inlet toward the Cove, moonlight flashing off the water as it reflects through the trees. And on through the native reserve, taking it slow as the speed limit is strictly enforced and he is, of course, without a valid driver's licence. Then on up the long hill past the marine works and at last approaching the lights of the intersection he'd recognized from the copter that signifies one has reached the Cove, and on past that and it's then, and only then, that he considers he's arrived at his destination devoid of any solid plan of action, devoid of even the actual address and location of Louella Debra Poule's dead mother's fucking townhouse, although he had been there once before but was so messed up he can't really remember its exact location. The only other time he'd thought he'd seen it is from the air, at night, and in the middle of a rainstorm.

THE CUBAN AND THE MICK, on the other hand, have no need of addresses. They need only to keep the green Dodge Neon in sight following it off the bridge exit to the Cove. They, too, see the flashes of the moon's reflection off the water through the trees, see the ghostly mists rising from the lights of the small refinery on the opposite shore. They keep a close tail up the long hill past the marine works and through the intersection that signifies one has ostensibly reached the Cove and then proceed to follow the Neon as it begins to meander the winding roads of the Cove, hugging a rock cliff one minute, then navigating tight residential streets the next. They appear to make three passes through the village centre of Deep Cove itself, each time going in a different direction before the Mick is motivated to remark: "This fucker know where he's going?"

"It would appear ol' Jimmy boy doesn't have a fucking clue," says the Cuban. "And why am I not surprised . . .?"

It's twenty-five minutes of seemingly random driving before the Neon ahead stops in front of a row of townhouses.

"About fucking time," says the Mick.

"One must be the girlfriend's place," says the Cuban.

They switch off the lights and park the car. Watch as Jimmy Flood exits the Dodge Neon and stands a moment, undecided, checking out the townhouses. He appears to make a decision and begins limping to the townhouse at the far end. He approaches the door, appears to ring the doorbell, and a moment passes. Then someone appears to be talking to him through the door, Jimmy Flood leaning his ear to it, suddenly more animated, his voice rising.

"It would appear," says the Cuban, "that the lady isn't having any of it."

"Have you noticed the poor bastard's grabbed his butt a hundred times in the last minute?" says the Mick.

"That I have, Mr. McFadden," says the Cuban. "He looks to be in a bit of pain."

The yelling escalates, Jimmy Flood putting a fist to the door.

"You think that dope drop could really have been this asshole's idea?" says the Mick.

"Well, it did happen somewhere in this neighbourhood, I believe," says the Cuban. "A bit of a coincidence, wouldn't you say, Mr. McFadden?"

"I would fucking certainly say, Mr. Rourke," says the Mick getting out of the car. "And this dinkshit's sense of direction as we've seen tonight is so fucked up that if anyone could drop a shipment in the wrong place, it'd be him."

The two of them stand by the car. Jimmy Flood is yelling, the door of the townhouse is not opening.

"Let's have a chat with ol' Jimmy," says the Cuban.

INSIDE DEAD MOMMA'S townhouse Louella Debra Poule holds the Petersville Slugger, peers through dead Momma's peephole. She closes the tiny metal grate and moves into the kitchen. She will let Jimmy Flood rant for a little longer and hope that Mona or someone else calls the police. She doesn't want to have to do that herself. And taking a coffee into the living room to curl up on the couch. From the metal wrought table against the wall, the new aquarium pump hums gently; a newly purchased orange clownfish, three Congo tetras, a spotted angelfish, and two black moor goldfish swim in the warmly lit clear water behind the newly cleaned glass. She switches on the TV, surfing the channels, and notices (with a certain amount of relief) that the yelling outside has stopped.

OUTSIDE DEAD MOMMA'S townhouse, the yelling has indeed stopped, Jimmy Flood overcome with an overwhelming feeling of futility, a feeling not that unfamiliar. And turning back toward the road only to see two familiar shapes coming toward him, the Cuban and the Mick now passing from the subdued nuance of moonlit shadows into the more theatrical brilliance of the street light. They see him see them and shout their favourite names for him, none of which are "Jimmy" or "Flood," Jimmy Flood responding in his habitual way whenever confronted with authority, that response being full and shameless flight and this night things are no different, Jimmy Flood turning and sprinting up the road toward the black unlit void a short distance ahead that he knows is a sports field of some kind, the field not a totally black void as it first appears, but lit almost romantically with moonlight, affording one at least some silvery perception of terrain, the angry pain of imaginary jellyfish stings along one's right thigh and buttocks momentarily forgotten, dewy night grasses spongy under one's feet until reaching the far edge of the field where a high, black wall of forest awaits, suddenly blotting out the moon and the stars. His footfalls sounding across a small wooden bridge, a small inky stream bubbling happily underneath and then new ground underfoot, totally black and pitted with unseeable and bone-jarring dips and modulations.

Jimmy Flood slowing, stumbling onward in the black. A light rain beginning to fall—no—that's one sweating one's guts out with fear and exertion. And thick, low-hanging branches trying to put out one's eyes, dense leafy arms grabbing at his pant legs. Then the sound of the two narcs' two pairs of boots pounding across the small wooden bridge behind, someone singing:

> Oh, Bridgit O'Malley, you left my heart shaken
> With hopeless desolation I'd have you know...

THEN THE SOUNDS of pursuit stopping except that of sporadic gasping and heavy breathing as the two narcs hesitate at the beginning of the woods at the end of the bridge, Jimmy Flood somewhere ahead in the darkness attempting to make headway deeper into the forest blackness, knees wet where they meet unseen damp earth, mysterious foliage clutching at his arms and his face. And best to just curl up where he's fallen under shelter of whatever growth this is that he's fallen into and listen to some mad flailing and twig snapping of the Cuban and the Mick, a sudden pause in the clamour, the dark woods still, save the sounds again of the two narcs' heavy breathing.

A pissed-off whisper, *"This is fucked, man..."*

Then more silence, the entire forest looming above and around Jimmy Flood listening. No movement, Jimmy Flood embracing fauna, flora, squeezing the life out of some unlucky bush that presses against his chest. The Cuban and the Mick sensed not too far away, but one is also able to sense that these two asshole cops are equally out of their comfort zone.

Then the Cuban: "Fuck him. Let's go..."

The Mick with voice raised: *"We'll be seeing you, dickhead. Don't think we won't!"*

And Jimmy Flood curled up tighter in nature's unfamiliar embrace, bristly leaves scratching his brow, head resting on an indulgent bed of decomposing forest bark and pine needles, the sound of some unseen forest creature scampering down a wooded ravine, cry of a night bird, and the unrelenting burn of jellyfish stings along his right thigh and buttock.

ONCE BACK AT the car the two narcs pause a moment, both leaning with arms on the roof and both staring back up the road to the black void of the sports fields.

"Well, that was one waste of time," says the Mick.

"It would seem," says the Cuban.

"Think we ought'a call on the girlfriend there?" says the Mick, looking towards the townhouses.

"Can't really think what for," says the Cuban. "Don't really give a shit what she's up to . . ."

"No, can't say I do either," says the Mick.

Headlights appear down the road, approach and stop in front of the townhouse complex. A guy gets out of the car carrying a hot foods delivery bag, the words *Abruzzi Pizza* can be seen along the side of the car. The two narcs watch as the man goes to the townhouse on the end. The door opens and Louella Debra Poule is there, takes the pizza and shuts the door. The guy returns to his car lighting a cigarette on the way, opens the driver's door as the Cuban's voice rumbles the night air.

"Hey, you. Get the fuck over here . . ."

And Vincent Julio Prevost feels the pre-winter November chill a little harsher than he had a minute ago.

43

The Hills of Connemara

CONSTABLE DUSTY YORKE has been able to concede that for a night of the full moon, the evening hasn't been all that crazy. One domestic disturbance (the intoxicated spouse was long gone when police arrived on the scene); one complaint of a loud party on Indian River Drive that was easily managed; a minor traffic accident on the Parkway; and a reported possible B&E in the Rendell Apartments on Jubilee that turned out to be the tenant himself, inebriated and trying to break into his own residence, having lost his key. No, it hasn't been all that crazy this night as she cruises the Cove deciding to make one last pass by the townhouse complex and the house where that botched drug drop had occurred some weeks ago.

The street is quiet as is the rest of the Cove, two cars illuminated in her headlights parked opposite the townhouse complex and both parked on the wrong side of the road. There appear to be two individuals sitting in the car nearest, no one in the car farther up, Constable Dusty Yorke pulling over a few yards short of the occupied car and relaying her location to dispatch before getting out of her car.

She does not approach the occupied car alone, however, as it may appear to any passerby. In her line of work, Constable Dusty Yorke is never really alone, being in the habit of invoking the fanciful support and protection of her heavenly white-haired benefactor above, who, as He always does when she imagines Him up there, leans forward over the billowy crest of a cloud and keeps an eye on things. So Constable Dusty Yorke is assured that He, too, catches a glimpse of reddish hair, a pale unshaven face above an all-weather work vest over a tattered jean jacket sitting in the passenger seat of the near car as she taps on the window.

Inside the car both the Mick and the Cuban have seen Constable Yorke coming, although both are no less startled when the full blinding effect of the beam from her police-issue flashlight explodes off the glass of the passenger side window as she peers inside.

"Jesus Christ!" says the Mick.

"Easy..." says the Cuban.

The Mick rolls down the window.

"Good evening," says Dusty Yorke. "But I'll need to see some ID."

"Not a problem, constable," says the Cuban. "Must look pretty suspicious, but we're Vancouver PD, plain clothes. Not here on official business, of course."

Dusty Yorke scanning their police identification badges, her benefactor (she imagines) scanning them, too, over her shoulder as inside the car both men know what's coming; both men know what's coming and both men think they're ready for it.

"A bit out of your jurisdiction, aren't you?" says Constable Dusty Yorke.

Now, maybe it's the disappointment of not busting Jimmy Flood. Maybe it's just a general discontent and frustration with their very lives, or maybe it's just the full moon suddenly coming to force, but at any rate and no matter what both men think they're ready for, neither plainclothes cop is ready for it.

"*Jesus shit! There's that word again!*" says the Mick, losing his cool and smacking the dashboard.

"*Aye, that fucking word again, Mr. McFadden!*" says the Cuban also losing his cool. "*Ya know, I'm seriously thinkin' of havin' me dear ol' Ma stitch it RIGHT INTO ME FUCKING UNDERWEAR!*"

Dusty Yorke takes a step back from the window at the sudden outburst. The Mick lapses into a fit of coughing as the Cuban issues just one huge hack and spits a large wad of sputum out his window. His voice comes winded and raspy.

"Sorry, constable. We're not on the clock. Just checking in on a witness in a case who lives out here. We were just leaving as a matter of fact."

"Oh," says Dusty Yorke. "And who might this witness be, you don't mind me asking?"

"Sorry," says the Cuban. "Officer McFadden and myself are not at liberty to say. Confidential."

"Yes, very confidential," says the Mick.

"I see," says Dusty Yorke. "It's not the lady in the end townhouse, is it?"

"Um—well, we can't really—"

"Yeah, okay. Can't say," says Dusty Yorke.

"Yup," says the Cuban, "can't say."

"It just seems a little..." says Dusty Yorke.

"You know," says the Cuban, "you might want to check out that green Neon up there. Saw a man running from it when we pulled up. It could be stolen, don't you think, Mr. McFadden?"

"I do think, Mr. Rourke," says the Mick.

"Well, thanks..." says Dusty Yorke. "I'll check into it."

"Oh, and one more thing, constable..." says the Cuban.

"Yes?" says Dusty Yorke.

The Cuban leans over and hands Dusty Yorke a scrap of paper.

"You might want to check out this guy. We think there might be drugs involved, and it is, well, it is in your jurisdiction..."

Dusty Yorke looking at the crinkled paper.

It reads:

Vincent Prevost
Abruzzi Pizza

They pull away, watching as Dusty Yorke moves to check out the green Neon.

"Now that's what we could've used tonight," says the Mick.

"What?" says the Cuban.

"One 'a those honking fucking flashlights," says the Mick.

"We used to have flashlights," says the Cuban.

"Yeah, but we broke 'em," says the Mick.

"Be damned, we did?" says the Cuban.

"Yes, we did," says the Mick. "You broke yours on that crackhead Bobby Wescott's head, I think. And I broke mine on the skull of that pimping scumbag Jeffery Dugas."

"No kiddin'," says the Cuban. "You sure?"

"As sure as..." says the Mick, "the excise men will dance all night..."

The Cuban joins in.

They sing:

> Drinkin' up the tay 'til the broad daylight
> In the hills of Connema-a-a-ra!

44.

Accumulated Dread

LOUELLA READS:
Gardening on Concrete: In such cases it is a Herculean task to break the concrete, cart it away, and replace it with soil...on the debit side, the site may be too open with little privacy, or the aspect grimy and depressing.

AND WHO IS TO SAY when it is, in a time frame relative to the mental and emotional state of a specific individual, who, beset with an accumulated dread of each coming day begins not to dread their coming days so much but begins to find them, at least in some small way and with a diminished amount of fear and cowering, interesting. And a common thing about such a transformation is that it will be almost imperceptible to the subject, so subtle and sublime the manifestations, as in Louella's case, as one begins to fill one's days with long walks through the Cove that eventually turn into long jogs after purchasing a spiffy pair of cross-trainers and a really cool two-piece nylon windsuit with cargo pull-on pants. There are also long drives of informal exploration along the coast or far out into the valley in dead Momma's powder-blue Toyota, and one discovers that one can almost avoid the downtown part of the city entirely by simply driving around it. She even finds herself signing up with a local group called Basic Plant Care for Dummies, hosted by Mona's friend Sheila Van Beekum. This she does out of an uneasy deference to one's dead Momma's obvious interest in cultivating plants and a hope perhaps that by better knowing something of the plants one is surrounded with, one will better come to know something about one's mother. She also attends regular 12-step meetings with Meagre Deerstone and, at Meagre's suggestion, begins browsing the 'net on dead Momma's laptop, checking into healthcare training courses and registered nursing programs.

"You'd be good at it," says Meagre Deerstone.

"No, I wouldn't," says Louella.

"Your mother was," says Meagre Deerstone.

"That was Mom," says Louella.

"The fruit don't fall all that far from the tree," says Meagre Deerstone.

"That's a white man saying," says Louella.

"And lifted originally, I don't doubt, from some Indian," says Meagre Deerstone.

And there are regular visits with Aunt Inga and Mona Rose, and even a fair number of get-togethers with one's new-found neighbour, Marie Philena Jereni Papadopoulos, who brings over jars of liquid honey dripped right off the comb.

"Good for cuts and burns," says Marie Papadopoulos.

"And tastes fucking good, too," says Louella.

"That, too," says Marie Papadopoulos.

And it's after one of Marie Papadopoulos's visits that Louella notices another name added to the list in dead Momma's kitchen:

Loida Nicolas-Lewis—Filipino CEO of a two-billion-dollar corporation that is the leading manufacturer of potato chips in Ireland.

"My, my," says Alcina scanning the list on one of her visits. "Who would have known that?"

"Exactly," says Louella. "And what really blows my mind is, who would know that the women I know would know about even half of these women?"

"And who would know anyone who would know even half of what you just fucking said, my dear," says Alcina.

And Alcina promptly adds to the list:

Marie Rollet—Canada's first farmer's wife.

"And that's gotta be bullshit," says Louella.

"Don't ask me, but it's a fact," says Alcina. "A recorded fact."

"And how would anyone know that?" says Louella.

"Put down for the record by some government statistician with naught else to do back in the day, I guess," says Alcina.

"And you know this—" says Louella.

"Everybody knows this, don't they?" says Alcina.

"But how could you figure out who was actually the first wife of a farmer in the whole country, for Christ's sake?" says Louella.

"Well, somebody's got to be the first, don't they?" says Alcina. "And I don't suppose it'd be that hard to notice some poor woman standing around in the first godawful settlement completely surrounded by equally godawful men, one of whom steps forward ankle deep in mud and horse manure and pops the question . . ."

"Marie fucking Rollet . . ." says Louella.

"It was actually probably a pretty big deal," says Alcina. "Hey, Pierre! Jean up the road's just got hisself a wife just in time to help with the harvest!"

"Funny," says Louella.

"It's always a bit unclear about what's important and what isn't, isn't it?" says Alcina. "Obviously some retard thought this was important. Nothing is ever as it seems, it seems . . ."

"Oooo, very mysterious, Alcina," says Louella.

"Now let's not get snarky, my dear Lou. Feel bad for Marie Rollet, the first in the new country to fall. History is full of the trivial. I think my forefathers ate the heads and the testicles of their enemies, but you can't go putting that in a textbook. Now make some coffee, an act that we can both agree *is* of importance," says Alcina Omojolade Ajunwa.

WINTER OFFICIALLY ARRIVES, heralded by icy rains and occasional dumpings of thick wet snow, Louella standing in her recently acquired jogging attire, windsuit jacket zippered to the neck as one shivers under a blue spruce, attempting to wait out a particularly nasty downpour along a park trail, and the thought occurring that it's no longer that pleasurable attending to the outdoors for the season. It gets dark earlier in the Cove than elsewhere on the Lower Mainland one has discovered, the sun sinking sooner behind the high crests of the North Shore mountains and the surrounding partitions of tall forest. It also rains more on the North Shore and in the Cove (documented data from the Weather Bureau gleaned from the internet), prompting one to rustle out one of dead Momma's winter coats from the mirrored closet in the front hallway, a strictly utilitarian-looking thing, heavily insulated and weatherproofed such as a Russian farm worker would be happy to wear, but who cares. Look cool or be warm—those are the choices.

And so, too, with the onset of the new season does approach ever closer *that* season, Christmas, that highly pressured time of year that inevitably raises the question of how exactly is one going to spend it? It's never really been an issue when one was using: there are no special days or times. But now, living in dead Momma's townhouse in Deep Cove and confronting veritable waves of seemingly daily changes in one's life, what does one do? Go carolling? Volunteer at the Sally Ann serving Christmas dinners to the needy? A nice idea, but one is still pretty needy oneself. Or maybe one is just to go to Horst and Aunt Inga's and hang out for the duration?

And so it may be this growing and unexpressed sense of confusion and season-inflicted pressure that helps explain why one finds one-self parked in dead Momma's powder-blue Toyota outside the house on St. Catherines Street a few nights before Christmas Eve, seeing that the lights are on in the house, which means Blacky Harbottle is likely home.

She turns the engine off. Sits.

A hard rain drumming the car roof, assaulting the windshield. The odd wet snowflake spattering against the glass. She's driven in from the Cove with the sole purpose of scoring a hit and getting high, and it's not a desperate craving that suddenly overcomes her while potting one of her newly purchased indoor plants, a wide-leafed goosefoot *Syngonium*. No, it isn't like that. And one can't even say it's just a moment of temporary insanity, a natural-enough occurrence for anyone trying to kick a drug habit. No, it isn't crazy-like; it's much quieter than that. More like a meditative and reflective steering toward what seems a logical thing to do when one's mind and emotions have been so ravaged, when the brain won't stop shuffling images of past and present, and one's emotions play hide-and-seek, lying low for a time and then when not expected, leaping from the bushes to scare the hell right out of you. And after all these weeks and months—the realizations, fears, and anxieties—well, one simply needs to quiet it all. One needs to get out of dead Momma's powder-blue Toyota and climb those steps to the house on St. Catherines Street and talk to Blacky Harbottle, even though one suspects he had something to do with the Truman brothers and that asinine kidnapping attempt. But that's not a real problem, the code of the street being that anyone who's holding something one wants is immediately forgiven all betrayals and underhanded plots as Louella Debra Poule stares out through the windshield of dead Momma's powder-blue Toyota, watches the slanted rain.

Her lips move: *"Oh, sweet Matilda Goomba..."*

45.

The Man with Two Crystal Balls

WHILE LOUELLA DEBRA POULE thus sits outside the house on St. Catherines Street, struggling with the demons that threaten to undermine her resolve, Jimmy Flood sits soaked to the skin at Blacky Harbottle's kitchen table inside the house on St. Catherines Street struggling with a roll of paper towels, having just come in the back way from the tempest outside. Water can be heard gushing down onto the back porch from the unmaintained, overflowing eaves and a windowpane rattles sporadically with gusts of wind. A pile of wet, crumpled paper towels lies on the table in front of him, a small puddle forming on the floor under his chair.

"Take your fucking shoes off," says Blacky Harbottle staring at the kitchen counter. An open package of bologna, a jar of yellow mustard, and a loaf of white bread are spread out before him, Blacky Harbottle poised with butter knife in hand, his brow furrowed.

"I've forgotten something . . ." says Blacky Harbottle.

"What a shitty night," says Jimmy Flood.

"Something... something... " says Blacky Harbottle.

And possibly it's the influence of the very nature of the wild weather outside, indiscriminately flipping ions about and manipulating pressure zones that could, to some, suggest omnipotent powers of some kind at work, a window to unconscious premonition, perhaps, for what else could explain that on the last night of his life, and although somewhat befitting and apropos, that on the last night of his life Jimmy Flood should be taken suddenly with otherworldly contemplations of a sort? And, just as Blacky Harbottle contemplates what's missing in this world from the bologna, yellow mustard, and loaf of white bread, the bottom-line ingredients essential to providing a decent late-night sandwich, what else could cause Jimmy Flood to suddenly fess up: "I think I saw God last night..."

And, in this case, what else could cause Jimmy Flood to think (somewhat stupidly, such is his muddled state of mind) that this last remark in turn causes Blacky Harbottle to shout, *"The fucking mayonnaise!"*

Neither of them is able to hear a car start and pull away on the street outside as Blacky Harbottle scrounges in the fridge.

"Fucking mayonnaise..." says Blacky Harbottle again.

Jimmy Flood sniffles at the kitchen table, running another paper towel over his face.

"I think I—" says Jimmy Flood.

"Yeah, yeah. I heard you," says Blacky Harbottle.

The fridge door closes; Blacky Harbottle back at the counter with the mayonnaise but not all that comfortable after Jimmy Flood's last statement.

"God who?" he finally says.

"Just . . . you know," says Jimmy Flood. "*God* god."

"You mean, *the* God?" says Blacky Harbottle.

"Yeah, that one," says Jimmy Flood.

Blacky Harbottle is standing erect now, the lid on the jar of mayonnaise popping as he opens it. He stares into the jar a moment and exhales a breath.

"And where'd you see, um, the real God by chance, dear dipshit, sir? ..." says Blacky Harbottle.

"Well..." says Jimmy Flood. "The crack house on Fifteenth. I was there the other night."

Blacky Harbottle setting down the jar of mayonnaise, holding Jimmy Flood with an even stare. The sandwich momentarily forgotten. Jimmy Flood shifting in his seat, blowing his nose.

"You've heard of my crystal balls, Jimmy. I'm sure you've heard of them," says Blacky Harbottle.

"Yeah," says Jimmy Flood, "I've heard of them."

And who in the great local world of the street had not heard of

Blacky Harbottle's infamous crystal balls, purchased some years ago off a "Gypsy-like woman" (Blacky Harbottle's own words) one balmy summer night on East Cordova Street downtown. The story goes that Blacky had baked his brain on meth for fifteen days, stumbling the streets of Vancouver's lower east side skids before meeting the mysterious woman who promptly sold him two "crystal balls" that Blacky Harbottle to this day will swear were the real thing. (The truth, as told by seventy-two-year-old bag lady Janie Macintosh herself, a long-time denizen of the street and one prone to wearing head scarves and copious layers of scrounged dresses of assorted designs and materials as well as a wide, mismatched array of cheap costume jewellery, giving her a somewhat "gypsy-like" aspect, was that she herself had sold Blacky Harbottle the "crystal balls" that were in fact two glass Japanese fishing floats that sometimes can be found washed up on Vancouver beaches or occasionally even in the harbour.)

"Well, let me tell you a little about the world of 'seeing things,' my friend," says Blacky Harbottle. "Now, at least those crystal balls *worked*. Gave me a shitload of visions and general cosmic sort of information. In fact, I got so much information from those things, it was like to drive me nuts. It was too much to handle and that's why I got rid of them. I know a lot of people thought I was full of shit and it was all a load of crap, but the reality was that I just wasn't equipped to deal with the whole freaky business. But the messages were there, man, fucking *there*. And the visions, they were there, man. But this bullshit—seeing 'God' outta the blue—in a crack fucking house—"

"Well, I said I *think* I saw him," says Jimmy Flood.

"Okay, you *think* you saw him," says Blacky Harbottle. "And what'd he look like?"

"Well, I was kinda wasted ... " says Jimmy Flood.

"Please don't say the fucker had on a white robe, Jimmy boy. Please don't say he had long hair and a beard and wore sandals. That wasn't God, Jimmy boy! That was fucking Jesus, not God you saw! You saw His kid, Jimmy—you saw God's kid!"

"Christ, calm down, Blacky. I didn't think you'd believe it. I hardly believe it myself."

"Calm down? Calm down? You fucking saw God an' you want me to calm down? I'm calling the fucking newspapers!" says Blacky Harbottle. "Okay, blow job. Did He say anything? He say anything to you?"

"Well . . ."

"Did He? Huh? Did He?" says Blacky Harbottle.

"Well..." says Jimmy Flood, "I think He said, 'Bless you,' then something fuzzy . . . then 'One can run to or from, Jimmy my son . . .'"

"Jimmy, my son?' says Blacky Harbottle. "Good god, it *was* God!"

"Knew you wouldn't believe it," says Jimmy Flood. "But it must mean something regardless what you think."

"Everything in the fucking world means some fucking thing regardless of what I think, so that it must, dear dipshit, sir!" says Blacky Harbottle returning to his sandwich. A glob of mayonnaise hits the floor.

"What you think it means?" says Jimmy Flood.

Outside the rain's let up, a steady, heavy drip replaces the free flow of water from the eaves onto the back porch. The wind still rattles one of the windowpanes.

"It means, mumph," says Blacky Harbottle with his mouth full of sandwich and a smear of mustard along his upper lip, "that, mumph, mumph, even junkie dipshits like you, mumph, mumph, have hopes and dreams..."

"You think that's it?" says Jimmy Flood.

"Mumph, mumph," says Blacky Harbottle.

46.

Aspirations

LOUELLA REACHES HOME, pulls dead Momma's Toyota into the carport and cuts the engine. What appear to be undulating swirls of clear liquid swim in the corners of her vision, her head tilting to the right as she stares a moment through the front windshield. It feels better that way. One doesn't want to move, doesn't want to ruin this mild catatonic state. One has made it back from the house on St. Catherines Street, still clean and drug-free and not that much the worse for wear, although the true state of one's condition could, at a later time maybe, be up for closer scrutiny.

Then standing in dead Momma's carport, biting, brawny smell of pine and cedar, damp wood rot, and ocean air. Can smell brine (one thinks), decaying shellfish, mouldering brown seaweed drifting up from the Cove. And one thinks that one can even smell the granite cliffs, the flight of night birds, the glinting, wily stares of night-marauding raccoons.

Now standing in the open doorway of dead Momma's townhouse, neither in nor out, "on the threshold," and turning to look back out onto the night, the night of no colours, the night that holds everything, everything there can be. And the night that holds nothing. The night of no great mystery and at the same time the night that holds all great mysteries. The night that can brandish fear or put forth comfort; that can hide or reveal. And now against one's back, the flow of warm air; one suddenly aware of dead Momma's townhouse standing open— calm, maternal—waiting. And heard faintly the new aquarium pump resonating from the living room.

Louella turning, stepping in.

"And it's just another night isn't it, Momma?" she says. "*In a long line of nights from the days of the dinosaurs and before, a normality, nothing more."* And Christmas will be spent safely with Uncle Horst and Aunt Inga, it's decided right then and there; it'll be a sad time but bearable as at the exact time Louella Debra Poule decides this, somewhere in the Maplewood area of North Vancouver, RCMP Constable Dusty Yorke is unlocking at least one mystery that this very same night holds by busting one Vincent Julio Prevost for dealing methamphetamine and crack out of his pizza delivery car, an event that will lead to a whole sequence of subsequent busts and the eventual dismantling of an entire network of illegal meth labs across the Lower Mainland.

And this process will in turn promote Constable Dusty Yorke to virtual stardom in the law enforcement community. And no one will ever be able to tell her that it was just another night in a long line of nights (what kind of talk is that?) because Constable Dusty Yorke will also know that besides holding everything and nothing, the night can hold the answer to one's aspirations, can be completely devoid of any mystery whatsoever on the odd occasion when the turning point of one's life and career can rest simply on following the right hunch or a nondescript scrap of paper scrawled with the name of some drug-dealing scumbag.

47.

Of White-Capped Blue Horizons

AS FAR AS ANY Zen-like paradox of the night holding nothing and holding everything, holding all great mysteries and holding no great mysteries, the only mystery of the night for Blacky Harbottle this very same night that Louella Poule visits and just as promptly unvisits the house on St. Catherines Street is why it takes him so long to react when he hears the first dulcet lines of "Back Home in Derry" coming from the other side of his front door. And now, too late, the Mick is on his way through the living room to check the kitchen, punches him hard in the stomach, and leaves him on the living room carpet expelling a bellyful of air and curling into the fetal position while imploring silently: *"Dear fucked-over Jesus— will the harassment never end?"*

And as if in answer to this question the Cuban just as suddenly stands above him, planting a size thirteen Dayton on his shoulder.

"Ever feel we've done all this before?" says the Cuban.

"Little bastard's taking it up the alley again!" he hears the Mick.

"Then off on his sorry little ass!" the Cuban calls back as the size thirteen is removed and both plainclothes cops thunder through the kitchen to the back door and out through the backyard.

This, at least, leaves Blacky Harbottle alone to perhaps collect himself, even relax a bit, albeit in pain and taxed to draw a breath. He can relax as far as not having reason to worry that there are any illegal drugs on the premises, Jimmy Flood having grabbed what was on the kitchen table seconds before the Cuban and the Mick kicked in the door, and any other illicit drugs lie sealed in a WS 1-SC slot and combination safe, a neat little number weighing only

115 lbs and buried safely (face up for easy access) in the dirt floor of a nearby neighbour's unused garage half a block away.

Outside and also about half a block away but in the opposite direction to Blacky Harbottle's stash, the unwritten liturgy of the Cuban and the Mick's obsession is once again unfolding as both give what is now inexorable chase to Jimmy Flood, who has inexorably once again taken it up the alley, the Cuban taking the high road legging it west along Eighth Avenue while the Mick maintains the alley keeping the fleeing figure of Jimmy Flood in his sights, a cold cascade of mean rain pelting his face, trees along the way waving water-heavy branches in the wind. Jimmy Flood for his part performs a not-unremarkable feat, a tightly rolled five dollar bill jammed in a nostril and managing to snort five lines of coke while in a full sprint without spilling a grain from a small mirror cupped in his left hand that he scooped off Blacky Harbottle's kitchen table as soon as the two narcs gained entrance to the house on St. Catherines Street. And Jimmy tossing the mirror while crossing Prince Albert Street, the coke supplying a needed boost to body and mind, then on to Fraser, Carolina, feet pounding on across St. George and the familiar dash through Guelph Park succeeded by a risky, headlong sprint dodging traffic across Main Street to the other side and all the while attempting a smooth, steady gait to conserve energy, but this made all the more difficult by the sear of jellyfish stings that has begun to ravage his right thigh and buttocks. Then continuing on along Seventh Avenue, buoyed by fear, paranoia, and five hits of cocaine, and another sensation, nutty at best, that one is running across the country as one hits the cross streets named after the provinces—Quebec, Ontario, and Manitoba Streets—and so on until one hits another main artery, and here another headlong sprint dodging traffic across busy Cambie Street ("*And hardly breaking a fucking sweat,*" it seems to an exuberant Jimmy Flood), and still sprinting westward and now the sensation of running through forests, all the cross streets named after trees (had he ever noticed?), sneakers slapping across Ash Street, Willow Street, and Laurel Street, the sky brightening from the east ever so slightly with the early morning dawn behind low mean clouds as one crosses Oak, Spruce, and Alder and approaching another main artery that feeds into the downtown, Granville Street seen ahead and one is still strangely euphoric, wings on one's feet and thoughts of taking up running as an enjoyable and positive pastime as Jimmy Flood darts onto the newly painted traffic lines of Granville and once more timing the spaces between the oncoming and honking cars in one's third headlong sprint, dodging vehicles, when the heart gives what could easily be described as a gentle *pop* midway across, just a gentle *pop* and he drops dead on the spot, an inconvenience to others even in death as Granville Street will be blocked, morning rush hour just beginning, and the ensuing traffic snarl won't be sorted out until well past noon.

The Cuban and the Mick have long given up on the chase, pulling up way back at the juncture of Kingsway Street and Main, a crick in both their sides, chests burning and breath short; the twerp isn't worth the effort, not this time, and, as they both know, there will be another.

But back in the middle of Granville Street, north of Eighth Avenue and south of Sixth, there is that part of us all that never dies and that part of Jimmy Flood keeps running, leaving the body behind and with it the stinging heat of jellyfish barbs and other earthly afflictions and handicaps to continue on westward across Fir, Pine, and Cypress Streets (more trees), Maple, Arbutus, and Yew, and on through the Kitsilano area, his gait now smooth and fluid as freaking running water. Jericho Beach sighted and skirting the golf course through the University Endowment Lands as one leaves the residential areas to reach the end of land at the far cliffs of Point Grey and not stopping, just a moment of doubt as one's feet leave the beach and touch the water but don't sink in, instead continue to run atop the water, across the Strait, Jimmy Flood feeling no pain, no diminishing of energy and reaching land on the far side of the Strait, the stony shore of Vancouver Island where one heads up and overland through forest, mountain, and gorge, more trees again but these ones real, Pacific dogwood, lodgepole pine, Cottonwoods, and

Garry oaks, black hawthorn, and aspen, mountain hemlock, western larch, red alder, and how does one suddenly know all these names? . . . and reaching the western shore and now descending through blowholes, sandbars, excavated stone fish traps, and ancient village fortifications of the Nuu-chah-nulth peoples to the Broken Group Islands, as back in the bleak-feeling reality of the living the Cuban and the Mick, about to kick another door in, break out in a rousing rendition of "Who Threw the Overalls in Mrs. Murphy's Chowder?," the spirit of Jimmy Flood pounding out across a spit of sand into and over the crashing surf of the deep Pacific, where somewhere ahead, not that far over the whitecapped blue horizon of open sea, one knows lie Japan, China (that homeland of one's still-revered hero, Frankie Yin), and those other mysterious Asian places where one has heard one can live real cheap, like the Philippines, Laos, Thailand, and where someone has also heard the dope's the best in the world, or anywhere else for that matter . . .

48.

Even Junkie Dipshits Have
Hopes and Dreams

BLACKY HARBOTTLE REMAINS curled on his living room floor for some time, unaware of the demise of Jimmy Flood, the last act in a tragedy that could be titled, simply, *A Tragedy Called the Life of Jimmy Flood*. No, Blacky Harbottle has yet to hear of the end of Jimmy Flood, has yet to think up that title himself to be used in the future when relating what he will consider a morality tale of sorts, a tale that will begin with the words: "Let me tell you a story about this poor dipshit I call . . ."

But for now Blacky Harbottle lies curled on his living room floor, his physical discomfort at least subsiding. He is able to see himself, can see himself there viewed from above, of all places, and the image is not of a man curled there but a child, a little boy who's been punished, wrongly but still punished, and left alone to sob away his guilt and shame, reflect on things. And the adult Blacky Harbottle does just that, reflecting on the vicious and plain ugly circle one's low-life existence may have become, reflecting on the need, perhaps, to associate with a better class of people, and perhaps this is part of the reason that one has now formed an allegiance with Bobby Phat and the Tai Pai boys, less drug business and maybe get involved in "cleaner crime" like internet fraud, where you can just sit on your butt in a clean room somewhere in front of a fucking PC while eating high-end takeout and not even have to see the fucking street let alone deal with any of the shitfreaks out there. And although the fact remains that one may be in strong denial and even ignorance of the extent of one's own drug abuse and subsequent dysfunction and the damage it has caused,

Blacky Harbottle is not entirely cynical and disillusioned, even on occasion allowing himself hopes and dreams of another world, a better world, a better world for him (and why not?). A world where one could endure the rigours and downright horrible shit that accompanies a heavy drug habit and the basic criminal life, but *happily*. Why not happily? Why not a middle-of-the-road-type world where one basically has to give up nothing that one desires, no matter how destructive and downright evil those things desired may be, and still manage to live a contented, and if not a truly productive, life, at least a well-meaning one. Because in this world of Blacky Harbottle's, meaning well would be, well, better than nothing, and a lot less difficult and time-consuming than actually *doing* well.

And lying there on one's living room floor, viewed from above, and in some half-hearted attempt to take stock of one's life, one can attempt two lists of friends and/or acquaintances (it's unsure which are which sometimes) and sort them under two titles: The Desirable and The Undesirable. And as one compiles said lists (and does it with brutal honestly as there is no one there to deceive), The Undesirable side grows longer and longer, while The Desirable side doesn't appear to grow at all, and this is not in keeping with the dream of a satisfactory middle-of-the-road, consequence-free happy world. And all one really wants is to be safe, isn't it? Free from fear, from persecution, Blacky Harbottle gazing along the carpet toward his torn and battered front door that just days before one had had reinforced with escutcheon plates with wraparound door channels and three vertical drop deadbolts—and what good did that fucking do, I ask ya?

Dreaming up better worlds is perhaps more work than one supposes, Blacky Harbottle remaining prone on the floor and dozing a bit. In the half-sleep haze, another list conjured up, a list of the five safest places in Canada to live, read some time ago in a *Maclean's* magazine at the doctor's office while waiting to scam a prescription. And Caledon, Ontario, was one of them. Nottawasaga and York Region were two others, also in Ontario. And Maskoutains in

Quebec, not too far from one's hometown. And some European country far from one's own was deemed the safest country in the world, according to the Global Peace Index. And can one envision one's self moving to one of these places, selling the house on St. Catherines Street, belongings crammed in a U-Haul, cartoon style, and heading east in a dream within a dream, these goofy-named places all very small, somewhat remote; drug profits would plummet. And dreaming on, viewed from above, with the decrease in a viable drug trade, one would have to budget carefully, of course, make things last (especially if the internet fraud doesn't pay off), and one may have to work a part-time job or something to supplement loss of income.

And the body of Blacky Harbottle stirs, straightens along the floor. It's a voice that's made his body do this, made his body shake off the daze and attempt to get to its feet, a voice that interrupted the dream of a possible middle-of-the-road-you-wouldn't-have-to-give-up-or-change-anything-you-like world on the words *part-time job*, a voice that says: *"Jesus, dipshit, now you're really dreamin'. . ."*

And with that the dream is over, for now, Blacky Harbottle on his feet and moving to pick up pieces of doorstop, door jamb, door casing. Outside the skies grow lighter, the wind subsides, and one will leave the annoying little stuff until tomorrow; the sinkers, box nails, wood screws. In the meantime, can wear thick-soled slippers to protect against possible piercings, having never really thought of one's home as being dangerous enough to warrant the purchase of at least a simple first aid kit. And in those same thick-soled slippers, one can walk the few doors down the alley to the neighbour's unused garage before anyone's awake, remove camouflage from the 115 lb. WS 1-SC, and with the secret numbers only one's self knows, acquire some drug of one's choice to consume voraciously (in lieu of the night's trauma) and calm one's nerves, and, of course, to better keep the dream alive.

49

Inner Workings

THEY SIT AT THE white kitchen table. Above their heads the red of trailing fuchsias, pale mauve of spur flower, and the gold of creeping Jenny, dead Momma's hanging baskets rejuvenated and well tended. The sky outside rides low and dark, a West Coast rite of January. Rain falls steadily, Mona, Meagre, and Louella sitting around dead Momma's white kitchen table munching from two bowls, one of potato chips, one of Cheezies, chips and Cheezies used to scoop mounds of garlic dip, small plate of stuffed *Halkidiki* Greek olives and baby dills, the smell of fresh-brewed coffee. *The Complete Home Gardener* maintains its revered place open on dead Momma's table. Through the window the tops of tall, dark trees sway like drunken sentries in the wind.

"For instance," says Louella (referring to Marie Papadopoulos's property next door), "the smaller hedge circling the side lawn is a thorny *Elaeagnus* and the taller one lining the driveway is an American *Arborvitae*."

"I'm impressed," says Meagre. "From complete ignorance to expertise."

"I'm getting better," says Louella.

"Do you talk to them, too?" says Meagre.

"Actually I do," says Louella. "Plants are more interesting than I would ever have thought."

"Do they talk back?" says Meagre.

"I've not gone that far," says Louella. "But in the sixties there was some CIA interrogation expert who hooked a lie detector up to a plant, and apparently the polygraph showed a stress reaction when he told the plant he was going to burn it."

"You've got to be kidding," says Meagre.

"And there was also a Sir Jagadish someone who claimed to have recorded the screams of tomatoes being cut up," says Louella.

Meagre laughs.

"Herd has left," says Mona. "Just up and gone."

Louella holds a baby dill. The fridge hums. And Meagre will outlast her easily in the sudden silence.

"Jesus, I'm sorry, Mona," says Louella. "Kind of out of the fucking blue, isn't it?"

"Not really," says Mona. "Things have not been great for a while. But just the same, I can't really believe it."

"He just up and left?" says Louella. "He didn't say anything?"

"Didn't *say* anything. Just left a note..."

Silence. Meagre waits. Louella waits.

"What'd the note say?" says Louella.

"*I'm leaving.*"

"That it?"

"That's it."

The world waits.

"I think there's someone else," says Mona. "In fact, I'm sure. Someone at his work."

"For fuck's sake," says Louella.

"Exactly," says Mona.

And Louella looking at Meagre Deerstone who looks back and one knows they're both thinking: "*Herd Rose—what woman in her right fucking mind? ...*"

"Sorry, Mona," says Meagre.

"Yeah, fuck, Mona," says Louella. "Anything we can do?"

"Oh, I'll survive," says Mona Rose. "Nothing to do, really. Just feels a bit strange, I guess."

"How's Shamus taking it?" says Louella.

"Oh, who knows with kids?" says Mona. "I think he blames me for it. He'll be mad for a while, I guess. And that's okay. Everything'll be okay, I know that. It'll just be kind of weird for a while..."

Silence. Louella waits.

Meagre Deerstone's slow, measured voice: "Weirder than before Herd left?"

Mona bursts out laughing, Meagre's face spilling a slow smile. Louella again looking at Meagre Deerstone.

"Mona needs to see the pelican lines..."

"Yes," says Meagre Deerstone. "Needs to see something that knows what it's doing."

"What the fuck are you guys talking about?" says Mona.

"None of your fucking business, right now," says Louella. "Just be ready."

"Ready for what?"

"Don't worry about it," says Louella. "It's a good thing." And looking at Meagre. "Was thinking of Marie next door, too..."

Meagre nodding.

"Grandfather says it should be four this time."

"Ah, your grandfather..."

IT'S BECOME A common-enough occurrence in the past months for Louella and Meagre to spend a lot of time together, sometimes in almost complete silence, sometimes in easy, measured talk. The meetings and visits are seldom arranged in any traditional sense; they just happen as if the flow of one life to the other is supposed to occur with neither taking the lead or precedent over the other. The two will often do a smudging, then end up splayed out on dead Momma's blue leather sectional in the living room, the TV on but turned low and presenting either mindless movies or, more often, documentaries.

And it's no different this same evening after Mona has gone, the two of them sprawled on dead Momma's couch, the TV turned low and offering a computer-animated rendition of the inner workings of the western world's first water clock, invented by the Greek Ctesibius in the third century. For the two ladies watching animated water flow through a primitive metal cone, thereby powering this and that, their own personal inner workings may be, of course, much less obvious but are there nonetheless, and in the case of Meagre Deerstone any physical and emotional workings are really anybody's guess, being herself disposed to not give much away at the best of times. For Louella on the other hand, it can be said that at least any physical and emotional inner workings have become less severe, more like a gentle tilling of the soil now as opposed to earlier, more violent upheavals of earth and rock, and, as Ctesibius's water clock turns, these more gentle inner workings may enable one's self to grieve easier for the loss of one's mother and for the loss of other things, too. And it's into this more gentle and nurturing atmosphere of veneration for the proficiency of the ancients mixing with the possible healing qualities of the present day that comes again the measured voice of Meagre Deerstone.

"You going to England?"

"Can't, can't get a passport," says Louella.

"Right..."

"He's coming here, though. In March."

"That good?" says Meagre Deerstone.

"I think so," says Louella.

A silence. They're informed that Ctesibius was able to make his clock whistle like a bird or sound like bells.

Louella waits.

Meagre Deerstone's slow, measured voice: "Remember that night, Louella? Those guys and the pink Cadillac and then you ended up getting loaded overtown. You called me, got a cab..."

"Yes," says Louella.

"You mentioned someone..." says Meagre.

"I did?" says Louella.

"Tell me about Matilda Goomba," says Meagre Deerstone.

And to Meagre's, and her own, surprise, and under the dark January sky, Louella does.

50.

Of That Which Is Yet to Be Named

GORDY TRUMAN, in what could be perceived by anyone who knows him as a completely uncharacteristic and (in Butch Truman's mind, anyway) downright mutinous act, does not decide to abscond with the rented Volkswagen Cabriolet and take it to a chop shop just outside of Edmonton to sell it for parts, even though Butch Truman sees it as the obvious thing to do.

"It's in Harbottle's fucking name," says Butch Truman. "He's liable for it. It's a clean fucking score, for Christ's sake! You crazy?"

Gordy Truman doesn't really have an answer to that last question. A part of him says yes. Another part of him says nothing, just kind of ponders the idea. At any rate, he drops the car off at the rental lot early one morning, leaving the keys in it. He then returns to the motel where the four of them are staying while awaiting repairs to the Cadillac, and they all stay stoned for three days until the Caddy's pronounced repaired and roadworthy enough for the trip back home. Everything is compliments of dear Mrs. Truman, of course, thanks to her younger son's phone call, Butch Truman having added a hefty arbitrary amount to the estimate of cost to get the four of them and the car back to Edmonton.

"You wouldn't believe how expensive everything is out here, Mom!" says Butch when making the call. "Wire it right away, will ya? An' the sooner we'll be home."

"Good god," says Mom. "You'll need *how* much for accommodation?"

"I know, Mom," says Butch Truman. "It's freaking robbery, but you want we should sleep on the street 'til the car's ready?"

"Well, no, of course not—"

"Well, better get 'er done then, Mom. Better get 'er done!"

Butch is finally able to go pick up the Caddy, wheeling it into the motel parking lot with Baby sitting tight to his side.

"The lovebirds are back," says Gordy Truman, looking through the curtains.

"Oh, god," says Sherry. "I just want to get the fuck going, no assing around, away from this fucking place and with the fucking top *up* this time all the way."

"And no more fucking Daddy and Baby crap either," says Gordy. "They can do that shit after we're home."

The Caddy looks good, the driver's door reattached and the whole vehicle cleaned up. And Gordy Truman does put a stop to the whole Baby and Daddy crap, laying down the ground rules for the trip home.

"Those are our special names, man . . ." says Butch Truman.

"Until we get home they're not," says Gordy Truman. "Then you guys can do what you like. And no stupid signs on the car."

"Stupid signs?" says Butch. "Who says you—"

"It wasn't a stupid sign, was it, Butch?" says Baby, her eyes beginning to tear.

"Oh, god," says Sherry Kinsella.

"So let's just get in and get going," says Gordy.

"So, what the fuck's the matter with you all of a sudden?" says Butch. "It's my fucking car. Jeez, you think you can—"

"The sooner we get going, the sooner you guys can get back to your thing and we can get back to ours," says Gordy.

"Buuutch? . . ." says Baby.

A car guns it onto the street, setting off a crow on the motel roof. It lets go a squawk and pounds his wings into the air.

"It's okay, Baby," says Butch. "We'll get the jerks home an' then we'll hit the road again, just the two of us."

"Really?" sobs Tina Blout.

"Really," says Butch Truman. And then to his brother: "And I don't care what you fucking say, man, but me 'n Baby are gonna—"

"Oh, Christ, don't fucking start—" says Gordy Truman.

"Me 'n *Tina* are gonna stop when we want to if we gotta pee or eat somethin'!"

"Yeah, yeah, good. Can we get going?" says Gordy.

"Yeah, we can get going," says Butch Truman, "whoever the fuck *you* are, buddy!"

And the pink Caddy then at last back on the road, leaving what has now become an unpleasant place and heading out toward what has now had enough time to have become a much more pleasant place again, the foursome rolling eastward toward the more pleasant province of Alberta where hopefully any of the unpleasantness from a few months ago is no longer and the cycle of good things going to bad things can start again. Butch and Baby sandwiched together in the front seat, Gordy Truman and Sherry Kinsella flaked out in the back, Gordy Truman pensive and mulling over his brother's last comment before leaving the motel—*"Yeah, we can get going, whoever the fuck* you *are, buddy!"* And the truth be known in all this, one Gordy Truman is no longer sure who the fuck one is, buddy. In fact, this has been Gordy Truman's situation for some time, ever since the encounter a while back with that crazy clerk at the all-night convenience store in Wetaskiwin, home to the oldest functioning water tower in Canada.

Something had happened then, something had happened to Gordy Truman, criminal, heroin crackhead, ex-con, thug-bruiser guy. Something "shifted," not a lot but just enough, just enough to make one uncomfortable, uncomfortable with everything one's been doing since. The trip to the coast, then running around scoring, boosting, kidnapping, for Christ's sake—all pursuits that one would have felt just fine performing for years and years but all of a sudden seeming so, ah, *outdated?* Could that be the word? In short, Gordy Truman has not felt like Gordy Truman (the one he knows at any rate) since that early morning encounter with that crazy lunatic store clerk. Here was a guy as angry and desperate as one's self, *more* angry and desperate and not even strung out on drugs, a guy quite ready to have his life ended over a couple of hundred bucks or to hack someone to pieces for it, whichever came first. And one had known at the outset that it wasn't the money the guy actually cared about, it was something bigger, farther, deeper. One has become used to people being afraid, intimidated by the big, angry Gordy Truman, nuts himself and capable of no small amount of violence, and especially when he was sticking a fucking gun in their faces, for fuck's sake. But this guy wasn't afraid; instead he was just pissed. Insulted or something. And, yeah, one can admit, if only to one's self, that, yeah, the guy was fucking scary.

But regardless of any true clarity of explanation for this "shift" in the psyche and perhaps very soul of Gordy Truman, suffice to allow that a shift of some kind did happen, and, for Gordy Truman, there is no going back. So knowing this, it's of no great surprise to himself at least that he bids goodbye to Sherry Kinsella upon arriving in Edmonton, an act that he experiences as a truly terrible thing, suggesting lamely that she may want to reconnect with her family back east or something, get straight, go back to nursing. Sunlight is glancing off a fresh prairie snowfall as he suggests this, and tiny ice particles dance in the air before his eyes as Sherry Kinsella, no less as tough as the cons she administered to when a practising nurse at Kingston Pen and now fired by a ragged, soul-ravaging drug habit, punches him in the head and then tries to stab him, tears freezing on her cheeks.

"You're an asshole," she says.

"Sorry," he says.

"Like fuck!" she says, Sherry Kinsella staggering unsteadily through the snowdrifts to find her way downtown. (She does eventually find her way back east, back home, and receives the help she needs, kicks her habit, and returns to herself.)

The same, however, can't be said for Gordy Truman, who can't really return to somewhere that was never there in the first place. To him (to the best of his knowledge) there has only ever been the one "self," now becoming more and more uncomfortable to be with, but at the same time evaporating, misting around the edges, and becoming less and less defined and very possibly disappearing altogether unless some action is taken to preserve *something*. What that action would be, he has no idea.

Two nights later Gordy Truman sits in one family chair, Mr. Truman in another, both chairs and all the furniture in the house of the knobbly pseudo-Spanish style that is freely available at reasonable prices at the never-ending close-out sales at any discount furniture warehouse store.

Mr. Truman leans back in his chair, Gordy Truman leans forward in his. Their eyes hold for a total of forty-three seconds before Mr. Truman says: "And what the fuck brought this on..."

Eleven seconds.

"Not sure," says Gordy Truman. "But I'm ready..."

Thirteen seconds.

"Rehab, you said..." says Mr. Truman.

Another eleven seconds.

"But before I do it, I just want to borrow the car for a night..." says Gordy Truman.

"No fucking way," says Mr. Truman from his pseudo Spanish–style chair in the living room.

"That shouldn't be a problem," says Mrs. Truman from her pseudo Spanish–style stool in the kitchen.

GORDY TRUMAN, disappearing man, enters the all-night convenience store on Highway 2A in Wetaskiwin, Alberta. A young guy behind the counter looks up.

"Help you?"

"Um, there another guy work here nights? Black guy, older?"

"You mean Claver?"

"Ah, yeah. Claver."

"Nope, he don't work here anymore."

"Oh..."

"He quit. Opened his own business or somethin'. Works for the government, maybe? You know him?"

"Um, sort of did. Yeah..."

"Kinda funny. Was a whole bunch of robberies when he worked here. Cops thought he had something to do with 'em but couldn't prove nothing. I liked Claver; he was a nice guy. Last robbery they had was a smash-and-grab, eh? Someone backed their car right through the window there an' took off with the whole ATM machine as well as cash from the till... "

"No shit? Was, um, Claver working that night, too?"

"Yeah, he was workin.'"

"Must've freaked him out, eh?"

"Not really. He was always kind of calm about being robbed. He was a bit of a weird guy."

"Yeah, weird guy... "

"All the robberies have stopped though. Makes you think."

"Yeah, guess so... "

Seven seconds.

"You want somethin'?"

"Um, yeah. Bag of potato chips... "

And Gordy Truman is done talking, leaving the town limits with a hint of dawn low on the prairie sky as he rolls out past gold-skimmed prairie farmlands, fields of wheat, canola, barley. Sugar beets, dairy cattle, hogs, and cotton-batten bundles of sheep, the rich, warm colour imparted freely by the rising sun and painting all in the weave of a perfect picture postcard of contentment, beauty, and prosperity.

"That sonofabitch... " he says, with no little admiration.

And the next night asleep in his parents' home a day before checking into rehab does Gordy Truman dream, become a dreamer. Not the drug-muddled, comic book–style dreaming of younger brother Butch, of making movies or the writing of mawkish songs trumpeting the bleak and embarrassing in three chords, or even driving around in pink cars, but this be the clear and unrestrained dreaming of the new and unknown, things so new and unknown so as to not yet even have names, terms of reference. Fact is, in fact, that come the morning Gordy Truman, reappearing man, won't be able to tell you what he dreamed, only that it was new. And as yet unknown. And, well, dreamed...

END

ABOUT THE AUTHOR

John Thomas Osborne, aka J.T. Osborne, was born on Baffin Island in June of 1949. He has illustrated various books, including Mary Beth Knechtel's under-acknowledged *The Goldfish That Exploded* and *Social Credit for Beginners: An Armchair Guide* (Pulp Press, 1986). J.T. Osborne is also the author of several books of poetry, including *Under the Shadow of Thy Wings* (1986), *9 Love Poems,* and *Please Wait for Attendant to Open Gate.* His first novel, *Foozlers,* was published by Anvil Press in 2004 and was followed in 2006 by *Dead Man in the Orchestra Pit* (Anvil). Osborne grew up in Kamloops, BC and Vancouver, co-founded Pulp Press Book Publishers (now Arsenal Pulp) in the early 1970s, and currently resides in Maple Ridge, BC.